Advance praise for

NINE MONTHS IN AUGUST

"With sharp humor and an unflinching eye, Adriana Bourgoin shows us that pregnancy changes more than just a woman's body—it can upend her entire existence. *Nine Months in August* has it all: the "is-he-ready-for-fatherhood" husband, the career uncertainty, the friends with kids who talk to you in Mommy Voice, the friends without kids who don't talk to you at all, and, lest we forget, the grandparents-to-be gone right off the deep end. This book reminds us, though, that ultimately, happiness lies somewhere underneath that upset apple cart.

—Stacie Cockrell, Cathy O'Neill and Julia Stone, coauthors of *Babyproofing Your Marriage*

NINE MONTHS IN AUGUST

Adriana Bourgoin

KENSINGTON BOOKS
http://www.kensingtonbooks.com

KENSINGTON BOOKS are published by

Kensington Publishing Corp.
850 Third Avenue
New York, NY 10022

All Kensington titles, imprints and distributed lines are available at special quantity discounts for bulk purchases for sales promotion, premiums, fund raising, educational or institutional use.

Special book excerpts or customized printings can also be created to fit specific needs. For details, write or phone the office of the Kensington Special Sales Manager: Kensington Publishing Corp., 850 Third Avenue, New York, NY 10022. Attn. Special Sales Department. Phone: 1-800-221-2647.

Kensington and the K logo Reg. U.S. Pat. & TM Off.

ISBN-13: 978-0-7582-1731-8
ISBN-10: 0-7582-1731-5

First Kensington Trade Paperback Printing: June 2007
10 9 8 7 6 5 4 3 2 1

Printed in the United States of America

For Nicole Flanagan Ayers

1972–2006

Acknowledgments

I want to thank my husband, John, who in the spirit of healthy competition actually dared me to finish this book. John, without your expertise in *facilities, finance, foodservices* and, of course, *human resources,* Declan, Nate, and I would be lost.

I also want to thank my mother and my sisters, Marisa and Elena—I think Dad would be proud of all of us.

A special thank you to Melissa Moore, Katie Mason, Casey Taylor, and Susan Poulton; I appreciate your agreeing—though you might not have been aware of it—to support me through the writing of this book.

Thanks to Tracy Harrison Peixoto and Meghan Quinn—my favorite memories about growing up always include you.

Also, thank you to John Mason, Chris Johnson, Jason Golomb, and Bob Wooldridge (1961–2006).

Last, but not least, I want to thank Richard Abate, my agent at ICM, and John Scognamiglio, my editor at Kensington Books.

Chapter 1

*"Don't throw the baby out with the bathwater! Even
the strongest of friendships can be challenged when
one of you becomes a mother. Take the time to support your friend in her new endeavors and don't be
afraid to offer a gentle reminder that you have a life,
too."*
—From *Living Life* magazine, "What to Do When
   Your Best Friend Succumbs to Mommy Madness."

Every Wednesday I meet my two closest friends for coffee at the Java Joint. Meredith, now known as "Ryder's Mommy," is four minutes pregnant with her second.
Louisa, on the other hand, is more like me. After several
thousand hours of analyzing, we decided that it just doesn't
make sense to become a mother until you can honestly say
you don't hate your own.

"Ryder, look at Mommy. Ryder. Ryder. Look at Mommy. NO."

"Would he like a cookie?" Louisa asks.

"Thanks, but no refined sugar for us. Ryder, sit down.
Sit down, please. Ryder?"

We began this tradition five years ago, when I moved
back to Northampton from Washington, D.C. The three
of us met freshman year at Smith College, which rests on a

hill six blocks north of the Joint. The main entrance of the
school at the Grecourt Gates (erected in honor of the Smith
College Relief Unit, a group of graduates who went to
France after World War I) is visible from the window next
to our table. We're crammed around it to accommodate a
high chair Ryder abandoned immediately after he was placed
in it. He stands at the window, rubbing his fingers against
the glass; it's foggy from the cold. *Squeak. Squeak.*

"When do you leave for New York?" Meredith asks
Louisa. "Ryder. *No.* Mommy asked you to stop that.
Please?"

"Tomorrow morning. Gretchen, sure you don't want to
come?"

"Nah. I don't have a New Year's Eve in New York in
me."

"Lord knows I don't," Meredith adds, brushing crumbs
off her shirt. "But you have no idea how much I would love
a drink. To be drunk. To sleep." She yawns. "Time for a nap.
Ryder, it's time for you and Mommy to go home, for night-
night."

"No!" Ryder screams.

"Night-night!" Louisa says, laughing.

Meredith starts to bundle up Ryder. She forces his feet,
shoes on, through the narrow legs of a snowsuit. She Vel-
cros his mittens over his clenched fists and finally, covers
his head with a Cat in the Hat–like tower of knit.

"The hat has to be last," Meredith explains. "Otherwise, he'll try and take it off. I hate to stifle his gross-
motor-skills development with the mittens for even a
minute but it's so cold out!"

Louisa kicks me under the table.

"I saw that," Meredith says.

Meredith is an associate professor of anthropology at
Smith, and as such she is prone to overthinking. She spent
two happy years knee-deep in mud on the beaches of the

Black Sea in search of evidence of "the tiny people" tribe and has now turned the full, unbridled force of her intellectual prowess to a) Ryder, b) the state of her career post-child birth, and, c) a painfully earnest e-mail with the subject line "Just Gestating" that she and her husband, Alan, send out periodically to keep interested parties up-to-date on her pregnancy. In last week's letter, Meredith noted that she'd heard— in the waiting room of her OB's office—that a woman is more fertile *after* she's already had a child. I don't know enough about it to say that this is a medical fact but, really, why would I? I didn't even know Ryder was a name.

"What are you and Fredrik doing for New Year's?" Louisa asks.

"I'm working," I answer. "Not sure what Fredrik's doing."

My cell phone, which is set on vibrate, starts buzzing and moves across the table; it's headed straight for Louisa's latte.

"Sorry," I say to Louisa and Meredith, who are now shouting to each other in order to be heard over Ryder's demands to play with the phone. I quickly turn away and answer it, without checking caller ID; I'm desperate to get it out of Ryder's view.

"I want to exhume your father's body," my mother says, before I can eke out a hello.

"What?" I yell. "Why?"

I look to Louisa. She is mouthing, "Who is that?"

"I can't hear you, Mom," I say. "I will call you later."

I flip the phone shut and put it away in my purse. I sigh.

"She wants to dig up my dad," I explain.

"Not that again," Louisa says.

"On that note, I've got to get going," Meredith says.

She spends a few more minutes with Louisa and me, trying to coach a "bye-bye" out of Ryder, but she gives up, says it for him, and heads for the door. After she leaves, the Joint is quiet—except for a muffled screaming sound, coming from the parking lot. I turn my attention to the window. I can see Meredith struggling to put Ryder in his car seat. He is arching his back and kicking his legs wildly.

"Ryder is adorable," Louisa says.

"Do you think the defiance is innate?" I ask, chuckling.

"Meredith is so patient; she's a good mom," Louisa adds.

I think she is, but again, how would I know? I'm not sure my experience as a daughter, more specifically my crazy mother's daughter, puts me in a position to judge someone's mothering ability. And from what I've heard from Meredith, there is a lot, and I do mean a lot, I don't know about being a mom—like Back to Sleep, food allergies, and *1-2-3 Magic*. It is while I'm considering this, and my mother's announcement, that two women in matching gray fur-lined down parkas approach me. They remove their hoods and their gloves in unison. They look vaguely familiar.

"Gretchen! We met at Meredith's New Year's Day open house last year. I'm Char, and this is my partner, my fiancée, as of Christmas Eve, Kate."

Let me explain. I am the catering manager at the Northampton Grande, the town's largest hotel, and since same-sex marriages became legal in Massachusetts I've logged thousands of hours planning parties for the gay, lesbian, and transgendered "Just Married" crowd. Char and Kate look away from me to check out Louisa. Nearly six feet tall, with long black hair that curls downward past her shoulders, her eyes are bright blue and they twinkle against her fair, lightly freckled skin. She is striking. I, in contrast, stretch to reach 5 feet, 2 inches, and my hair flips under on one side, up on the other. My eyes are brown. My skin is olive—greenish really—prone to breakouts and, as a result, I'm not altogether unfamiliar with products that contain "the active ingredient benzoyl peroxide." I suspect they think Louisa and I are a couple, that I'm out of my league, and that I will never experience the pure, unadulterated joy of exchanging *matching* Tiffany classic-setting engagement rings. They are clearly enamored of their new sparklers; both women are admiring their hands in the Joint window, gesturing emphatically in a way only a recently engaged woman can.

"Best wishes to you," I say.

"Of course we want *you* to plan our wedding," Char replies.

"I'd love to."

I take two business cards from my card-carrying case and hand one to each of them. This is the safest route; it's hard to tell with two women who will do the actual planning. Nine times out of ten, it is four people: the two brides and their mothers. *I am surrounded by mothers.*

"I'm beginning to understand why you don't wear a wedding ring. Not good for business," Louisa observes after they've left.

I've often thought that it's too bad I'm *not* gay, because Smith would have been the perfect place to come out. As a Gold Key Tour Guide I'd explained to more than one prospective student's parent about how the college's tolerant atmosphere "fosters personal discovery." For some, that means playing with gender, though applicants have to be biologically female at the time of admission. For others, it's the freedom to experiment with same-sex relationships. But it's a nonissue. I'm straight, a "breeder"—a term thrown around by the more radical lesbians on campus. I never understood how lesbianism, feminism, or humanity could continue without *someone* reproducing, so I'm not entirely sure why this is a pejorative term. On the other hand, I am happy to postpone my participation in the great Disney Elton John Circle of Life until the timing is absolutely perfect.

Unfortunately, my period is five days late.

"I have scoop," Louisa says.

"What?" I ask. *Is it that obvious I could be pregnant?*

"Jason and I are officially, um, trying," she says, winking.

"Trying?" I ask. "Oh, no," I groan, laughing.

"Come on. You read that book. We're ancient, fertility-wise."

"We're in our early thirties!" I protest.

"We'll be mid, like any minute," Louisa says.

"We are solidly early," I insist.

"Come on, G, you have to try," she whispers as she leans across the table. "Otherwise you could get pregnant at an inappropriate time."

"What do you mean?"

"You know, like during regular sex. Or worse, during drunk sex, when you're pretending to be a nurse or something."

"A nurse?"

"A naughty nurse," she says.

"STOP!" I yell.

"When did you become such a prude?" Louisa asks. "I thought even those wacky nuns at your high school said it was OK to have sex when you're married."

"If you are referring to the Ursulines I should remind you that the order was named for the saint of consecrated virginity."

"Ah, right, the *superspecial* virgins."

"STOP!" I yell again.

"As much as I'm enjoying our sex chat, it's very liberated of us, don't you think? I have to go. Do you want a ride?" Louisa asks. "Jason and I could drop you off; I'm meeting him in ten minutes to grab dinner in Greenfield."

Louisa stands up, puts on her coat. I open my mouth to tell her that I may be a) a serious disappointment to the Ursulines, and b) a victim of an Improperly Staged Conception, but I do not. Doesn't seem fair to Fredrik. I pull my sweater over my head, wrap a scarf around my neck, and button my coat.

"Nah, I'll walk. Don't want to intrude on your fore-play."

"Don't you think that we have to stop obsessing and just do it?"

"I don't know" I hesitate. *What if I've already done it?*

"Come on, Ryder's Mommy would want it for us. She says there is no right time."

"She also says misery loves company!"

"True. OK. Gotta run. I will talk to you later."

Louisa leaves and I dawdle in the Joint for a minute. I want something else to eat. Fredrik is rarely home before seven and the fridge is empty so I'm on my own for dinner. Do they have anything that could be even remotely construed as a meal? Hmm. No. Round baskets piled high with homemadeish baked goods—Rice Krispies treats, brownies, and M&M bars clutter the register counter. This will be a snack, then, a large snack. I deserve it; think of the calories I'll burn walking home in the cold.

"I'll take this," I say, pointing to an M&M thing.

"You didn't like the cookie?" the barista asks me.

"What? Oh, no, no. This is for my husband. Thanks."

I push open the door, struggling against the wind. I wait until I'm around the corner and out of sight of the barista before I bite into the dessert. While I'm chewing—this is so much better than the cookie—I decide I will take a detour from my usual route home to go to Higger's Drug Store. I desperately need tweezers. And not the cheapies, either; after all, I am half Italian.

Once I'm in the store, I climb over the one-dollar discount bins that sit in the aisles, overflowing with cheap, garish Christmas toys, off-brand candy, and tinsel. The dark gray carpet can't hide the stains, and long fiber snakes coil intermittently across the floor. I wander back to the cosmetics aisle, grabbing a multipack of musical lights along the way. An ancient pharmacy clerk, whose egg-shaped age spots form a cluster on his forehead, is locked in head-to-head combat with a heavyset woman adorned in an ill-advised sweat suit.

"Spell it again, please."

"D.E.E. HYPHEN G. O. L. D."

"E.L.G.O.—"

"No."

While standing by the tweezers, my eye catches sight of a row of pregnancy tests, arranged directly to the left of the condoms (seems like an odd kind of up-sell, like, try this, but if it doesn't work, try these). I stumble over to the tests and I am about to grab one when a greasy teenager in a woolen skullcap asks me if I need help.

"Help?" I ask, stopping my hand in midair.

"Yes, help."

"No, but thank you," I say, smiling at him.

I turn my attention back to my hand, which has drifted to the right, toward the "XXXL Ribbed for Her Pleasure" ones. Oh, shit! He nods at me and walks away. Great. *Sigh.* Just as well, because now I'm free to examine the tests more closely.

It appears as though each one has its own method of breaking the news: blue lines, pink lines, one line, two lines, a plus sign. Which to buy? Should I get the most expensive one? Won't that mean it's the best? Maybe I'd better get two tests, just in case I screw it up. But they all say here, on the front of the packages, that they are close to 99 percent accurate. But maybe it's too early to even take a test; I'm barely even late. Oh, wait, this one says the test can measure hormone HCG four days before a missed period. *Before?* Maybe the pregnancy test people should just move into my damn bedroom. I decide on the test package priced squarely in the middle.

Why am I so nervous? Maybe it's the TCH coursing

through my blood! No, wait, TCH is in pot. *HCG* is what the test is measuring. Yikes, there's no way a good mother would confuse the active ingredient in a "gateway" drug with the hormone your body produces when pregnant. What's more, I think to myself as I make my way to the front of the store, *a real, good mother would not be afraid to bring her purchase to the cashier*. Oh, hell. Here I am. I put the tweezers and the test on the counter, but I do not make eye contact with the clerk, who has emerged from a back room, reeking of cigarettes, to assist me. Instead, I use this time to do a spot reorganization of my wallet. Credit cards, here, all forms of ID go here, membership cards behind here oh, wow. Done already! I thank the clerk, grab the bag, and run for the door.

I start back up Main Street. The gusts are getting stronger as I get closer to my house, which, like Louisa's, sits on the northern edge of campus. I walk through the Gates instead of going around campus, as I would if classes were in session, and head up College Lane to Paradise Lane. The dorms are dark, save for a few lights here and there, most likely from the rooms of students who can't or won't go home. Each dorm is a self-contained "house," complete with a living room, home to the weekly tea; a dining room; and a "smoker," where we smoked and voted on pressing community issues—such as, which of the three a capella groups should perform at the next formal and which floors should allow boys in the bathrooms. Knowing what I know now about men and bathrooms, I wish I'd argued to keep them out. The one I share with Fredrik in our house—his, really, since he'd bought and renovated the turn-of-the-century Victorian before I'd even met him—is a battle of the sexes in microcosm. Fredrik doesn't like anything crowding the sink ("Why do you need *two* ChapSticks?" he asked. "One is for day, one is for night," I explained. "The nighttime one doesn't have

SPF."). And I would prefer not to clean urine off the walls ("Would it *kill* you to try for the toilet? It smells like a stadium in here.").

By the time I reach our house, I'm so cold I can't breathe. Boo, my yellow Labrador Retriever, jumps on me, wags his tail, and whines for dinner before I've even taken the keys out of the front door lock. I fill Boo's bowl with "I Woof You," his organic dog food, and he gobbles it down. I run upstairs to hide the test behind my tampons and Maxi Pads; Fredrik will never look there. Boo and I then settle into our nighttime routine, both of us on the couch. I'm under a blanket; he's at my feet. We watch three episodes of *The Golden Girls* and are preparing for a fourth when Fredrik walks in the door. Boo stays put, staking his territory. Fredrik picks up the remote and throws his coat on the back of the couch.

"*Auto Week* is on," he says, changing the channel.

"I'm watching this."

"Yes, but we've seen this one before. This is the episode where Blanche decides to write a romance novel."

"You're scaring me, Fredrik. What's in the bag?"

He hands me a plastic bag filled with well-worn Tupperware containers, each marked with masking tape and blue ballpoint pen ("cheaper than labels," Mrs. Stirling, Fredrik's mom, says). I open one and jerk my head away; it smells so pungent.

"Beef stew and rice."

"The Land Rover Defender 110 has been restored to its former glory," the announcer intones, "and the rugged landscape of Chile is hardly a match—"

"Turn it back."

Fredrik holds the remote over his head.

"Make me."

There is little chance of that. He's a full foot taller than me and strong from his work at his father's general contracting firm, Stirling & Sons. My best bet is to outwit him, but I don't have the energy. I've been so tired all week. Last night, I went to bed at eight thirty. I leave the couch to hang up Fredrik's coat on the rack, careful to re-arrange mine so the smallest coat is on top, and climb the stairs.

"You feeling OK?" Fredrik calls after me.

"Yep. Good night."

"Good night."

Once in my room, I notice a car slowing down in front of the house. It's probably Louisa and Jason back from dinner. I move to the window and see Jason walking to Louisa's side of the car and opening her door. He helps her out of the car and I smile, thinking of how polite he is, even to me. Luckily, he's forgiven me for some rude comments I made to him early on in our collective relationship. A few days after he'd proposed to her, he answered the phone at her apartment. "Where will I sleep when I visit?" I asked. He said nothing. "In a guest room?" I pressed on. "Why would you be sleeping *here*," he'd finally replied, "when you have your own place down the street?" I thought we were doomed, for sure. Didn't he know I'd spent like a thousand nights at her apartment because a night with Louisa, Edy's Grand French Vanilla, and *Wings*— I only watch reruns and old movies—beat the hell out of a night at home alone with Edy's Grand French Vanilla and *Wings?*

I guess I was feeling a little territorial. After all, Louisa and I have been friends forever. By "forever" I mean since the first day of our freshman year at Smith, when she and I bonded over a visceral dislike of her roommate, who came to our orientation meeting in a wide-brimmed straw hat, on which she had wrapped an expensive-looking silk scarf—a look more evocative of the South of France than of southern Massachusetts. Then, during our psychology student-led sensitivity training—we had to take turns say-ing our names followed by a label, for example "My name is Gretchen and I am blind/vegan/Rastafarian" in order to preempt any kind of judging (They gave us examples, in case we didn't know what we were judging for.)—Louisa's roommate said, "Pass." You were allowed to say "pass" if you felt uncomfortable with the process, but it was the first day of college—*everything* about it was uncomfortable. After she said "pass" I had one of those moments when I can't control what sounds are coming out of my mouth, and I laughed. I had to cough to hide it. Then someone else started coughing to give me cover—Louisa.

In no time we were inseparable; she basically moved into my room. And my roommate, perhaps annoyed by Louisa's constant presence, started spending a lot of nights at her boyfriend's dorm, over at Hampshire College (She'd known the guy in high school, which, as far as I could tell, was the only way to get a date at Smith, you had to know the guy *before* you arrived on campus.), so we like to say that we were freshman-year roommates. It was our first mutually agreed upon lie. We have many of these that have come up over the years, including: I played field hockey in high school (Truth: I played for gym class, not on a team, I didn't even make JV.); Louisa can drive a stick shift (Truth: she cannot but she thought this made her sound cool.); and we love to travel to exciting, undiscovered places on a moment's no-tice (do the Berkshires count?). We didn't plan out these lies—they just happened. We instinctively knew, and con-tinue to know, when to back each other up.

Louisa was the kind of friend I'd been waiting for, after years of struggling in high school through the Ursuline Academy of Georgetown's *Lord of the Flies*-like atmo-sphere. The kind of friend who knows to turn the radio down when you're talking in the car, even though her fa-vorite song was playing, but who also knows when to turn

it up, because you are both tired of talking. The kind of
friend who takes everything you say seriously, because *you*
are saying it, no matter how inconsequential or how *con-
sequential* it is. I remember distinctly the first time I broached
the subject of my parents—what became of Mom after
Dad died—and she didn't dismiss it with an "Oh, everyone's
mother is a lunatic." Instead, she listened. And when she
met Mom some months later, Louisa was so *charming*, so
respectful of her, I knew from then on I could trust her
with anything, no matter how unpleasant or unflattering,
for instance, "Meredith is so smart it's irritating."

We discovered Meredith toward the end of our freshman year. She lived on another floor and was less involved
in house activities than Louisa and I were. She was too
busy doing her reserve readings at Neilson Library, or
writing for the *Sophian,* to waste a lunch hour analyzing
my across-the-hall neighbor, a senior, who made a series of
musical mixes entitled "Songs To Screw To." She was fully
engaged in college and she had little patience for our com-
placency. She'd ask us why we were there if we weren't
going to take "full advantage." "Why is anyone anywhere?"
Louisa would respond. Meredith was the first smart person I'd met who made no apologies for being an intellectual, for wanting to learn more—no one at the Academy
would ever confess to being interested in anything—and
over time, Meredith got us out there, *trying.* For example,
Meredith signed Louisa and me up for stage work as part
of a theater class she was taking, and while it was somewhat of a disaster—I forget the play, but the lead character
shouted: "Do I have diamonds between my thighs? Does
my vagina frighten you?" . . . which made me laugh out
loud, from stage left, during every performance—Louisa
and I happily added it to our ever-evolving personal lore
("We handled audio for an important Latin American the-
atrical production.").

The thing about college—and now, this seems like a luxury I didn't appreciate—there was all this *time*. Time to do stupid shit, like make proclamations about The Kind of Person You Were Going to Be ("I can see myself being a really successful Marxist feminist! But first, let me follow the Dave Matthews Band!"), and still there was time left over, to do *even more* stupid shit, like date. I use the term "date" loosely, in the same way I use the term "diet" loosely, that is, I was aware that other people did it with some measure of success. Meredith didn't care about the opposite sex nearly as much as Louisa and I did. She had a ton of guy friends. We weren't sure when she made them, as we were always together; we even went with her to the pornography versus artistic-expression debates (viewing of porn required, in order to decide). But these guys—cute guys whose physical appearance she *claimed* not to notice—were always coming by to study with her. We'd ask her about it and she'd say, "All I care about is if he is intellectually curious." *Groan.* "Is he smart enough to remember your phone number?" Louisa would tease.

Having two best friends—Louisa who loves me, just as I am, and Meredith, who believes *absolutely*, in my unlimited potential—suits me. And while I am surprised we ended up in the same place (Fearful travelers have limited options.), it's nice to be able to grow up together. But Louisa's declaration that "it's time" has unnerved me. Is there something wrong with me that the only thing I'm "trying" to do is *avoid* pregnancy? Of course, Fredrik and I have discussed starting a family but only in a vague, *we'll know when the time is right* kind of way—that is, *not now*.

And, geez, what about this naughty-nurse thing? That was kind of a surprise. I wonder if they wear costumes. Argh. I can't think anymore. I must go to sleep.

I will take the test first thing in the morning.

Chapter 2

"Stop the attack of the killer hormones! It happens to the best of us, but new treatments are available. If medication isn't your style, keep track of your cycles so you're not caught by surprise when the inevitable carbohydrate loading, irritability, and stomach bloating strikes."
—From *Living Life* magazine, "The Facts About Premenstrual Syndrome."

"Are you about to get your period?" Fredrik asks. Fredrik is just out of the shower and stands before me, preening. He is dripping wet and wearing a small towel that barely makes it around his waist. I am in bed in no hurry to do anything, as I have the day off. Boo is dozing on the floor.

"It is *so* like you to attribute legitimate annoyance to hormones."

"All I said was that a nose ring on someone your age is silly."

"Unlike your towel?"

"But no one sees me in my towel. Everyone would see you in your nose ring."

"Not a ring, Fredrik, a stud. A tasteful diamond stud."

"Whatever."

Fredrik drags his towel over his back. I sit up, flip the covers to the side, get out of bed, and approach him. Boo barks, sensing a confrontation.

"And what about this?" I ask, tapping his upper right arm where an ink drawing of something (I'm not sure what) appeared last spring, after a particularly late night with his brother, Andrew.

"What about it," he says, "is that I am a man. I work with tools. A tattoo is practically a job requirement." Fredrik strikes a he-man pose and makes a muscle. "Besides, I was the only one on the crew without one."

"Let's just all jump off a bridge, then," I suggest as I lean up to kiss him. I think better of it and snort instead.

"Again, are you—never mind. I love you despite your hormone-induced delusions. And *you* love *my* muscles. And my tattoo. *My tat.* That's what we call it, we tattoo people."

"Oh, my goof," I say, laughing.

I climb back into bed and consider how grateful I am that Fredrik doesn't take himself too seriously. It's one of his best qualities. He doesn't care if he's the butt of a joke (his own, his brother's, mine) because he knows exactly what kind of person he is (a "tat" person, apparently) *and* what kind of person he is not ("I am not fit for employment in the corporate world. I could never kiss ass."). I think this is the result of being confident—not arrogant, but confident. Lucky bastard.

Fredrik finishes getting dressed and after striking one more pose, kisses me on the forehead. "Gotta run, be home around nine," he says.

I yawn. I'm exhausted. I was up most of the night thinking of reasons why I am not ready to become a mother—beyond total and obvious ignorance about how to care for a baby. For starters, I've not done anything spectacular, like climb Mount Kilimanjaro. Second, I don't have any talent of any kind—I can barely apply mascara. The end result, I think, is that (a) I'm not that interesting a person, and (b) I have nothing to "pass on" to my children. The nose piercing seemed like a nice, quick fix, but in retrospect, how would that help me be a good parent? Doesn't matter now because Fredrik's accusing me of PMS can mean only one thing: I'm getting my period any minute. I can practically feel the cramps starting. No need to take the pregnancy test, then.

Maybe I should double-check my calculations. I sit up and take my brown leather Filofax off my bedside table. The Filofax has been my constant companion since I was in the ninth grade. Everyone at my high school had one. Everyone was always having something (Remember the "Add a Bead" necklace and L.L. Bean Blucher moccasins?). I bought mine the day after Ann Newhouse and I crashed Bethany Hamrick's seniors-only party, which we attended *not* because we wanted to meet the boys—who, in our opinion, were smelly and obnoxious—but because we wanted to be at the house of a Popular Girl, to get some pointers. We left the "rec" room, where most of the kids were hanging out, and made our way toward Bethany's bedroom, which we were sure would be ground zero for coolness (This is all sounding very *Single White Female* and it wasn't, at all!). We got past her dad, who was standing guard at the stairway, by claiming we had a problem of a feminine nature.

Once we were in Bethany's room, which featured an impressive collection of 11x14 inch photographs of Bethany and her boyfriend, Johnny Johnson, we weren't sure what to do. It was while we were examining the photos, mounted on the wall directly above her bed in plastic box frames, that we spotted the Filofax, on Bethany's nightstand. Adolescent impulses being what they are, we "allowed" the calendar to open and fall to the day-by-day recall. After quickly flipping through the pages, we noticed that a hand-drawn black heart accompanied each entry about Johnny—"met J2 @ Mazza Galleria"—and that some of these entries had three or four. Ann and I looked at each other and it occurred to us, simultaneously, that Bethany was keeping track of their hookups. And you don't keep track of going to second base; you keep track of s-e-x. We were stunned. *It made no sense.* Bethany was prim, preppy, and popular (Did I mention popular?); she so did *not* need to be, um, hooking up with J2 in the Roy Rogers' parking lot. So why was she?

For the record, I figured it out on February third, my sophomore year of college, and promptly black-hearted it.

For the record, the Filofax did not make me cool.

Anyway, I will look at my monthly calendar again. Here's the December Month-At-A-Glance and, again, I don't see a little circle (my own invention—a logical follow-up to the heart). Maybe I forgot to write it down? Here's one on the twenty-second. I got it on the morning of Thanksgiving, in the truck, on the drive to upstate New York to visit Fredrik's aunt and uncle. I remember worrying I'd have it at Christmas. But Christmas was last week. I should have gotten it. I counted the weeks. I counted again.

Wait a minute. Didn't last month's *Living Life* have an article about missing your period? I'll read that; it's sure to have an explanation. I reach for the November issue—I keep the magazines stacked on my bedside table, in reverse chronological order—and start fanning through the pages. Where is the damn table of contents? Here it is! I turn to page 72, "When You Hear Hoofbeats, Think Horses, Not Zebras." *Right.* Possible causes of a missed period (other than pregnancy, which is listed first), include:

- *Stress:*
  Negative. My only source of stress right now is my late period.

- *An eating disorder or compulsive exercise:*
  Impossible. I'm not one of those "oh, no dessert for me" types and I'm too squeamish to purge. I'm active, yes, but mostly out of necessity because I don't have a car. But *exercise?* No. I've bypassed the fitness crazes of the past decade because I won't invest in an activity-specific wardrobe. If a T-shirt and an ex-boyfriend's basketball shorts aren't appropriate, I'm not doing it.

- *Menopause:*
  Unlikely.

It's just inconceivable (Why can't I stop using this word?) to me that I could be pregnant. I use my diaphragm every single time we have sex. I am certain of this because, after all these years, I still don't quite have the knack of inserting it and more often than not, it springs out of my hands and bounces off the bathroom wall. So it's not something I do without considerable thought and effort.

But now I'm less certain. It's still not here.

I was sure that the act of buying the test would smoke signal my mind that I have total acceptance of a pregnancy and as a result, I would relax. And everyone knows that the minute you relax or put on a bathing suit you get your period. *Now where the hell is it?* You know what? I will prove I'm not pregnant by taking the test. This will be such a good story: "The minute after I took the test, I got it. What a waste of twelve dollars." *Ha ha.* Here I go, then, into the bathroom. Why can't I get the plastic off the package? Shouldn't the package-making people plan on you having weak, sweaty hands when you try to open this damn thing? Where are my nail clippers? Shit. Here's Fredrik's Leatherman, I'll use that.

Dammit! I don't even know my own strength. I've

pressed so hard I've ripped both the box and the English instructions. All that's left are the German ones.

Step 1. *Entfernen Sie die Kappe.*
    Is "*stellen sie a dar*" Figure A? This is worse than the IKEA instructions.

Step 2. *Legen Sie saugfähige Spitze in Urinstrom für 5-7 Sekunden.*
    Urinstrom must involve urine. Gross.

Step 3. *Wartezeit 5 Minuten.*
    I consider the following: I will never make it five minutes.

How to pass the time? Since I'm in the bathroom, I conduct a quick check of my skin. Always, always, always a good indication of impending hormonal changes. I have a little ritual, which I will in engage in now, as a time killer. I line up my skin care products. I put my hair into two braids. I am now ready for intense facial therapy. I step up onto the toilet and climb onto the counter. I sit down and put my feet in the sink basin; my knees are nearly at my chin. I look in the mirror for any possible pregnancy-and/or PMS-related changes. I pinch, prod, and press my face. It's now red and blotchy but otherwise the same. Since I'm here, I apply my Teen Kleen 24-hour Emergency Mask. I dot heavily on my troubled areas. A few extra hours of the mask should do me good.

All of a sudden, I feel sick. My heart is racing. I climb down from the sink and go to the bedroom to lie down. This can't be happening. But if I am pregnant, it's OK, right? I am married. Fredrik's a good guy and I should know because in my search for the One, I've spent some time with some real losers. Being fatherless left me particularly vulnerable to a certain kind of guy, the kind no one

else wants. And really, I wasn't picky, I just wanted someone who *wouldn't*:

- Make out with Ann Newhouse, now my *former* best
  friend, at the world-famous Levine Family After-
  Prom Party despite technically being my date; ignore
  me and my new best friend Margaret O'Malley's
  amazing musical talents, which we showcased by ma-
  nipulating the DRUMS function on Dr. Levine's large
  Yamaha keyboard, which is located in the basement,
  not far from the couch you are sitting on with you-
  know-who; ignore my soulful rendition of the *Les
  Miserables* soundtrack ("I had a dream my life would
  be / So different from this hell I'm living"), which
  Margaret set to a salsa beat. (Doug)

- Insist on double-dating with a girl from my house and
  her boyfriend and after approximately one hundred
  Jell-O shots, make a proposal regarding a collective
  sexual act and then, when realize we couldn't understand because of the loud music playing at the bar,
  gesture to explain suggestion; bleed profusely over
  everyone after being socked by housemate's boyfriend;
  force all parties to conclude evening in the ER of Coo-
  ley Dickinson Hospital; tell all his friends that while
  there, he met my therapist, who *happened* to be on call
  that night and who *happened* to have been asked by the
  ER staff to take stock of the situation. (Philip)

- Decide that I should be more involved in our nation's
  esteemed political process as I am living at home
  postcollege graduation, and he is a legislative assistant for a congressman who is going to make a difference; become depressed when said congressman is
  sidetracked by a mail-fraud scandal that involved a
  young intern and an off-shore account; do not appre-

ciate that "I saw it coming"; cancel romantic weekend at George Washington National Forest to mourn
death of congressman's career. (James)

Ah, *James*. He took the congressman's flaws so personally. The congressman was a short, stocky, and unassum-
ing man with a predilection for young, busty women
who'd appeared in *Girls Gone Wild* videos and gambling.
Bang.
The front door. Why does Fredrik do that? I bet all the
coats have fallen onto the floor. *Wait a minute*. He's here.
And he's talking. To Andrew. They're both here! I jump
out of bed and run to the bathroom. I quickly close the
door and look at the test, which I left on the counter.
There it is. The test spells it out: PREGNANT.
Knock knock.
"Gretchen? We need to get in there."
"What? Why? I'm taking a shower."
"I wanted to show Andrew the leak behind the sink."
"Can it wait? I'm not dressed."
"Come on. It'll take two minutes."
"OK, OK."
I scoop up the instructions and the empty box, and
wrap them in toilet paper and shove it all in the trash can.
My hands are shaking. I put the test in the waistband of
my pajamas. I open the door. It's a small bathroom, so I
have to squeeze by them to make room for them to get in.
As I do this, the test slips from my waist, through my pa-
jama leg and to the ground; it rattles as it settles on the
hardwood floor.
"What is that on your face?" Andrew asks.
"Nothing," I say, bending over to retrieve the test.
Andrew beats me to it.
"I'm serious, you have something on there," Andrew
insists.

"It's my acne mask," I answer.

"And what's this?" Andrew asks as he waves the test around in the air.

"Um, uh . . ." I stammer.

"Says, 'pregnant,' " he observes.

Fredrik stops banging at the pipes and turns around. "What?"

"It's a miracle! Andrew can read," I say. I turn to Andrew and continue, "By the way, that has my urine on it." Andrew pitches the test at me, which I catch. I look to Fredrik and smile. My heart is racing. I hold the test up, above my head.

"Oh, my God!" Fredrik shouts.

"I should go," Andrew offers.

He does not.

After an awkward second or two, I back out of the doorway and into the hall. Fredrik pushes past Andrew, picks me up at the waist and lifts me into the air.

"Put me down," I say.

"We're having a baby!" Fredrik shouts.

"I think so. But I should take another test."

"Why? They're like one hundred percent effective," Andrew adds.

"YOU ARE SO NOT HELPING!" I yell.

"Sorry," he says, adding, "I should go."

He does not.

Instead, the three of us make our way downstairs to the kitchen where Andrew and Fredrik start rummaging through the cabinets, looking for something to eat. Since I am unable to convince either of them to go to a drugstore and buy more pregnancy tests, I announce that I'm going to call the "If you have a question (*fragen?*)" number listed on the side of the box.

"Why?" Fredrik asks.

"What if the test is wrong?" I answer.

"It's not. You can take it before you've even missed—" Andrew starts.

"Thank you," I say in my best Ryder's Mommy voice. "I think I'm familiar with the testing, uh, um, methodology."

"You're late, right?" Fredrik asks, his mouth full. "What's to discuss. You had sex and now you're pregnant."

Andrew makes a fist and pumps it in the air when Fredrik says "sex."

I am about to remind Fredrik about the diaphragm, as well as bring him up-to-date on the other causes of late and/or missed periods—perhaps Andrew could be of assistance here—but I stop. "Wait, what?" I ask instead.

"You've had sex," Fredrik says slowly. "And now, you're pregnant."

"Oh, my God," I say.

"Does that stuff on your face sting? You just got really red," Andrew says.

"No, no. It's just when you said that—Fredrik? Are you listening? Could you stop chewing for one minute, please? Or, at least put the sandwich down?"

"You're being knocked up doesn't change the fact that I'm hungry," Fredrik says.

"FREDRIK!" I shout.

"What is the problem?" Fredrik asks.

"Everyone will know that I've had sex!"

Andrew's fist is in the air again. Fredrik bursts out laughing.

I continue, "*Everyone* means my mother. And *your* father, Fredrik. And, oh, God, Front Desk Bob."

"I suspected it all along," Andrew says.

I glare at both of them.

"This is so embarrassing," I say, looking over at Andrew.

"What, the shit on your face?" Andrew asks.

"Why are you still here?" I ask.

"It's lunchtime," Andrew says, offering me a sandwich. I accept. My secret is out. I might as well eat.

Later that night when we climb into bed, I turn to face Fredrik, instead of the wall, as I normally do.

"I'm beat," he says, smiling at me.

"All I did all day was eat," I say, laughing. "It's all so surreal. You wake up, take a test—and I am going to take another one tomorrow—and then, there it is, you're pregnant. And pregnancy means a baby and a baby means we're someone's mother and father and—Oh, my God."

"I'm sure we'll be *excellent* parents," Fredrik says. "Look how well we take care of Boo. It can't be that different."

"I said that to Meredith once and she got really angry. She said—and I quote—'Having a dog is like looking down a hallway, that leads to a door, that leads to a room, and in that room there is a dresser, and in that dresser, there is a drawer that contains a box, and if you can make it all out from the hallway—the room, the dresser, the drawer, and the box *inside* of the drawer, then, yes, you've had a glimpse of parenthood.' Or something to that effect."

"Does that mean you can't leave a baby in a crate with a chew-toy?"

"Probably not."

Fredrik turns to lie on his back.

"What?" I ask.

"It's exciting," he says up to the ceiling.

"But scary."

"But exciting."

"But scary. And it's change. I'm not good with change."

"But still, this is great news," he says.

"It is!" I shout a little too loudly. I'm giddy.

"We're ready for this."

"When Louisa said she thought we were ready, Meredith commented that no way in a *million years* can you even *begin* to prepare. I am pretty sure she said 'begin to prepare' instead of 'prepare'."

Fredrik turns back to me and places two fingers across my lips.

"Enough of Meredith," he teases.

I smile at him.

"I love you," I say.

"I love you, too."

"Maybe we can't prepare," Fredrik says.

"*Begin* to prepare," I correct him.

"And maybe we are nervous," he continues.

"I am," I whisper.

"But we'll be fine. I know it."

"If you say so." I laugh.

See? There's that confidence. Comes in handy.

He kisses me on the lips and we fall asleep, facing each other.

Chapter 3

"Make it a date! Don't pressure yourself, or your man, to go crazy on New Year's Eve if it isn't your style. An evening spent together, eating dinner or watching a movie, can be just as fun (and definitely more romantic) than hanging out with friends or a big crowd."
—From *Living Life* magazine, "How to Have a *Hot* Holiday."

I'm walking south, down Main Street, on my way to work. I'm stepping slowly, careful to avoid patches of ice and rushed shoppers. It's late afternoon and the sidewalk is crowded with people dashing in and out of stores to get last-minute provisions for New Year's Eve parties. We have no plans for the night. Fredrik and I typically don't celebrate New Year's because I'm usually working. (I'm on call when the rest of the world is off. Sort of like being a doctor, I suppose, except without the prestige, pay, and/or power to make life-and-death decisions. Maybe I'm more like an OR orderly.) But having low-key holidays hasn't been a big sacrifice for me because I'm not a big holiday person. Fredrik isn't either; he stubbornly refuses to acknowledge any event that has a greeting card associated with it. While his antiholiday stance is a logical extension of his contrarian nature, I secretly would like nothing more than to be festive, and now, finally with a baby, maybe I can be. This time next year, perhaps *I* will host the kid's party, which Meredith noted cannot start before three but must end by seven ("But the New Year starts at midnight," Louisa pointed out. "You don't get it, seven o'clock *is* my midnight," Meredith responded.).

I'm not a Scrooge—honestly, I'm not, no one *wants* to hate Christmas—I'm just on a holiday hiatus that started the first Thanksgiving after Dad died, when I was sixteen. Dad was killed in a multiple car pileup on the Capital Beltway, which began when another motorist suddenly slammed on his brakes. A curve in the Beltway had obstructed the driver's view of a long line of nearly idle cars. A few weeks after the accident, the *Washington Post* published a report on local highway safety. The series revealed that that portion of the Beltway had been designed that way *on purpose* to protect the natural habitat of the Flathead fish, which scientists had thought was near extinction. They were wrong; millions of them lived, undetected, apparently, in Tampa, Florida. To make matters worse, the local news stations picked up the story and for the week of Thanksgiving, we were bombarded with broadcasts about our "DEADLY HIGHWAY," some of which mentioned Dad—"I'm reporting live from the Connecticut Avenue exit, which, if you are not careful, may kill you. Only a few weeks ago, a forty-nine-year-old father of two . . ."

"Two and two" my dad always said—two parents, two kids, easily divided into two: Mom and Peyton, my younger sister, and Dad and me. That's how we'd play Monopoly, that's how we divided up Saturday chores: Mom and Peyton inside, Dad and me out. We mowed the lawn in the summer—I particularly enjoyed the precision of edging—and shoveled the walk in the winter. And when Mom and Dad came upstairs to tuck us in, Mom always went right to Peyton's room and Dad came straight to mine. He always smelled like laundry detergent. The first night after he died, I waited in the bed for him to kiss me good night. I didn't know how to do anything else. I waited for over a year before I realized I'd never get tucked in again, because, really, who wants to give that attention up? I never felt special after that.

Except in a bad, freakish way—because of how he died. It was so violent and random. When I closed my eyes, I could see the accident—my father in our car—and I saw him suffering. I saw him dying alone. I didn't talk about any of it with Mom, who seemed more comfortable soothing Peyton than soothing me—that was Dad's job, after all. When Mom wasn't with Peyton, she was immersed in a new cause: to convince the transportation agencies of Maryland, the District of Columbia, *and* Virginia to shut down the Beltway, which carried millions of cars around the city daily. One of the newscasts had dubbed her the Beltway Widow, a moniker she took to heart. She memorized all kinds of numbing statistics that she'd announce when I least expected it, like when I'd be standing in front of the fridge thinking about how empty it was—just containers of take-out, instead of a flank steak marinating for a family dinner—and then she'd start talking about *highway fatalities* and *government accountability*.

I preferred to just sit in my room and watch television. This is when I started to seek out reruns of sitcoms in earnest. Reruns because it meant I might have seen the episode with Dad ("That Theo—such a troublemaker!") and sitcoms, because I liked how neatly everything ended, in twenty-three minutes, no matter how serious the plotline. A young mother died? Get the two whacky uncles to move in and turn those frowns upside down—better yet, use cute twins! I watched TV all day and I slept with the set on. When the first Christmas approached, Peyton and I begged

Mom to take us away. Going through the motions of celebrating seemed impossible on both a theoretical and prac-
tical level (Who would put the tree on the car? Who would
devise the codes on the bottom of the packages that deter-
mined which gift belonged to whom? Who would shop for
Mom? *See, Daddy did all that.*). So Mom planned that
Christmas vacation to a warm, sunny, "News You Can
Use"-free destination.

   She chose Death Valley, California.

   The grim name was bestowed upon the desert by miners
who, attempting to reach the Gold Coast, lost loved ones,
livestock, and hope to the harsh terrain. "Good-bye, Death
Valley," they cried, when they finally escaped. "Hello, holiday fun," Petyon said when we arrived at the Furnace Creek
Inn, where we were issued pamphlets on the park's history.
"I read it's the hottest place on earth," Peyton said, after we'd
turned out the lights at eight o'clock because there was
nothing else at night to do—no TV, no phone. "I knew it!"
I replied. "We *are* in hell."

   It was a long two weeks. Subsequent holidays weren't
much better. And while Peyton and I bonded each Christmas
over Mom's general weirdness, we were happy to pursue
alternate holiday plans the minute they presented themselves (because whatever sadness you could effectively mute
during the year—through work, booze and/or Beltway
boycotts—came rushing back). And while Peyton could do
no wrong in Mom's eyes—she's driven, successful, a Rising Star at the State Department—I seem to consistently
cause her Great Worry. "I'm worried about you. Won't you
get frustrated being in a job that doesn't make the most of
your education?" *Um, no.* She always hated my job. But
then, sometimes I do, too—especially on New Year's.

   Oh, my God, what is that smell? Now, I'm walking on
Ryland, an alleyish side street that serves as the employee
entrance to the Grande. I descend the stairs to the base-

ment, where I encounter the full effects of the olfactory affront of tonight's " 'Auld Lang Syne' Extravaganza" special, Seafood Mariscada. My eyes are watering. *It's horrible*. It smells like wet dog.

Mrs. Torrez, the Honduran head housekeeper, and her deputies, Isabella, Carlotta, and Esperinza, stand in the hall. Mrs. Torrez looks warm, motherlike. I want to sit in her lap. She is teaching me Spanish.

"Buenos días, Gretchen, ¿Como es usted? ¿Cansado, no?"

"Soy bueno, gracias, Señora Torrez. Ah, casado? I don't *entiende 'cansado'."*

"Tired, little one. You look tired."

She puts her hand to my cheek. Carlotta points to me, tilts her head to the left, and rests her cheek on her folded hands.

"¡El oh, su marido ronca y le mantiene despierto!"

Carlotta fake-snores as Eliza, the only daughter of the hotel's owners, the Henry "Hank" Singletons, walks through the hall and greets us, resplendent in her headset (I'm sorry, do I work at Old Navy?) and an anonymizing black pantsuit. A recent graduate of the Wharton School, Eliza is the director of sales and catering. She is a blessing to her parents, ensuring a hassle-free retirement in Naples, Florida, but an annoyance to the entire hotel staff.

"Yes, I've got her. Repeat, I've got Gretchen," Eliza reports to the front desk. "Over. Señora Torrez, Carlotta, Esperinza, Isabella, *BUENOS DÍAS.*"

Eliza robotically gestures and raises the volume whenever she speaks Spanish. She turns to me and says, "Two potential clients are here to see you. They're seated in the Coolidge Library, enjoying Earl Gray tea, with our compliments." Eliza loves to dole out treats "with our (her) compliments," and remind the staff that we are in "the business of hospitality" as we "provide a memorable experience for our guests and *enjoy professional satisfaction for ourselves.*" (From the "Northampton Grande Mission Statement," created last summer, during a six-hour "brainstorming" session hosted by Eliza. I didn't contribute; I was busy consuming seven hundred Blue Peppermint Ice Cubes.) She hustles me toward the lobby, which is overflowing with white floral arrangements, in keeping with Eliza's black-and-white theme for tonight's event, which is the first in a series of events Eliza has planned to introduce the hotel to a more "upscale" audience.

I walk toward the library (just an area off the lobby) where two women in green "Scentsational" oxfords water plants. I smile at Char and Kate, who stand up from their seats at a faux-marble table.

"Gretchen! We came to see the hotel in action," Kate begins.

"Everything is lovely. *Lovely.* Isn't it, Kate?" Char adds.

"Would you like a tour? I could show you the ballroom," I offer.

"That would be lovely," Char says.

"Stop saying lovely," Kate whispers to Char. "It's driving me crazy."

I nod to Front Desk Bob, a recent graduate of Massachusetts State, who can recite *Old School* in toto, as I lead Char and Kate through the hallway leading to the ballroom, where the porters are piecing together the dance floor. Hundreds of black-and-white balloons hover at the ceiling, straining to be freed. The effect is supposed to be modern but it is utterly at odds with the decor of the room, which features a hunter green rug and wrought iron light fixtures as an homage to the colonials who settled Massachusetts.

"The room can accommodate up to two hundred guests, and we can arrange it any way you'd like. These are rounds, tables of ten, but we also have rounds of twelve and eight, and smaller cocktail tables. If you're thinking of creating a more intimate feel, we can also subdivide the room—maybe even set one long rectangular table? What did you have in mind? Let's start with time of year," I say.

"Char? I love the balloons. What do you think? Let's definitely do balloons."

"It's not a birthday party. I was thinking of something more refined."

While they debate the overall tone of their wedding, I gaze off to the middle distance, a trick I've honed after being privy to too many engaged couples' intimate conversations ("What do you mean you don't want a DJ? I feel like I don't even know you. DON'T TOUCH ME!"). After a few minutes, they remember I'm here. I reassure them that there's no hurry to decide anything. I give them a few hotel brochures and send them on their way. I hope Char and Kate don't look at our promotional materials too closely. While I love the Singletons, they preferred to barter with local service people rather than pay for anything outright, so when it came time to print new brochures, they got a friend of a friend of a friend to handle the pictures in exchange for wall space in our lobby. It wasn't the ideal trade. For one, the photographer rushed through the shoot and didn't notice that the same two employees appeared in every room he happened to be photographing (some kind of a race between the guys in Room Service) and for two, his specialty is portraits of pets and their owners, so we've got a poster-sized picture of a blind man and his parakeet greeting all of our guests.

I say my good-byes to Char and Kate, who apologize several times for not being "prepared." I reassure them that this is all *very* normal (Wedding planning is one of those once-in-a-lifetime events when you'd benefit from previous experience.) and do not share any of the harsh realities I refer to as the Truth About Weddings. Interestingly, the sexual orientation of the participants has no impact whatsoever on this phenomenon, because regardless of whom you're sleeping with, once you've set your sights on the "big day," a wave of irrationality will overcome you. It's as though you've been whacked over the head with a frying pan.

I myself experienced this firsthand, after I became engaged.

But let me back up, so you can see where all the trouble began. When Fredrik proposed, he and I had already been a couple for almost three years, although each of us has a slightly different method of counting. For me, "we" started on June 15, at our first meeting, when a water pipe burst at the Grande, and Stirling & Sons was called to fix the damage. The near cancellation of a two hundred-person-black-tie wedding reception I'd spent eighteen months planning—yes, *a year and a half*—made me curiously vulnerable to Cupid's strike. By the time he'd finished blow-drying the paint on the faux—everything in the hotel is fake—crown molding, I was wishing desperately that I could change into a better bra or, at a minimum, shine my brass name tag, in case passion should strike. Correction: in case passion should strike *him*. I was in for sure. I was entranced by his legs. He spent most of the night on a ladder, so his sculpted, tanned calves were level with my eyes and his casual, I carry-heavy-things-for-a-living look stood in contrast to the men I spent most of my day with, covered as *they* were in black polyester, iron-free uniforms. The repairs on the back of the house, the part of the hotel not seen by guests, continued during the party. I was all too happy to provide him with unlimited imported beers from the bride's top-shelf open bar while he worked.

Fredrik, however, does not sanction "dating" anniversaries. I discovered this the hard way, the first year we were together. I bought him a watch and had it engraved with a heartfelt passage: "Never the time and the place and the loved one all together." Before he had even slid a

finger under the flap of the understated, masculine wrap-
ping paper, he blurted, "What on earth is this for?" The
day ended without my receiving so much as a card. Hours
and hours of debate did not alter his view on the subject.
Today, if he's asked how long we've been together, he says
"two years." He does not mention, as I might, our dramatic
meeting, his then soon-to-be-ex-long-term girlfriend, her
confronting him about their future, and a nail biting period of uncertainty in month one; the first vacation in year
two; the wave of friends' engagements that Christmas; the
decision that marriage was not for me, it was just so pedes-
trian, and wasn't *Beauty and the Beast* having an open
casting call for the new season? never mind, I can't sing,
and, finally, in year three, the announcement that I'd like
to "see other people" (a bluff).

Thirty-nine hours and sixteen minutes later, he proposed.

As is typical, the proposal didn't go down exactly as I'd
imagined. I was at my desk at work when he called to tell
me I'd forgotten my "lunch" pack at home. We always
used air quotes around the word *lunch* because, despite
my best intentions, I often grazed on bits and pieces of it
during the morning so the food became more of a *supplement* to the lunch rather than a lunch (I failed to save
money, yet succeeded in gaining weight), so going without
the old snack pack for a day was hardly a tragedy. But he
insisted on driving it down. After an hour or so passed, I
grew tired of sitting at my desk, so I went to the vending
machine and bought some cookies. I was returning to my
desk, and was mid-chew, when I noticed him sitting in my
chair.

"You bought a snack?" he asked accusingly.

"Yes, I'm sorry—I forgot." My mouth was full.

"Clearly," he said, as he stood to go.

"What's the problem?" I asked.

"You've just eaten a cookie," he hissed.

"Yes, but I will eat again. I'm sure of it," I said, laughing.

"Forget it!" he shouted.

"What is wrong with you?" I asked.

He didn't answer. Instead, he stood up and started practically racing through the hallways of the hotel. I followed him. He didn't turn around—although he knew I was behind him—and he didn't stop walking until he was in the parking lot, at the truck. He still had the stupid pack on his shoulder. He looked ridiculous, trying to get the truck door open with the pack flying about. I ran to him and put my hand on his arm. He pulled away.

"Have you gone INSANE?" I shouted.

Fredrik paused, turned to me. He was sweating.

"Get in the truck," he ordered.

"OK," I said. I figured he was breaking up with me in response to the ultimatum (I usually assumed the worst—an emotional shortcut of sorts), and I took my time walking around the back of the truck. When I got to the passenger side door, he leaned across the seat to unlock it. But he wouldn't look at me. I climbed in. Then, we stared ahead (at the trash Dumpsters) in silence. We watched as the busboys came outside to sneak a cigarette, before the lunch rush began. I thought about how, if I wasn't with Fredrik, I could really embrace smoking—he hated it—*and I would be free to get lung cancer*. I winced. What would I do without him?

Fredrik turned to me. "I wrote you a letter," he said.

He opened the lunch pack and took out a piece of paper, torn from his sketchbook. He handed it to me. I opened it. It read, all caps:

DON'T DATE OTHER PEOPLE
DATE ME
MARRY ME

"I was worried you'd throw it away," he explained.

I laughed. I read it again. I started to cry.

"Yes!" I shouted. "I will marry you, Fredrik Stirling."

"Thank God," he said. "Because I've never been so nervous in my life."

We kissed and as the busboys hooted in the background, I felt a great sense of hope—something I'd not felt, ever, as an adult—a hope that the future would not only be OK, but good. A future that I was sure would start with the world's most perfect wedding because, unlike other brides-to-be, I was a wedding planning *professional*.

Of course, I was wrong. But anyone who has been married knows that. Though I was able to maintain excitement about my long-term future with Fredrik (and I don't care what the cynics say, it felt very different to be engaged, versus just dating), I quickly lost confidence in my ability to plan anything that would prove meaningful to anyone, as it involved facing two harsh truths: (1) my father wouldn't be there, and (2) my mother would. In fact, in no time Mom was turning *every conversation* about the wedding into referenda on my life.

"What do you mean no assigned seating?" she'd asked. "It's so hurly-burly."

"But place cards are too formal."

"A wedding is supposed to be a *grand* occasion."

"But we are not grand people."

"I guess if you'd stayed with that James from the Hill, this would be a *much* different conversation," she added. "You had so much more in common with him."

"No, Mom, I didn't. *You did*."

In the end, Fredrik and I decided to have a quick ceremony at the courthouse and a reception at our home. This made exactly no one happy because (a) Mrs. Stirling had *very* much wanted to host it (but I knew her doing so would make my mother absolutely miserable and I'd never hear the end of it); (b) my mother kept insisting it was not a "real" wedding, as a red-nosed priest had not blessed the union; but mostly (c) because it made me miss my dad all over again. A bride—even one wearing a Banana Republic suit down a three-row aisle—is supposed to have a father. Several viewings of the *Father of the Bride* confirmed this. Fredrik was great about it, he never asked "Why are you so sad?" because he knew. It's not just the death that's hard. It's the fact that I kept living, and Dad didn't come with me.

"Gretchen," Eliza says, jolting me back to reality.

"Yes?"

"You were daydreaming. Our guests are arriving. Please report to Station 4A."

I look at her blankly—I can't seem to keep our new way-finding system straight. In case you didn't know, way finding is a more upscale term for "signs."

"By the main entrance, please," she adds.

"Why don't we just call it the goddamn front door?" I ask as I take my place next to Front Desk Bob. "Why Station 4A?"

"It's all about the way finding, baby. Gonna get fucked up later?" he asks.

No matter the time of day, Front Desk Bob appears as though he just woke up *startled*. His black, thick, curly hair stays in place when he moves his head, which he does a lot, because he gestures with it. His eyes are perpetually bloodshot. He owns an endless supply of offensive T-shirts; his favorite, which he is wearing under his uniform, bears the slogan FRESHMAN GIRLS: GET 'EM WHILE THEY'RE SKINNY.

"If one more person says "way finding" to me, I'm going to scream."

"You're too uptight, man. Too uptight. Gotta drink. GOTTA POUND."

The arrival of a bus from the Hadley Senior Village—

their activity planner had purchased thirty or so tickets to tonight's event—puts us at full attention. Eliza, who has joined us, looks crestfallen as the riders disembark. When she announced the black-and-white theme, she'd described some party Truman Capote had for Katharine Graham in the sixties in great detail. By the looks of things, some of our guests would have been on the older side even back then. The men wear leisure suits and wide ties. The women sport elaborate corsages and are dressed to dazzle, with lots of sequins. All of them wear sensible shoes. Their excitement is infectious and my mood is immediately bolstered by their glee (and Eliza's corresponding horror). She wrinkles her nose as she catches a whiff of the antiseptic-smelling cloud that accompanies the group. I happily escort them to the ballroom.

Once it's clear that the event isn't a smash hit ("I thought we'd sell more tickets at the door; this is so disappointing," Eliza cried.) and I am able to confirm that at least one member on staff knew how to perform CPR (Dirty dancing is apparently appropriate for all ages.), I go back to my locker to collect my things. Mrs. Torrez, whose shift has ended, offers to give me a ride home. I accept. We walk out to her car, a maroon Maxima, and wait a few minutes for the engine to warm up. The rosary dangling from the rearview mirror is beige, and the beads are cracked. I want to touch them but they look too delicate. I gaze out the window. I see Eliza in the ballroom, shaking her head and mumbling to herself.

"Thanks so much for the ride, Señora."

"*De nada*, Gretchen. You need a car. ¡*El congelar*!"

Her breath is visible in the cold. My not having a car has come up with Señora before. I have explained to her that I *like* to walk everywhere—that's why I live in a small town. But to her, not having "wheels," as she sometimes refers to cars, is utterly anti-American. Mrs. Torrez spends a lot of her time chauffeuring her kids around—the mall, color-guard practice, and what not. She regularly scours the classifieds for used Jeep Cherokees, as her oldest feels strongly that she must, must, *must* have this exact car the minute she turns sixteen. Señora has told me, repeatedly, that you cannot have kids without a car and, wow, maybe she's right. My daughter can't be taking the bus to color-guard practice. Whatever that is.

A horn honks. There's Fredrik, in the truck, pulling into the hotel driveway. He opens his door and walks to the hotel, leaving the truck running. I roll down my window.

"Fredrik?" He turns toward me. "What are you doing here?" I ask.

He walks to the window. "Hello, Señora," he says. "I came to pick you up."

"Great," I say as I thank Señora.

"It's too icy for you to walk," Fredrik observes as we cross the parking lot.

"I know; that's why I asked Señora for a ride." I reapply my ChapStick.

"Andrew and I were worried about you," he says.

"There is nothing wrong with walking when you're pregnant."

"But not on ice."

"I'm not going to fall," I say, forgetting I'd had the same worry only hours ago.

"I'm sorry I came down here," Fredrik whines.

"OK, OK, yes—honey, *thank you for the ride*. Let's start over."

"It's too icy for you to walk," Fredrik says again, smiling.

I laugh. Fredrik is always one step ahead on matters of "operations," like travel. Initially I thought this impulse was strange, very bossy and controlling (Did it *really* matter if we were on time?). But that's not why he does it. He does it because he thinks he is making something easier for me. He doesn't want me to have to take the weather into account when I'm calculating travel time—not that I would, I cannot obsess equally about everything—he wants to do it *for* me. So I let him check the Doppler. And now I'm quite prompt.

Anyway, as Fredrik had noted (Northampton's traffic cameras are online; he has bookmarked the site.), the streets are empty and we make it home in record time. Once inside, I change into my pajamas and join Fredrik on the couch. After three minutes of watching "Dick Clark's New Year's Rockin' Eve" live broadcasts from New York and Los Angeles, both of which are hosted by "stars" from reality TV shows that I do not, on principle, watch (Why would I want to see people *like me* on TV? The whole idea behind television is to *escape reality*.), I yawn loudly and announce I'm going to bed. Fredrik turns off the TV and follows me up the stairs. We get into bed. I face the wall and he lies behind me with his arms around my waist. They quickly move to my breasts.

"Ow!" I yell.

"What?"

"That hurt."

"Sorry."

He moves his hands back to my waist. We're silent for a few minutes. He is pulling me toward him—closer, closer, closer. His arms are rubbing my legs.

"Whatever you think is happening here is not happening," I say.

"It's New Year's," he says.

"I thought you didn't acknowledge holidays. Besides, I'm tired."

"Not too tired to resist me."

I turn around to face him. He takes my cheek in his hands. Damn him! He knows I'm a sucker for that move. Doesn't matter.

"I think we should wait to talk to Dr. Blankley, first, honey. Just to be sure."

"Oh, right."

Fredrik yawns. I kiss him on the lips and I turn back around to the wall.

"Tomorrow I'm going to call Dr. Blankley to make an appointment," I begin. "Wait, tomorrow's New Year's Day. Her office will be closed. What's your schedule like on Tuesday? I have a menu-tasting but I don't remember if it's before or after lunch. I could probably do the morning. But it would have to be early. Maybe Wednesday is better. What's your schedule like on Wednesday?"

I pause and notice Fredrik's breathing has become a steady in-and-out, in-and-out; he's asleep. *I thought he wanted to have sex?*

"Fredrik?" I ask again. Silence. "Great. Tuesday it is."

Chapter 4

"You're not alone! Today's expectant dads want to be involved in every step of the pregnancy. By taking him with you to your prenatal appointments, starting a journal together or creating an intimate ritual of reading from this book, you will reaffirm your bond as a couple."
—From *Ready or Not, An Expectant Mother's Guide* (Week 7, page 34)

Today is the day of my first OB appointment but it's not with my usual doctor after all. When I called Dr. Blankley's office, I learned she is a GYN not an OB/GYN. Turns out the OB part is optional (Clearly, I need to pay more attention during *ER*.). I was so embarrassed that I hung up on the receptionist before I could ask her for a recommendation. I wasn't sure what to do next. I don't know any other OBs besides Meredith's and she has a *serious thing* for hers, Dr. Mitchell. Meredith talks about him a lot. As though he was some kind of god. "I'm not kidding you, Gretchen, he has the *softest* touch; you don't even feel the speculum," she advised me after a particularly, I don't know, "good" visit. Her obsession aside, Meredith did have an easy labor, perhaps owing to what she described as Dr. Mitchell's "awesomely low episiotomy rate." Louisa and I use this phrase sporadically, inappropriately, as a way of endlessly teasing Meredith. "What a pretty sweater," I'd say. Louisa would add, "*And look.* It has an awesomely low episiotomy rate." "I hate you," Meredith would say and laugh.

Anyway, after I realized that I cannot pronounce "obstetrics" (I practiced in the mirror.) and thus could not ask anyone else for referrals, I went ahead and made the appointment with Dr. Mitchell, which is why I find myself, now, sitting next to Fredrik, in his waiting room. The room is mauve with tasteful, if dated, wallpaper. Nine chairs line the perimeter, and of these, half are filled with patients or husbands. Fredrik takes a *Fly Fishing for Fun* magazine out of his back pants pocket and begins to read. I glance over at a table with assorted parenting magazines, all of which appear to feature articles about screaming infants ("Ten Tricks to Soothe Your Crying Baby" and "The Secrets of Your Baby's Wails"). I find a *Fit Pregnancy* and pick it up. I breeze through an article about "Looking Your Best Nine Months Through" and turn the page to a photo spread. Wow, these women do look good. This one is doing squats in a matching maternity workout outfit while she balances on a large yellow exercise ball. Hmmm. Forget it. That is so *not* happening.

I toss the magazine aside.

"Gretchen Stirling?" A young nurse in teddy bear–adorned scrubs is holding a clipboard, calling my name. I stand and she walks toward me, smiling. "Dr. Mitchell will be with you in a few minutes, but first, you need to fill out these forms—about your medical history. If you have any questions, the receptionist can help."

I sit back down next to Fredrik and review the form. My permanent record.

Onset of menorrhea
I was fourteen and in the ninth grade, new to

the Academy; I'd transferred from a more down-market parochial school. I was painfully self-conscious and grateful for the popular uniform-bastardizing technique: boy's boxers worn under our kilts. Surely, they hid my Maxi Pad (though probably placed undue emphasis on my butt).

Sexually Transmitted Diseases
Ah, no.

Smoking
I haven't smoked in—let me think. When is the last time I drank? Was probably Christmas Day. However, I didn't smoke then because Fredrik's parents were around and despite being thirty-two, I still think of them as being the "adults" and I didn't want to "get in trouble."

Alcohol
1–2 drinks / week
3–5 drinks / week
6–10 drinks / week
I round down to 1–2 drinks / week.

Illicit drugs
I never actually *paid* for the drugs I took in college, so negative on this one.

Family medical history
Hmm. Nope, no heart disease. No cancer. No diabetes.

I'm not sure how to describe my parents except to say that while they are (were?) relatively physically healthy, they are (were?) crazy, given their tendency to treat every aspect of their lives as some grand social experiment—an approach they concocted while getting their PhDs, Dad's in criminology and Mom's in economics, her major at Smith. For example, they prided themselves on being hip, liberal, smart-thinking people *but at the same time* they were practicing Catholics and thus wanted their daughters to experience a religious education. And the best Catholic school in D.C. was the snooty Ursuline Academy where money—not discussions of how the Vatican could eradicate world hunger by deaccessioning Raphael's *Stanze*— ruled the day. As a result, I was doomed to social failure. I was totally, one hundred percent out of it. I didn't know that when referring to Nantucket, you say "on," as in "I was *on* Nantucket." ("It's an island," Bethany explained.) And since I was never, ever, not in a million years going to get a credit card, not even for emergencies, because my father didn't *believe* in credit cards and paid for everything with a check he'd pull from a large three-ringed binder, I was forced to spend my free time in a variety of money-making schemes—including drafting submissions to *Reader's Digest* "Life in These United States" column—instead of doing my homework. Needless to say, I didn't do very well.

Hold on. I flip through the remaining pages of the questionnaire. Why aren't there any questions about Fredrik? Why doesn't anyone want to know about *his* past or current drug, alcohol, or tobacco use (some, some, none)? Or his medical history? This would be an oral recounting, though; no medical records exist for Fredrik, given his strict adherence to the first of the Stirling Family Guiding Principles: Weakness is for the Weak (Never mind the cast, just keep playing!). What about the remaining Stirling beliefs—The Less Said the Better; Paying Retail Is Giving Up; and A Recipe from the Back of a Soup Can Is As Good If

Not Better than One Found in a Cookbook—should I make a note of those in the margins?

I stand up to hand the clipboard back to the reception-ist. Fredrik and I are then led to a hallway with a small nook. The walls are covered with pictures of babies, all kinds of babies: tiny, raisinlike babies, porkers, sleeping babies, babies midscream. Some of the babies have red hair, some have weirdly long, black wisps; others are completely bald. There are babies in pairs and in threes, being held up for the camera by bleary-eyed parents in hospital gowns.

In the nook I see a scale and the nurse gestures to me to get on it.

"Each visit, we'll weigh you," she says.

AWESOME.

I step on, wishing I'd removed my bundling. It's 12 de-grees outside so I have layered as follows: T-shirt, an ox-ford, a cardigan, a large wool scarf wrapped jauntily around my shoulders, tights, and pants. My watch is a man's model, heavy, close to fourteen pounds.

"One hundred forty-two. Now, step down. There you go. Go ahead into the restroom now, and leave a sample. When you're done, come to Exam Room 3."

I enter the bathroom and lock the door.

I take the permanent marker and scrawl my name on a sterile plastic container.

I push my pants and underwear to my knees.

I open an antiseptic wipe—with my hands, not my teeth.

I wipe, front to back, three times to facilitate "sterile" collection.

I unscrew the top of the container while scooting over to the toilet.

I throw the used wipes away in a trash can and not the toilet.

I pee.

I pull up my pants and rearrange my outfit.

I vigorously wash my hands.

I exit the bathroom holding the sample, victorious. The cup is warm. The nurse smiles at me. Fredrik averts his eyes.

"You can leave that behind the little door there in the wall of the bathroom, and a technician will pick it up; no need to carry it out."

OK, then. Fredrik and I walk silently to the room. His eyes immediately take stock of the tools of the trade—the pipe cleaner Pap smear thing, a tube of K-Y Jelly, and speculums of all sizes, neatly arranged on a paper towel. For some reason, he starts taking his own blood pressure, *pump, pump, pump.*

"Mr. Stirling, have a seat. We'll start by taking your wife's blood pressure"—she nods toward the cuff and begins to remove it from his arm—"then blood for the lab. We'll test for hormone levels, STDs—all routine. The urine is examined for blood sugar levels."

Five needle pricks later I think I'm done. I'm ready to meet Dr. Mitchell—in his office, I guess—which is a nice, dignified way to start our relationship.

"Now, remove your clothes and step into this gown. Dr. Mitchell will be in shortly for your internal exam."

Shit.

Fredrik, who is not a chit-chatter by any stretch, starts making painful small talk. "She was nice," he says, which I take to mean as code for: *Will I have to look at your vagina?*

"Yeah." Code for: *God, I hope not.*

Knock knock.

The fabled Dr. Mitchell enters. He appears to be utterly average—dark-haired but balding, normal physique. *I'm not sure I get it*, I think. He shakes Fredrik's hand, introduces himself. Looks over my file. He takes a cardboard wheel out of his lab coat pocket and tells me, "You are about eight weeks, due September first."

I lie down on the table and Dr. Mitchell examines my breasts.

"They're sore," Fredrik says from behind me. *Oh, my God.*

Dr. Mitchell looks at me and says, "Breast tenderness, normal for pregnancy." He gets up, walks to the phone, and speaks into the intercom: "Beth, Room 3 please."

The nurse returns. Torture time.

I'm midexam when Fredrik's walkie-talkie beeps. "FRED-DDDDIE. Send lawyers, guns, and money."

Dr. Mitchell pauses. I know this because I see him, between my legs, with a headlamp on. I'm in no position to explain that it's Andrew, quoting a Warren Zevon song, their standard greeting.

"Could you turn that off?"

"Sorry," he says as he shoves it back in his pocket.

Dr. Mitchell resumes his work.

"Gretchen, can you scoot do~n? Your cervix is hard to see."

"Is that bad for the baby?" Fredrik asks.

"It's an anatomical quirk, Fredrik," I hiss.

"Not to worry. Everything looks great. Time for the sonogram."

Nurse Beth turns on a machine and slips a condom over a long wand. Where is *that* going? Fredrik walks over to the window, not wanting to wait to find out.

"It's a bit early," Dr. Mitchell is saying, "but I like to try for a heartbeat. This is your uterus," he explains.

"Oh," I say, wondering how it is we are all conversing normally, despite the presence of an object that in other circumstances would be considered a "sexual aid."

"How long have you been in this office?" Fredrik asks, his back to us. "You've got a great view."

I'm considering how it is that my husband has morphed into a complete idiot when I hear it—like an echo of a pulse, distorted, underwater. Fast. Dr. Mitchell points to the screen. I look closely; it is tiny, beating.

"Dad?" Nurse Beth says to get Fredrik's attention. "Want to take a look?"

"At what?" Fredrik's voice cracks.

"The *baby*," the nurse says.

Fredrik tears himself away from the captivating Northampton skyline and walks over to the screen and squints. "What's that?"

"It's your baby's heart. See?" Nurse Beth says, pointing.

"Wow," Fredrik responds. He looks down at me. He inches closer to the monitor. "That's our baby?"

"Yes. Good heartbeat, too. Nice and strong," Dr. Mitchell answers.

"Nice and strong," Fredrik repeats. He kisses my forehead.

"Any questions?"

"No," I answer.

Fredrik coughs into his hand.

"Just one, Dr. Mitchell," Fredrik begins.

Dr. Mitchell and I are silent. Fredrik looks at me and raises his eyebrows. *Oh, my God, he wants me to ask this man about sex*. Code for: *I'm horny?*

"Um yes, uh," I stammer. "Dr. Mitchell. Is it, I was just wondering, or really, Fredrik was, what I mean to say is, we both wanted to know if we can have um, intercourse."

"Yes. But if you have any bleeding after, which can occur, give the office a call. Usually nothing to worry about. Most women don't have a problem."

"Great!" Fredrik says, a little too enthusiastically.

"See you in a month, then," he says, as he leaves the office.

"That was fun," I say to Fredrik.

"I'll go get the truck," he says, laughing, leaving me alone in the room.

I mop myself up with one hundred scratchy paper towels, make another appointment with the receptionist and head out to the front of the building, where Fredrik is idling in the truck. I tap on the window; the passenger side door is locked. Normally, he'd just unlock the door. But he surprises me and gets out of his seat and helps me in. Once inside, I fidget with the glove compartment. I find a black nylon CD holder, with the disks in alphabetical order, a first aid kit, some rope, a flashlight, and an up-to-date owner's manual, with each oil change noted in the same black ballpoint pen. Hmm. I wonder if he will start keeping raw meat in here now that he has proven himself to be a complete and total Neanderthal.

"What did you think of Dr. Mitchell?" Fredrik asks.

"I liked him. I'm sure *we* made an excellent impression," I snort.

"When is the next appointment?"

"I've got to call," I lie. Code for: *You ain't coming with me, buddy.*

"I'm getting busy at work," he says. Code for: *Don't worry, I don't want to.*

"I'm sure we'll work it out," I say.

Chapter 5

"Can't keep your eyes open? Fatigue is a commonly experienced symptom of the first trimester. Stay rested by retiring to bed early and sleeping late. Nap during the day if you can. Remember, there's nothing in the world more important than the work your body is doing."
—From *Ready or Not, An Expectant Mother's Guide* (Week 9, page 54)

"Gretchen. Gretchen. GRETCHEN! Wake up."

"What time is it?"

"Eight thirty," Fredrik says.

"I don't have to meet the girls until eleven. Let me sleep."

"Your mother is on the phone."

"Tell her I'll call her back—"

"I did. Yesterday. And the day before."

"I can't talk to her right now."

"You always say that."

I clear my throat and pick up the phone. "Hello?"

"Have you spoken with your sister?" Mom starts.

"No." I yawn.

"She is up for another promotion. Can you believe it? I wonder if there will be a ceremony."

"Can I call you back?"

"Why?"

"I just woke up. I need to get ready for work."

"You were still asleep? I've been up since four this morning. Why would he wake you? I told him not to." *On and on.* Finally, I hang up.

Mom always calls Fredrik "him." And to my knowledge, Fredrik has never called my mother by her name, Faye Fox. She is "f-squared"; or the old standby, "your mother," as in "Your mother keeps calling, why don't you just talk to her?" Mom is a communications-assault expert; she makes the most of any and all available methods (e-mail, FedEx, UPS, USPS, cell phone, work phone) to reach me. She is always going on about "how hard it is" to get in touch with me. It's not hard at all, it's just that I don't want to talk to her. Because if I stayed on the phone for even one more second, I will get sucked into some long conversation—possibly about relocating my father's grave, which she threatens to do every year or so. My theory—actually Louisa and Meredith's theory (Fredrik lost interest in analyzing Mom long ago.)—is that this makes her widowhood a more urgent, more current matter. I'm sure she's thinking the *Post* would want to do a profile (Maybe they'd send a photographer, too!) to answer the burning question: "*Whatever happened to the Beltway Widow?*" (Answer: She is resting comfortably with Helen Hunt.)

I turn over in bed, trying to get comfortable. I want to go back to sleep but I can't; my mind is bursting with images of how Mom will react to my pregnancy. Will she want to call a press conference? Would anyone in his or her right mind attend? Crap, no way can I sleep now. Might as well get up and face the day.

At the Joint, I notice two things before I open the door. The first is that several Smith students have stolen "our" table, so Louisa and Meredith are in the back, near the

bathrooms (not an altogether bad thing, given my new fre-
quency of use). The second is that Meredith is clapping
and jumping up and down, which is most unlike Meredith
because she has huge breasts, even when not pregnant.
After she had Ryder, her boobs were OUTRAGEOUS.
And when Louisa and I got a peek at her nipples—she was
in the awkward, new-to-breast-feeding phase and her shirt
was always stuck up in her bra—we nearly died. They
were bizarrely large, tribal-like. Now Meredith is taking
books from the small wooden table between their two
deep-cushioned purple chairs and handing them to Louisa,
one by one. Meredith's freckled cheeks are flushed red
with excitement. Her blonde hair, which has become
curlier with each pregnancy (another e-mail tidbit), is in a
bun and tied with a pencil. "I bet you're wondering where
Ryder is," Meredith shouts at me.

I take a chair from another table and sit down. I had
not, in fact, wondered. God, I'm horrible. Will I lose track
of my child? Correction, daughter?

"Where is he?" I ask.

"My in-laws have him. You will so learn to love your
in-laws, Louisa."

I take a seat. Meredith is handing Louisa *Ready or Not*.

"This was by far my favorite. The authors, a husband
and wife, are both doctors. But they get the emotional
stuff, too."

I raise an eyebrow.

"Tell her, Louisa," Meredith says.

"Meredith guessed," Louisa says. "I'm pregnant."

"Can you believe it, Gretchen? Isn't this wonderful?"

"Oh, my God!" I shout.

"Turns out, we didn't need to try. I didn't even know I
was late!"

"Oh. My. God!" I shout again. "How many weeks are
you?"

"I'm almost eleven," she answers as she cocks her head to the left and squints at me.

"Now, Gretchen, we should talk," Meredith says.

"About how misery loves company?" I laugh. I take Louisa's hand and squeeze it. "I'm so happy for you." *Why do I feel so emotional?*

Meredith starts in, "I know I complain, sometimes, a lot, but honestly, it's the best thing I've ever done, which is not to say I'm good at it, but I—" her voice cracks. She takes a deep breath. "Gretchen, all I can say is you must—"

"Have sex tonight," Louisa interrupts.

I ignore Louisa's demand. "Tell me everything. When did you take the test? How many did you take? What did Jason say? Have you told work? Who's your doctor?"

"Dr. Mitchell, of course," Louisa says.

"And I'm OK with that," Meredith says, wiping her eyes with a tissue.

Louisa and I laugh.

"*I am,*" Meredith insists. "I understand that he has other patients."

"Why did you want to know how many tests I took?" Louisa asks. Without waiting for an answer, she continues. "You're pregnant, aren't you?"

"No."

"Yes," she insists.

"Why would you think that?" Meredith asks.

"Nobody counts by weeks unless they're pregnant," Louisa declares.

"They don't?" I ask.

"That's a very good point," Meredith observes.

"ADMIT IT!" Louisa shouts. "YOU'VE HAD SEX!"

The Smith students look at us. No doubt they are thinking that we are too old and too unfashionably dressed to be having "*Let's stay up all night long because I've never been as turned on as I am right now*" sex. And maybe they're

right, because at this point in your life, the point at which
you are supposed to be starting a family, you don't "screw,"
you start telling your doctor you want to have INTER-
COURSE.

"Stop shouting," I whisper.

"Why?" Meredith asks. "We have nothing to be embarrassed about. It's perfectly natural. The Fulsasi clan of
Africa celebrates—"

"I'm pregnant," I say, desperate to avoid one of Meredith's lectures.

Louisa smiles at me. "I guess this means you're NOT a
superspecial virgin."

"It did not happen while I was *in costume,*" I joke.

"This is incredible," Meredith says, reaching out for
both of our hands, tears in her eyes. "We are all going to
have babies the same age. In the beginning a few weeks
will feel like a lot because so *much* happens developmen-
tally. But when they get older they'll be in the same class
unless the county changes the cutoff date for kindergarten.
Anyway, they'll be best friends, I'm sure of it. Like us."

"Like us," I say.

"Like us," Louisa adds.

Just then, Louisa's cell phone rings. "Hello? Yes, I feel
fine, honey. Stop worrying. No, no—listen, you'll never
believe who else is pregnant." Louisa winks at me.
"Gretchen. I know, wait, hold on." She hands the phone
to me. "He wants to talk to you."

"Hello?"

"Gretchen—tell Freddie that I always knew his boys
could make it uptown."

"Um, right. Thanks. Congratulations to you, too." I
hang up.

"What did he say?" Louisa asks.

"Something about 'his boys,' " I answer.

Meredith chuckles, adding, "I should warn you—husbands get this weird 'I am man, I can procreate,' thing going. Alan was insufferable."

Meredith thumps her chest and Louisa laughs.

A woman then enters the Joint, pushing a double stroller. She is sighing loudly and grunting a lot, trying to get through the door. After a few seconds, she is in. But several clueless Smithies block her path to the counter—there is an awkward standoff. Meredith stands up, walks over, and moves a chair out of the way. The mom says, "Thank you. It's so hard with a double stroller."

"I bet," Meredith replies. "I can barely maneuver my single. Do you like yours? I am in the market for a good one. I'm due with my second in July."

"How many months apart will your kids be?"

"A little under two years."

"That's a good break. These two are eleven months apart and my third is due in June."

"Wow, well, um, congratulations," Meredith stammers.

Meredith returns to our table looking deflated.

"I've just lost *another* hand of pregnancy poker," Meredith says.

"What?" I ask. "What's that?"

"Pregnancy poker. The game?"

Louisa and I look at each other and then at Meredith. We shake our heads.

"A woman with two kids, under two, less than a year apart, with a third on the way? She trumps me big-time. I only have one child."

"I don't understand," Louisa says.

"The more young kids you have, the closer in age, *that's* your hand."

"You're making this up," I say.

"I'm serious. I've played it at baby showers," Meredith insists.

I try to remember Meredith's baby shower but cannot

due to some unfortunate overserving (Louisa and I hosted and we were very, very nervous.). But I think I'd remember if we'd played a card game. I want to confirm this (Really, how drunk was I?) but cannot speak. There is something in my throat. I need to burp. My mouth is watering; I feel something come up in my throat. I've got to spit! But where? In a napkin? I leave the table and run to the Joint's bathroom. I'm spitting, spitting into the toilet—no relief. I hear Meredith and Louisa approaching. They knock and proceed to open the door, which I didn't have time to lock.

"G?" Louisa asks.

"*Nausea*. The term 'morning sickness' is a misnomer, as pregnancy-related nausea can strike at any time of the day or night," Meredith reads from *Ready or Not*.

"Helpful," I say as I dry heave.

"What have you eaten today?" Meredith asks.

"Nothing, really," I answer. Thank God this toilet is clean.

"No wonder," Meredith says.

She tucks my hair behind my ears. I have a flash of her doing this in college and then, a memory of my own mother comforting me when I was six or so, and suffering through a bout of the stomach flu. I'd wept when I realized I'd miss the Ice Capades.

I stand up and throw some water on my face. "I look awful," I say.

Louisa remarks that since we're all in here, we might as well go to the bathroom. We each take a turn on the toilet and then walk back to our seats. Louisa pulls a peanut butter and jelly sandwich and some crackers from her bag.

"Jason calls this my survival kit. Here—have it. You'll feel better if you eat. I keep food on my bedside table, at my desk, and in the car."

"That's a good idea," I say. I take a bite of the PB&J. It is *delicious*.

"By the way, is it normal to feel this tired?" Louisa asks.

"Yeah—it's like all-consuming fatigue," Meredith adds.

We stand up to go and each of us, in turn, yawns.

"Definitely one of those days when my biggest accomplishment will be staying awake," I joke.

We laugh and leave the Joint together. Louisa, Meredith, and I partake in an awkward group hug and giggle. I feel so lucky. Lucky to have my friends going through this with me.

Louisa's phone rings; it's Jason again. "I'm leaving now. I promise. Yes, I *know* I said that ten minutes ago," she says as she walks toward her car arm in arm with Meredith.

"Bye," I shout.

I smile at an older woman who is walking past me. Suddenly, I feel a toxic wave laced with peanut butter roll through my stomach. I burp.

"Excuse me," I say quietly.

"Excuse *me*," she responds, shaking her head.

Chapter 6

"Not tonight, honey! It's true; sex when you're pregnant isn't going to be the same. But we'll let you in on the best-kept pregnancy secret: There's a chance you'll find sex even more pleasurable than you did before. Some women experience multiple orgasms for the first time."
—From *Ready or Not, An Expectant Mother's Guide*
   (Week 11, page 104)

It's Valentine's Day, the single-worst holiday in the food-and-beverage industry. It's not a great day in the Stirling household either. Without fail, I spend the days leading up to Valentine's vacillating between accepting Fredrik's refusal to endorse "Hallmark holidays" and harboring a tiny but persistent belief that this year he will put a canary diamond on my English muffin. The reality is, he is *much* better when unprompted. He likes surprises, like buying a wallet I'd admired in a store window and hiding it in the refrigerator, so I'd discover it when pulling out the orange juice. Early this morning, when Fredrik made "the moves," I doubt he even knew it was Valentine's Day. When I protested that I wasn't in the mood, he suggested we "do something else." Meredith warned Louisa and me that *this* might happen—this being the dreaded sexual advance.

As I understand it, I can take one of several approaches:

- Do it. This is off-limits if I'm on pelvic rest or have a cerclage (sewing up a cervix to prevent premature labor because it's "incompetent" or weak and, yes, that is the medical description for the condition).

- "Do something else" (for him). God, can you imagine with the gagging? Anyway, Meredith lectured Louisa and me in her best, most stern Ryder's Mommy voice that oral sex on a pregnant woman is not permissible—there is a medical reason but I forget exactly what it is. Since I don't like it, I didn't care.

- Watch him. This is a low-commitment kind of "intimacy," in that it is not at all intimate. When I mentioned this to Meredith, she replied, "That's the point."

- Wish him well; short of cheating on me, Fredrik's free to do what he wants.

I'm leaning toward the latter. I feel so gross. I took stock of myself on the walk to work this morning. I noticed that my powder blue "Stop Winter in Its Tracks" Thinsulate coat, bought by my mother-in-law during a Christmas in July "seconds" shopping spree in Freeport, exaggerates my middle pudge. I'm ghostly pale—think Helena Bonham Carter suffering from consumption—and my mouth is permanently open, as my nasal passages are blocked. I've got circles under my eyes despite nearly fourteen hours of sleep last night. I also look like a bag lady; my purse is overstuffed, packed with the day's essentials—saline nose drops, tissues, Blistex, anti-motion sickness wristbands, three PB&Js, breath mints, and a bottle of ginger ale.

As soon as I get to my locker at the hotel, I realize I need to fix my makeup so I can be presentable for a final contract review for an interfaith, same-sex wedding reception wherein I must negotiate with the couple and their mothers. I sneeze as soon as I hit the lobby; it's bursting with red flowers of all varieties except roses ("Roses are so down-market," Eliza had said. Is she clueless or what?). At a table I find the brides, their mothers, a priest, and a rabbi; they are seated close enough for their legs to touch. The men stand, offering their hands. I shake, smile, and sit, waiting, clutching my clipboard. I cannot fathom why they'd be taking part in a discussion of our cancellation policies.

Bride A begins: "Laura and I have brought Rabbi Gold-berg and Father Flynn to ensure our reception honors our collective religious and cultural identities."

I nod in agreement and make a mental note: no garter toss. An hour later, we've decided Father Flynn will bless the meal, which will be kosher-style (that is, traditional Jewish dishes but not prepared in a kosher kitchen) and served after sundown, but before the Hora, in which both mothers will be lifted in chairs (not the fathers, as Bride B's has vertigo). The head table will consist of immediate family, which is defined as: the brides; Bride A's former partner, who is the biological mother of seven-year-old twin boys whose biological father is Bride A's brother; and the brides' remaining siblings, parents, stepparents, stepsiblings, and one half sister. The table centerpieces will acknowledge the families' Russian and Cuban heritages; the china, crystal, linens, etc., will be provided by *yada, yada, yada*. I need a bathroom.

"I'm so glad I was able to meet you," I say, hoping this will signal that the meeting simply must end. It does. Nonetheless, by the time I see the group to the front door, I have to pee so badly I half-walk, half-run across the lobby to get to the bathroom. *Thank God,* I think when I finally get to the stall. Back at my desk, I'm bored. Eliza's got some people in her office—lots of random meetings lately—

thereby preventing me from doing anything worthwhile, like making a personal call. I'm really, really good at making personal calls from work (e-mail and instant messaging are fine, but why not use the damn phone every once in awhile?). It's a talent. My advice to those who wish to learn:

- Place the **Personal Call** to a person who can follow a conversation despite being put on hold repeatedly for indeterminate amounts of time.

- Ensure that the *caller* and *callee* have similar shorthand. For instance, "Going forward, we should collectively ideate" must be obvious to both parties as meaning "We can plot revenge later, over Cheetos and a box of wine."

- Prioritize your **Personal Calls.** Repairing your relationship with your mother should take a backseat to discussing the new cover of *Star* magazine.

"Gretchen?" Eliza stands at my desk.

"Yes?"

"I want you to meet Jeremy Wilson, of Concorde Consulting." I stare at the guy. He is young, maybe late twenties, and fresh-looking. He is not wearing a wedding ring. Hmm. I absentmindedly put my hand down my shirt. Eliza looks at me, aghast. I pretend to fix my bra strap. "Your guest is here," she says. "Why don't you take Jeremy with you?"

"What guest? Oh, right, I know who it is," I lie. "Ready, Jeremy?"

I grab my composition notebook. Neither Jeremy nor I speak as we walk; I take a circuitous route, out of our basement office to a hallway that leads to the underground garage. I open an unmarked door to Room Service, nodding to Carlos, who is folding a stack of white linen napkins, and Jeremy and I hop on the ancient staff elevator up to Reservations. The two "reservationists" are seated in ergonomically correct chairs, as stipulated by union regulations, and wear headsets to ensure they are "standing by now, ready to serve you." I make a point to say hello to each of the middle-aged women because you never know when you'll need access to the hotel's 1-800 number.

We arrive in the lobby to find Meredith. I thought we were meeting for lunch at Thornes Mall, not here. Meredith has Ryder in some kind of elaborate backpack, the straps of which accentuate her chest. Front Desk Bob can barely contain himself. Ryder has a tumbler of Cheerios, which he is arranging in Meredith's hair.

"Hello, Meredith," I begin, hoping that the use of her name conveys the professional nature of our relationship to Jeremy. "This is Jeremy. He is a consultant," I say.

Meredith offers her hand to Jeremy. "What is your specialty, Jeremy?"

"Cost reduction," he answers.

"Right," Meredith says, looking at me as if to say *I understand you may be the "cost" to which Jeremy is referring.* "Gretchen, I apologize. My sitter canceled but I didn't want to miss our appointment."

"Jeremy, will you excuse us? We're going off-site to discuss a birthday party for Ryder. Hello, Ryder," I say, tousling his hair.

"OUT!" Ryder screams. "ME OUT!"

"We'd better get going. You know how kids are, Jeremy," Meredith says.

"Sure," he says, though I suspect this is the closest he has ever been to a child.

"I'm sorry for the confusion," I say.

Jeremy walks away toward the empty Front Desk since

Bob has disappeared into the back. Jeremy rings the bell and takes a stopwatch from his pocket. He watches it until Bob returns to the counter and offers to help him.

"Louisa told me to meet you here," she whispers. "I'm sorry."

"Please—don't worry about it. I didn't know that guy would be here."

"Are you worried?" she asks.

"Only about the ease with which I can lie," I laugh.

Fifteen minutes later, Meredith, Louisa, and I are shopping in the Thornes Mall, at the shoe store. Louisa and I wear our improvised "transitional" outfits. The genius behind the HELFPUL HINT to "use rubber bands to accommodate an expanding waistline" assumed, wrongly, that my ass and thighs have remained as is, pre-pregnancy. WRONG. I've gained about four pounds, but in all the wrong places. I'm in vintage (circa 2003) Gap pants, black with an elastic waistband. Underneath, my body-shaping opaque tights are growing tighter by the minute. My white oxford is stretched a bit over my breasts and the lace of my bra is irritating my sensitive nipples (Earlier, I thought it was sexy—now it's just annoying.). Louisa is tugging down the waist of her "fat" jeans, under her stomach, and her black sweater is riding slightly higher in the front than it should. Frankly, we've looked better. Worse, we're not even comfortable.

"What's this called again?" Louisa asks, pointing to a brown velvet shoe.

"A 'kitten' heel. What about soft cheeses?" I ask.

"Right—no soft cheeses. Do you think our feet will grow?" Louisa is a size 10.

"Yes, they will," Meredith answers.

"No, no, no," Louisa cries.

"Is it pasteurization-related?" I ask as I take a knee-high bone-colored leather boot with a five-inch heel from the display and peer into it, assessing the width—can I get my calves in?—and put the boot back on its Lucite holder. It falls twice so I drop it gently on the floor.

"No, listeria. A 'kitten' heel? Are you leaving that there?" Meredith asks.

"I can't get it to stay. What the hell is listeria?" I cry.

"Here, let me put this back. The elderly, pregnant, et cetera, are more susceptible—" Meredith starts.

"WAIT," I interrupt, "you forgot to give me the recipe for the organic do-it-yourself acne mask. I need it—my skin could not be worse."

"Do pregnant women wear boots?" Louisa asks Meredith.

"Sure, some do." Meredith is getting impatient.

"I can't concentrate. Is that normal? Today I had this bridal party"—I tilt my head toward a sneaker-mule combination and I raise my eyebrows. Louisa nods approval. I then make eye contact with a shoe salesman, point to the shoe and hold up seven fingers, all the while talking— "and I tuned OUT while making the list of crap I need to do to honor their, and I quote, 'collective identities.' They're focused on all the wrong things—will their announcement appear in the *New York Times* or should they keep their names professionally? But what about what really matters, like matching the napkins to the bridesmaids' dresses?"

"I don't know how you deal with these people," Meredith says.

"Argh, I need to go to the bathroom, again." Louisa laughs.

Louisa literally runs out of the store, toward the bathroom.

"For once, *I* don't have to go," I say, proudly, right before I realize I probably should go. But I'm too tired.

"I'm going to go pick up Alan's Valentine's Day gift downstairs. Come with me?" Meredith asks.

"No, I'll wait here for Louisa," I say and I flop down on the couch.

"Fine, I'll be right back," Meredith says.

The camel suede couch is deep and comfortable; if they had one in my size, I'd like to buy one. A woman pushing a stroller with twins stops at the store window. Twins, oh, a two of a kind! Or is it a pair? Who cares? I'm so tired I close my eyes.

"GRETCHEN!" Louisa's voice is shaky.

"What? What's wrong?" I look around. How long have I been sitting here?

Louisa stands before me, her face blotchy and red. She has her cell phone to her ear, kept in place with her shoulder, while she digs through her purse for a tissue. I can hear the *beep beep* of the automatic redial; there's no cell signal inside the store.

"I'm spotting and I have terrible, ouch! Cramps."

"Like period cramps?"

"No, no—worse, oh, my God. It hurts."

"Let's get you out of here," I say, putting my arm around her.

Where is Meredith? I have no idea what to do. I walk Louisa out of the mall and to the curb so she can get a cell signal. She is hunched over in pain. In a matter of seconds, Louisa has Dr. Mitchell's office on the phone and spits out replies to the nurse. In rapid order, she is on with Jason, her sister, and her mother. Her arm is wrapped in mine and I stand with her, my body ricocheting with her silent sobs. We stand there for a few minutes and then Jason arrives, idles the car and comes around to her, arms outstretched, and guides her to the passenger seat. I reach to open the back door, but Louisa won't look at me. I stay where I am. They leave without a word. I can't move. What do I do now?

My cell phone rings and it scares me half to death.

It's Meredith. "Where are you? I'm back at the shoe store."

"Come outside," I plead, near tears.

Meredith and Ryder join me on the curb.

"What's wrong? Where's Louisa?" she asks.

I tell her what's happened.

"Was it dark blood? Was it enough to soak a Maxi Pad in an hour?"

"I didn't ask. Or know to ask," I answer. "What does this mean?"

"It could be nothing. Spotting during pregnancy isn't unusual. And she's had a sonogram. Once you've heard the heartbeat, the rate of miscarriage is much lower."

"Oh," I say, glad that Meredith has been through this before.

"Dr. Mitchell will see her and tell her to go home and rest and that will be that."

Ryder starts to cry.

"Ryder, please, honey, calm down," Meredith says. "I should go—it's almost one o'clock and I still need to go to Higgers. If Ryder falls asleep before I can nap him in the crib, the rest of my day will be shot."

"Please don't go," I say.

"She's going to be fine, G, don't worry."

"If you say so. But call me if you hear anything."

"Yes, and you, too, call me."

We hug and Meredith walks up Main Street. I head back toward the hotel. I hate this time of year. Christmas is over. The snow is no longer quaint—it's dirty and annoying. Since it is dark at like four o'clock, everything looks bleak and lonely for most of the day. Valentine's Day isn't turning out to be much of a reprieve.

Nine hours later, I've read everything in my pregnancy books about miscarriage. There isn't much, really. It's more common than I realized—happens to one in four women or something—but they don't say how to know if it will happen to you or what to do to prevent it or anything *useful*. I'm in the window seat of the bedroom, in flannel pajamas, slathering Vaseline on my irritated waist. Fredrik is in bed, reading. I look out toward Louisa's. Both cars are parked in the driveway; the lights are out and I know the worst. No phone call to assure me otherwise. Where can I get more information? I need to talk to *someone*. I decide, unwisely, to try the Internet. I know how to do this because Louisa works—I'm not sure exactly what this means— "online."

I traipse downstairs to the kitchen. The dishwasher is clanking. *Whirl, clack, whirl, clack.* I go to the computer and the screen comes alive with a touch of the keyboard; it's already on. Fredrik's been using it. I close the following pages: Travelocity—price shopping for our tickets to D.C. next month (Isn't this the right thing to do? I always end up trying to do the right thing with Mom; invariably I regret it.); Treecyle—how to find and reuse wood, an "entrepreneur's guide;" Epicurious—high-protein meals that can be prepared one or two days in advance; The Note—a political newsletter; Psychology Today—Join Our Memory Boot Camp Today!

I type in "pregnancy" in a search box and get links to pregnancy and baby-magazine sites, an article about stem-cell research and pornography. I somehow make my way to message boards, where women tell of their struggles with fertility and miscarriage. I'm hysterical in minutes, which exacerbates my congestion.

Climbing the stairs back to my room, I run into Fredrik, who is shirtless, wearing only flannel pajama bottoms. His nearly hairless, lithe chest is level with my eyes. I look up.

"I'm going to bed," I say, my voice cracking.

"Honey, please don't assume it's bad news."

I throw my arms around his waist; the force of my body

pushes him backward. He steadies himself and I bury my face in his chest, crying.

"Come on, let's get you into bed," he says.

Fredrik leads me into our room and tucks me in on my side. He then climbs in beside me, and pulls me close. He's going to be a good father, I think; I never noticed how well he takes care of me. I close my eyes, hoping for sleep, but all I can think of is how worried I am for Louisa and, I'm embarrassed to admit, for myself.

"What if I have a miscarriage?" I ask.

"Try not to get upset over something you can't control."

"I hate when people say that. Not having control is exactly what I worry about. If I had control, I'd just prevent it from happening," I say as I start to cry. I take a deep breath and continue, "You don't understand—it's all abstract to you."

"No, it's not."

"It's not your body."

"But it is my baby, too." Fredrik squeezes me tighter. "I have a confession to make."

"What?" I ask.

"I bought the baby—our baby—something."

"You did?"

"Do you want to see it?"

"Yes."

Fredrik gets out of the bed, turns on the light. He goes to the closet and pulls a brown paper bag from a stack of dark blue Carhartt T-shirts. He pulls out something wrapped in plastic and then takes out a white shirt. It's tiny.

"What is that?" I ask.

He places it over his chest. It's a onesie and it reads: HOLD ME.

I burst out laughing. "Where did you get that?"

"I saw it—at a baby store. I couldn't help myself."

"Even though it's a holiday?"

"Even though it's a holiday."

Fredrik gets back into bed, chuckling to himself.

"I love you," I say. "I can't help it."

"I love you, too, then."

"No matter what."

"Yes."

I close my eyes and then I remember: he is still holding the onesie.

Chapter 7

"Make it memorable! Announcing your pregnancy to your family is just the beginning of a lifetime of love between the old and new generations. Just sit back, relax and enjoy the attention."
—From *Ready or Not, An Expectant Mother's Guide*
   (Week 14, page 122)

"After Mom picks us up, Peyton is coming over for dinner," I explain to Fredrik, who is crammed uncomfortably into his seat, during minute sixty-two of our seventy-five-minute flight to D.C.

"We are beginning our descent into the nation's capital. The local time is quarter after three. It's an unseasonable 57 degrees today, but breezy with a bit of cloud coverage," the captain announces. Earlier, he'd introduced himself as "Captain Robert."

"I don't want to know his name. But I would like to know why there is no food on this flight. Or *air*," I complain.

I'm in the middle seat; Fredrik's on the aisle and a filthy teenaged boy is by the window. I can't stand the smell of him. I twist the fan above me and then a blast of air hits Fredrik in the face.

"Quit playing around with that."

"I'm so hot. I need to go to the bathroom."

"Again?"

"Dr. Mitchell told me I should walk around anyway, for my circulation."

"But the seat belt sign is on."

"Tell that to my bladder."

"Lower your voice," Fredrik hisses.

I guess the word "bladder" freaked him out, but it's not like our row mate could *possibly* have heard us; he's cranking The Killers on his iPod. Fredrik stands up to let me out to the aisle. He rolls his eyes at me. I walk uneasily to the back of the plane. A flight attendant blocks my path and tells me to return to my seat. I want to explain that I'm an exception, I'm pregnant, can't you tell? But I don't have a chance; Fredrik is already leading me back to my seat. He's sure I will fall.

"Now put your seat belt on," he says impatiently.

Once off the plane I'm panting; too many layers. I rush to the first bathroom I find, and then I turn my cell back on. My mother is habitually late, so when the message signal beeps, I assume it's her, letting us know she is lost in the parking lot, or at the wrong airport. But no, it's a message from Louisa. "Sorry I missed you. Hope you're doing well. Let's talk when you get back." This is the first call of mine that she's returned in three weeks, since she miscarried. I return the call and hope she's there. Voice mail. *Fuck.* "Louisa. Hi." Pause. "It's me, Gretchen. We just got here, at the airport, to visit Mom for the weekend. Typical Mom, she's twenty minutes late. I have my cell. Give me a call." Pause. "If you've got time."

Ugh. That sounded so queer. But I don't know what to say! Right after the miscarriage (which Jason confirmed), I called her as I always had—approximately every six minutes. But when the calls went unreturned, I worried. I left messages, sent e-mails, walked by the house with Boo and knocked on the door and *nothing*. I thought she must be distraught, so I kept hitting redial, almost obsessively. When I mentioned to Meredith that I was concerned that Louisa was not relying on her friends and thus must be seriously depressed, so should we involve Jason, or a medical professional? etc., etc., etc., I was shocked to discover Meredith and Louisa had spoken *in person* and *over coffee*. "I don't understand," I muttered. Meredith explained that Louisa was still upset and wanted something low-key. I was shocked. Isn't it *my* job to report Louisa's state of mind? When she didn't make the final round for a professional award a few years ago, *I* called Meredith right away with a situation assessment, "She came very close; I agree the judges are complete idiots. Baja Fresh is obviously in order. I will call Jason." Ditto when Dr. Blankley found some weird precancerous cells during Louisa's annual checkup (Meredith actually gives herself breast exams, and she insists Louisa and I have annual checkups).

We took care of each other because that's what friends do (I am ready to step in whenever—even now I'm bummed that her message didn't have specific instructions, e.g., come over and bring me *Birdcage*). Certainly, that's what Louisa and Meredith had done for me; they mitigated the impact of my being parentless, which is how I felt when Mom was spending all her time obsessing over the Beltway instead of counseling me on how to manage adjusting to life as a quasiadult ("Divert 10 percent of your income to a savings account on your direct deposit form," Louisa instructed. "That is what my dad told me to do. You do have a savings account, don't you? We can set one up if you don't."). After Meredith told me that Louisa was fine, I was very relieved. But that emotion, like many others, did not last long (I am in my first trimester, after all.) and it was soon replaced by a less rational, less *charitable* feeling. I had felt so restless, so incomplete, without having her right there all the time that when I realized she might not feel the same way about me, I started to feel foolish. And then I was mad. Why didn't she call me back? Why is Meredith all of a sudden *so special?*

I close the phone, annoyed.

Where is Mom? Fredrik is checking his watch. He taps it with his finger. I hear Mom before I see her.

"After my husband died, I was afraid to even get on the Beltway. But I had no choice today—my daughter and her husband are coming for a visit—"

"MOM!" I shout.

"HI, HONEY!" Mom waves good-bye to a business-man, who has a newspaper in front of his face as he walks, unaware he was deep in conversation. She puts her arms around me to hug me and steps back and squints. "You look tired. Are you working too hard?"

"I'm fine."

"Hello, Fredrik."

"Why were you late?" I ask.

Fredrik shoots me a look as if to beg, *Please don't do this.*

"Never mind, where's your car?" I ask.

"In the hourly lot," she answers.

We head toward the lot and end up walking through the aisles, twice, trying to find her car. When we did finally see it, we realized that it was parked in the valet section (She did not recall handing her car keys over to another human being.). As I climb in, I prepare for severe nausea. Mom is a *horrible* driver and pumps the gas; fast, slow, fast whoops! Better brake! Fredrik fake-sleeps in the back. I share the passenger seat with nine half-empty water bot-tles, of the sports cap variety (though she's never exer-cised) and take a good, hard, look at her. Her dark brown wavy hair is a reliable indicator of her overall mental state. When I was younger and life was calm and easy, it was smooth and glossy; then, for several years, it was as manic as she was, curling outward from her head, defying gravity and dry to the bone. It's somewhere in between today. At sixty-six her skin is nearly wrinkle-free, except around her lips, owing to the clenched expression she adopts when deep in thought or when singing.

"—riding on the midnight train, oh, it's very late at night," she sings along with her tape of Gladys Knight & the Pips. She only has this one tape. The same one she's been playing for twenty years. Why can't she get the words right? And why can't she go any faster? She's driving under the speed limit; cars are whizzing by us. I grip the door handle and wonder if the Tidal Basin, resplendent in too-early-blooming cherry blossoms will be the last thing I see before—

"MOM!"

She's missed the exit off the George Washington Parkway to the Beltway, not her fault. D.C.-area roads—an odd mixture of National Scenic Byways, highways, and raggedy side streets—are poorly marked. I fear we are surely headed into Northern Virginia, where we'll surely experience death by "Mixing Bowl," a portion of I-95 where three or four major highways collide. Mom catches herself, cuts into a lane exiting onto Memorial Bridge, as an empty, hot-pink plastic basket smacks Fredrik in the head.

"Let's take the long way home, on Canal Road. So we can stop at Peoples," Mom suggests.

"It's CVS, Mom; they bought Peoples, like a thousand years ago. Remember? Can we just go home? I don't feel well."

"What's wrong? Fredrik? Are you awake? What is going on with my daughter?"

Mom pulls off at the Exxon, right after the bridge. She's giving me her "full attention," and before I can enjoy the memory of stopping at this exact gas station for cigarettes, right after I'd quit my job at the Wickford Hotel and decided to move back to Northampton, she turns to me and says, "*Wait a minute,* you're pregnant." Her turquoise reading glasses rest at the tip of her nose. "I'm your mother. Tell me. Yes or no?"

"I am. I'm due September first. Why are you wearing reading glasses to drive?"

Mom screams, "Oh, oh, oh!" and wipes her eyes. "That is wonderful, wonderful news. How do you feel? The glasses are to help me see, dear. Are you resting? Are you sick?" Mom honks the horn, to get Fredrik's attention. "Congratulations, honey. Of course, I had terrible, terrible nausea with you and when your father and I went to Mexico City for a conference, I couldn't get out of bed—the smells. Have you seen the doctor? You're sure about your due date?"

"Reasonably sure."

The car is creeping forward; Mom left the car in DRIVE and is neglecting the brake pedal. We lurch.

"GREAT. Because before I picked you up Pat called— it's why I was late—and Cathy's wedding has been moved to early August, in New York; you can still go—"

"MOM, Jesus, please, let's discuss that later."

Does your mom have a friend's daughter that she talks about regularly, even though the two of you are not friends? I'm always getting Cathy updates. "Cathy took a trip to Mexico." At my wedding reception, Mom complained to Peyton that it was such a shame that Cathy wasn't invited, when in fact we'd never spoken more than five words to each other. We arrive in Takoma Park, Maryland, relatively unscathed. Mom bought this house after I'd moved to Northampton. The one I grew up in, only a few streets away—the one I still dream about—was sold shortly after Dad died. I don't have any friends from the neighborhood, though; not one of my Academy classmates lived here. (It's only seven and a half miles from Ursuline's campus in Georgetown, but it might as well be 700. While Georgetown is populated by corporate lawyers, attorneys here in Takoma Park keep busy drafting friend-of-the-court briefs on behalf of death row convicts. *And* Takoma Park has been a nuclear-free zone since 1983.)

The moment we walk in the door Mom announces that I should nap. Am I four years old or pregnant? I pick up our bags and Fredrik takes them from me; we head upstairs toward the guest room but cannot move past Mom, who is body blocking the door. "Not in there. *I* sleep in the guest room," Mom says. "You two kids can have my room." I open my mouth to ask why she is sleeping there, and decide against it because, really, it won't make any sense and does it matter? But I know that Fredrik would rather *die* than sleep in Mom's room, even if she herself does not sleep there. So we retreat to my room with its chaste single bed, where I make a little pallet for Fredrik on the floor.

My old room has a stale feeling; it's decorated with second-tier memorabilia because I took anything of real value long ago ("value" being a subjective term, I learned, as selling my Cabbage Patch Doll collection on eBay yielded little, cash wise). The TV on the dresser is a boxy 13 inch and the two channel dials, vestiges of the hardship of life pre-remote, spin only to network television. Piled next to the TV are books—test prep guides for the GMATS, GRE, and LSAT exams; Mom has never given up the expectation that I'd continue my education. She still sends me the *U.S. News & World Report*'s annual graduate school rankings. On the wall above my bed hangs a collage I'd made as a sophomore in high school—photographs of my girlfriends interspersed with catchy headlines from teen magazines: BEST FRIENDS CONQUER ALL and THE HOTTEST PRIVATE

SCHOOL GIRLS. It emits a phantom smell of rubber cement, Giorgio perfume, and Boardwalk French fries.

"This should be fun," Fredrik whispers.

"You only have to see her a few times a year, Fredrik," I whisper back.

"Why does she sleep in the guest room?"

"I have no idea."

"It's crazy."

"It is *not*," I snap.

What is wrong with me? Why am I regressing? Why is it that I walk into this house, not even my childhood home but a smudged, barely readable copy of the original, and I become righteously indignant in a way only teenagers can? And why is it that Fredrik feels free to criticize my family? Mom may be crazy, but she's *my* crazy. If I so much as breathe a word about his mother ("Would it kill her to spend a dollar?"), father, or Andrew, he becomes apoplectic.

"Kids?" Mom asks from behind my bedroom door.

"Please stop calling us kids, Mom, we're adults," I insist as I look down at the floor from the vantage point of my bed. Fredrik is sprawled out on the floor and his feet stretch way past the edges of my Laura Ashley comforter. He looks at me and I stick my tongue out at him.

"You kids decent? Peyton's here," Mom says.

Peyton pushes open the door, walks in, and hovers next to Mom. At first glance, Peyton and I don't look much alike either—the color scheme is off. She is blonde and blue-eyed (and, damn her, taller and thinner). But the devil is in the details. Our thick "I-come-from-the-Old-Country" nose and full, hot-dog-bun mouths are identical. Our fingers are short and our nails are weak and crack easily. Our second toe is longer than our big toe. We both snort and laugh simultaneously and can raise one eyebrow, a trick we perfected by studying Vivian Leigh in *Gone With the*

Wind; as prewar Scarlett, she'd held her left eyebrow in place for over a minute and a half, in two separate scenes.

My first memory of us together is when I'm five and Peyton is about three; we are in the backyard, in the summer "painting" with water. Mom had given us a bucket of water and paintbrushes. We'd dump the brushes into the water and start slopping the water all over our wooden fence. Mom and Dad watched us from the brick patio, where they, too, had buckets of water (only theirs were filled with boiling-hot water, as they were trying to kill the weeds that had sprouted up between the bricks, via some ecologically correct, noneffective method). As soon as we'd finish our masterpieces, the "paint" would dry up and we'd shriek, and Mom and Dad would tell us to do it again. And we spent all day doing that. Or maybe it was five minutes, who knows? It was fun. And for a lot of years, really up until Dad died, Peyton and I had fun. For as much as you love your parents (and we did, we were kind of nerdy that way), they didn't Get It. They were the ones who told us we had to turn off our flashlights and go to bed when we were reading *Deenie* in my bed and discussing the very real threat of scoliosis, *way past our bedtimes!* And they were horrified when we confessed we could suck on a Now and Later in the pool for a full forty-five minutes— from one adult swim to the next; they said we'd choke. We thought that was hilarious. Didn't they know that you never *swallowed* a Now and Later? Why *would* you when you could just leave it stuck on your teeth and not think twice about it unexpectedly dislodging because we knew it would disintegrate over time?—time as measured by half-lifes. And having Peyton with me at the Academy, where I walked the halls in a constant state of "what did I miss?" panic, was reassuring—like having a little piece of home with you in a war zone.

We didn't get along all the time, though. We fought like

crazy over toys, specifically dolls (a certain Sally Doll met a violent end when we literally pulled her apart fighting over her), and we frequently stashed stuff under our beds to prevent the other from finding it. But our most awkward times were when Mom and Dad were fighting. This didn't happen very often, but when it did we divided right along the lines you'd think we would. Dad didn't rag on Mom, of course, but he would try to put things in perspective. "Your mother is very emotional, very passionate, and as hard as it can be sometimes, it's why I love her," he'd explain. "If you say so, Dad," I'd reply, skeptical, because all this love was *ruining our dinner*. At the same time, Peyton and Mom would act—in my view—conspiratorial. I always felt Mom was at fault, so I'd get into it with Peyton, defending Dad. "She's so selfish!" I'd scream, and Peyton would run to her room, furious. Then, if she was really mad, she wouldn't answer the knocks on our shared wall and I'd have to knock louder and louder until she'd yell "shut up!"—which is how I'd know we weren't in a fight anymore.

After Dad died, we stayed close to each other. We didn't feel like seeing anyone else (Again, his death was so unexpected and everyone kept saying, "It was a FREAK accident and the thing with the fish is SO WEIRD," which, over time, we abbreviated to mean, simply, "YOU ARE FREAKISHLY WEIRD PEOPLE!"), and we weren't really in a position to make new friends. But what drove us apart, I think, was that while Peyton felt badly for herself, and for Mom, *I* found Mom irritating in a way that defied explanation. Not just the Beltway thing, which was, yes, insane, but her very presence: every word she spoke, every sigh she made, even the way she shook her feet as she watched TV—it was maddening. I hated her. And I didn't hide it. And after a time, they didn't want to be around me, which I thought suited me fine. But here I am today, regardless.

"Mom says you're pregnant?" Peyton asks.

"Yes, I am!" I exclaim.

"Congratulations," Peyton says halfheartedly.

Before I can really analyze Peyton's reaction, or rather nonreaction, we are enlisted to help with dinner. So much for my nap. The guests are due to arrive any minute and Mom's done *nothing* to prepare for an elaborate four-course meal. "We're a family that cares about food," she announces to Fredrik, "and I don't understand people who don't." Neither Fredrik nor I acknowledge the thinly veiled reference to my in-laws. Mom, Peyton, and I fall into our old roles without thinking, even though it's probably been five years since we've all been here together. Mom is babbling, and rather than listen, I reorganize the ingredient lineup. Peyton is off in the corner, reading a folder with TOP SECRET stamped across it, making marks with a highlighter pen. Fredrik is left with nothing to do and nowhere to sit; the house is *violently* feminine and every chair has at least one silk shantung pillow on it.

There's a knock at the front door. Fredrik answers it and two women from Mom's Widows Club, Mary Margaret and Mary Beth, walk into the house. Mom has so many friends named Mary I've lost track of who's who. I've also forgotten the particulars of their personal tragedies, which Mom has recounted to me repeatedly over the years. I think the taller one's husband died crossing a bridge. I want to ask Peyton but she's still huddled in the corner. Shortly after, there is another knock. It's Mom's hairdresser, Jorges, long ago forgiven for a hideous experiment at frosting, which took place days before my college graduation. The dinner—the actual meal is not served until nearly nine thirty—drags. Fredrik is drunk but quiet, no doubt wish-

ing he could go read *AutoTrader* magazine in peace somewhere else, like in another state, and Peyton periodically
glares at him. Peyton doesn't *get* Fredrik. She's mapped
out her entire life; Fredrik likes to dabble. Before he committed to working with his dad at Stirling & Sons, he
worked for a few months as a cook on an Alaskan fishing
boat. For a few years after that, on weekends, he helped
out in the kitchen of Amherst's oldest Italian restaurant,
which is still family-run after eighty years, while he learned
to weld. He does not, to Peyton's annoyance, have a college degree. When I called with the news I was engaged
(after I explained, no, I didn't need or want a ring), she ex-
pressed concern about his "long-term" earning potential.
Why isn't she happy for me? Mom obviously is. She can't
leave me alone; she fusses over me, serving me first and
asking me repeatedly if I need anything.

"I have an announcement," Mom says as she clinks her
glass with a spoon, an unfortunate habit she'd picked up as
president of her house at Smith (To get the students' attention
at meals, she'd bang on her water glass with an engraved
silver fork). "I have decided that I would like my grandchildren to call me"—she pauses for effect—'Mother Fox.' "

Fredrik kicks me under the table.

"Oh," I say. "OK."

"What a wonderful name," Jorges adds.

"Are you going to get a car?" Peyton asks.

"What?" I ask.

"Are you going to get a car?" Peyton asks again.

"I can get around without one," I answer.

"Can you afford it?" Mom asks.

"Mom!" I shout.

"That's none of your business," Fredrik slurs.

"But it is, Fredrik. This baby belongs to all of us," Mom
says solemnly.

"Hear! Hear!" Mary somebody says.

"Why do they try and hide actresses' pregnancies on TV? Like we won't notice? It's like when they switch out people on soaps—there is no mention of the fact that the role is now played by an entirely different person!" I joke, trying to change the subject.

"You *still* watch *General Hospital?*" Peyton asks.

"Is something wrong?" I ask.

"Didn't Mom say you were thinking about a hotel management program?"

"I'm not sure where she got that idea."

I glare at Mom because that was *her* plan, not mine.

"Oh," Peyton says.

"Oh, *what?*"

"Girls, please."

"It doesn't sound like you've planned very well," Peyton says.

"She can still attend Cathy's wedding," Mom interjects.

"*Mother,*" Peyton and I say in unison.

"Stop that," Mom orders.

Someone changes the subject, something about Northern Ireland and, finally, the Marys and Jorges leave.

"I'm headed up to bed," Mom says, "*Letterman* is on. Sleep tight, kids."

I look around at the kitchen and survey the damage. Every surface is covered with something: dirty dishes, pots, pans, wineglasses; there are *four* spatulas wedged in the sink. Fredrik starts putzing around but I want to talk to Peyton alone, so I send him to bed.

"How about you clear the table and I'll load the dishwasher?" I suggest.

"OK."

Unfortunately, there is nowhere to put the dishes from the table; the dishwasher is already full. Peyton stays behind me as I take things out of the sink and put them to the side.

"What are you doing?" she asks.

"We'll wash them by hand."

"Why? Just leave them."

"Gross."

"This is going to take forever and I have to get up early for a riding lesson."

"You're taking bike lessons?"

"No, horses. I ride horses."

"You have a horsey?"

"No," Peyton sighs. "The horses are at the stables."

"I didn't realize we'd become a family of equestrians. How fancy."

"Are you being sarcastic?"

I put down the sponge and turn around to face her.

"Were you being sarcastic when you said I hadn't planned well?"

"No."

"Then me either."

I turn back around.

"Forget it, *I'm* leaving," she says. "THANKS FOR DINNER, MOM!" She yells up the stairs louder than she needs to "SEE YOU LATER, FREDRIK!"

Fredrik shouts a good-bye but Peyton doesn't hear him. She's already out the door. Alone in the kitchen, I wonder how it is that Mom managed to get saffron sauce on the ceiling fan, and then, as I disinfect Mom's toaster, I wonder why I'm in a fight with my sister. I hate that we aren't close. My eyes start to water as I mop the floor. At least the kitchen looks good. I put the mop away, briefly consider reorganizing the pantry, and finally trudge up to my room to go to bed. I climb over Fredrik, who has covered his face with a living room pillow adorned with beads and tassels.

"Fredrik," I whisper. "Are you awake?"

"Hmmph."

"Fredrik. *Fredrik*."

"What?"

"Did you hear Mom say she wants to come when the baby is born?"

"No."

"She does."

"Come where? To the delivery room?"

"I don't know."

"To the house?"

"I'm not sure."

"You should ask," he says.

"I guess so. Well, good night."

"No, correction," he says, "great night. Great night."

"It's so weird to see Mom excited about something *I'm* doing," I say as I had no real intention of going to sleep.

"Something tells me it doesn't have anything to do with you."

"What do you mean?"

"I mean a baby is a chance for Mother Fox to start over with someone, and maybe she's hoping she will do a little better with her grandchild than she did with her own daughter, the one who didn't—"

"Marry a college graduate," I finish for him.

"Exactly."

"I'm sorry she said that."

"Don't be. If I wanted to go, I would have."

"I know—that's not it. It's just, I wish she were more normal."

"What's normal?"

"Come on, Fredrik. This isn't. My own sister doesn't think I will be a good mother."

"She didn't say that."

"She might as well have. I can't believe a *sister* would think such a thing."

"You're convinced every family is perfect except for yours."

"That's not true," I reply.

"OK—every family except yours *and* mine."

I laugh. "It's just I have this vision of how I think things should be happening and it never works out as I had expected. And even though I am consistently disappointed by these visions, it never occurs to me not to have them."

"Visions? I think you mean you hope for the best."

"Ah—I wouldn't go that far. It's not just that today sucked—it's that I'm not even sure how my family *got* here, from where we started. You wouldn't know it, but we were actually a good family. You'd have wanted to come for dinner . . ."

"I don't know. You know what I always say," Fredrik reminds me.

"It's not your mother, it's *any* mother," we say in unison.

"Right," Fredrik says.

"And this whole thing with Louisa. Why isn't she calling me back?"

"I don't know."

"I feel like a loser," I half-joke.

"Hold me," he teases.

"Hold me," I say back.

"I hate this pillow!" he shouts as he tosses the pillow up in the air.

I laugh as the pillow smacks against the wall.

"Kids?" I hear Mom ask. "What is going on in there?"

"Nothing!" Fredrik and I shout in unison, giggling.

Chapter 8

"Get the facts! It's important to educate yourself about your rights under the Federal Medical Leave Act (FMLA) and your employer's maternity, disability, vacation and sick leave policies before you tell the office. Most importantly, make sure the news comes from you; it will reassure your boss that you take your job seriously, even if you don't plan to return."
—From *Ready or Not, An Expectant Mother's Guide* (Week 15, page 144)

I'm absentmindedly waving my hair dryer back and forth, mentally cataloguing the day ahead. I have an eleven o'clock meeting with Eliza to discuss my quarterly goals and career path, during which I will reveal my condition. I will be calm and professional. I will reassure her that the pregnancy will not impact my work *at all*. To prove my dedication, I will stay late tonight to supervise a cocktail party for the Calvin Coolidge Society of Notary Publics (Coolidge, who started his political career in Northampton, was sworn into office by his father, a notary public).

I've got it completely under control.

I'm so *hot* in this little bathroom. I unplug the dryer and relocate to my bedroom. I'm starting to sweat. I remove my shirt. My bra is too tight so I take that off, too. I turn to look at myself in the full-length mirror and *Whoa.* What is going on? My nipples are enormous, giant, brown saucers. Like Meredith's! And what's this on my stomach? A dark brown line from my belly button down to my pubic hair. Like, baby will emerge from here? *I hate nature.* This is horrible. I can't be thinking about my body browning like a crown roast right now; I need to prepare for the most important meeting of my adult life! Must refocus. *Must check notes.* I take out my Filo and sit down on the bed.

Family Medical Leave Act (FMLA)
The gist of this law is that I can take up to twelve weeks off with job protection and when I return I will get my old job back or a job of similar status. (Oh, you're not going to promote me when I'm out? Shocking!) Meredith explained that the FMLA has nothing to do, whatsoever, with whether or not I receive pay during that time. That decision is left to my employer, Eliza. We agreed that this is unfortunate.

Company Maternity Leave Policy, *unknown*
Not surprisingly, a Xerox of a Xerox, masquerading as a human resources pamphlet for nonunion employees, did not mention any policy of any kind. The Singletons were kind of loosey-goosey on these kinds of issues—perhaps a downside of working for a small, family-owned business.

Vacation, sick leave, unpaid time off, *unknown*
This is tricky. Hotel work is cyclical—either you're working a lot, or not at all. I wish I'd kept track over the last few months but, oh well.

I close my Filofax with a bang, stand up and walk to the mirror. I put my bra back on. It's tight—I'm on the last row of hooks—and as a result, my boobs are smashed together. I'm not altogether unpleased with the result so I decide to take it up a notch, so to speak, and replace the underwire bra with a slightly larger, padded version. Damn. I look *hot*. Unless you look at any other part of me. Oh, well. Not much more I can do here—which seems to be the story any time I'm getting dressed these days; might as well go to work.

Once at my desk, I can feel my confidence evaporating. Eliza's office is empty. I sit down, open the Notary Society file, and review the event details for the one hundredth time. That takes all of fifteen seconds. Time to use the bathroom. As I'm about to head in, I hear someone shout my name.

"Gretchen," Eliza says. She is with Front Desk Bob.

"Yes?" I have my hand on the women's room door.

"A few notaries are at check-in, asking for a complimentary room and additional rooms at a reduced group rate. Do you know anything about this?"

I remove my hand and take a step back. She does not suggest I go ahead and use the facilities. Now all I can think about is that I need to go.

"No—they're local. I didn't negotiate a block of rooms. Who's at the desk?" I ask.

"It's Mr. Andrews, the organizer," Front Desk Bob interjects. "He wants a room comped."

"I'm not sure their total food-and-beverage order warrants that," Eliza replies, opening a war-torn leather folder with CONCORDE CONSULTING emblazoned on the cover, "given our new policy—"

"And the rooms, who wants those?" I ask. *Please, make it quick*.

"The notaries," Bob answers. "They are going to PARTY

HARD and they'll need rooms in case they need to nota-rize, LATE NIGHT."

I blink and Eliza rolls her eyes.

Bob adds, "Hey, heard you were knocked up."

"What?"

"Susan told me."

"Who is Susan?" I ask.

"The hot chick from Accounting," he replies. "She saw you at the doctor's office and guessed. You *are* looking kind of um, *breastacular,*" he adds, staring at my chest. He runs his hands over his own nipples, mock twirling them for emphasis.

"Bob, thank you," Eliza says. "I will speak with the no-taries. Gretchen, do you have a minute?"

"Yes, of course. Just let me use the restroom?" I ask.

I dash in, without waiting for an answer. I'm hustling to undo my skirt, pull down my tights, *Jesus, this is not off to a good start,* and take a seat. Once I'm finished, I put my-self back together and return to her office. Why is it so warm in here? I know my internal temperature has risen almost one degree since I became pregnant, but this is def-initely fear induced. I stare at an enlarged photograph of Eliza crossing a speed-walking race finishing line; she is flanked by her tanned parents. God, I miss them. *They'd* be excited for me. Mrs. Singleton would knit booties for the baby—it was her favorite Front Desk activity. Depart-ing guests with complaints that the toilet ran all night re-ceived a pom-pom-topped hat as an apology.

"Gretchen, I'm disappointed I didn't hear this news from you."

"I'm so sorry."

"I just updated the hotel's human resource policies. Here is a packet for you to review; I'd planned to give it to you today anyway. These are the revised grooming guidelines," Eliza says as she looks at my shirt, which I took, in a moment of nothing-fits desperation, from Fredrik's closet. "This is an explanation of the new electronic time-card system, and here are the 'paid time off' policies."

"Thank you. And maternity leave?"

"We will not be offering any maternity leave or short-term disability pay. You may use any remaining vacation or sick leave during your absence. I reviewed your time sheets, Gretchen, and if my calculations are correct, and they *always* are, you currently owe the hotel fifteen hours."

"I do? Are you sure?"

"Positive," she replies.

I sit back in my chair. It's no use. It's my fault I didn't keep track of my hours—but really, I didn't know I'd need to. Besides, she hates me. I hate her. Don't get me wrong, I care about my *job*. I care about the clients; I pride myself on enjoyable, hassle-free events and I spend hours dreaming up "special touches" to make the rituals of life special. But maybe I should rethink this line of work. I'm not sure crawling around on the floor, looking for additional outlets because the AV guy didn't show, is a career.

But then career implies planning and I've done exactly none. I fell into this line of work right after graduation from Smith, as was required by the friendly coupon-issuing people at Sallie Mae. Desperate to make money (and unclear of how to harness my sociology degree into something other than graduate work), I answered an ad in the paper for a catering manager at the Wickford, a 1970s-era steel box masquerading as a Washington, D.C. hotel. As a girl Friday for the chef, I received *excellent* training in the field of indentured servitude. I checked coats (Amazing the furs people had—I loved to wear them in Chef's office as I smoked his Marlboro Reds and perused *Hello!* magazine.); I waited in line for a visa to the Ukraine (I have no idea why); I helped businessmen to the bathroom, so they wouldn't vomit in front of the other diners.

I was feeling pretty good about my job, and myself, until I received a flyer for a two-year reunion at Smith, which I was against in principle, as it seemed to be little more than a fund-raising scam. After all, I'd kept up with my class-mates via the *New York Times* wedding section ("Vivian Hawthorne and Richard Hutchinson were married yester-day at The Wauwinet inn, on Nantucket. The bride, 25, is a graduate of Smith College. Dr. Hawthorne, who is keep-ing her name professionally, is a third year resident at Co-lumbia University College of Physicians and Surgeons, where she received recognition for her isolation of a gene that pro-cesses trans-fat, unique to the indigenous people of Suma-tra.") and The *Alumnae Quarterly* (Samantha Hall enjoys her job as associate editor of *Travel + Leisure* magazine and keeps in touch with housemate Katherine "Kiki" Lan-ham, a curatorial specialist in the Portrait Miniatures group of the Fine Art department of Christie's auction house, New York), so why did I need to see them? I didn't speak to them when we were in college, why start now? I called Louisa, who'd stayed in Northampton, to let her know I was definitely *not* attending. "Has *no one* answered phones for a fucking living?" I asked.

"Stop. You're going," Louisa declared.

"We graduated one minute ago. It's not even a real re-union. Why bother?"

"To see people. You don't talk to anyone."

"I talk to people here."

"From high school?"

"No," I said, though I lived with my friends from the Academy, which she knew, as I was constantly gossiping about them, "*new* friends."

"The accounting department of the Wickford doesn't count."

"That's elitist," I protested, not meaning it.

"What I meant to say is that they are not mutually exclusive," Louisa said.

I went. In the end, it was good that I did, because it was time—past time—for me to leave Washington and the clutches of the Beltway Widow. The Widow had become so consumed with her Sisyphean effort, that she'd neglected every other part of her life. She couldn't help me out financially after I graduated (which is reasonable), but I needed it, because she stopped paying *all* of her bills (which is not). And guess whose phone number her creditors had?

My born-of-frugality diet of Marlboros Lights, Diet Mountain Dew, and dinosaur-shaped macaroni and cheese, suited my roommates fine, but I had a hard time keeping up with my employer's dress code (most hotels have them). As a result, I often resorted to raiding my roomies' closets. I admit I wasn't such a good "borrower" in the sense that I often failed to return the items. One girl's beige DKNY snap-at-the-bottom bodysuit held special allure; I kept it for weeks, tucked away in my boxer-shorts-and-tank-top drawer. Forcing her to retrieve it, on a morning she was late for her junior buyer's job at Bloomingdale's when she was nursing a hangover *and* a sneaking suspicion her boyfriend was cheating on her, effectively shut off access to her employee discount.

This didn't faze me until a few months later, when a walk to work in the freezing rain shrunk my polyester blazer into a rumpled, crumpled trash bag-like mess, prompting snide comments from French waiters ("She is like Courtney Love in the homeless dress, no?"). I needed a winter coat. I should have scoured the Junior League's Georgetown store for a gently used second, but what if I needed to join one day, to further James's political career? So, I did what any stupid, insecure yet *incredibly* entitled twentysomething would do. I stole one.

I passed the J. Crew on M Street every day, on the walk back and forth to the Wickford, and I'd spent a thousand Saturdays there with my roommates killing time before the date, party or trip that cried out for a new skirt, boot, or thirty-dollar tortoise-shell hair clip. "J. Crew cuts me all wrong," I'd say, burning with jealousy, plowing through the racks while they tried on clothes. It wasn't that I loved the clothes; I didn't—my preferred style is more eclectic—it was more what they symbolized. Christ, if you can buy three pairs of pants in what was essentially the same color— stone, rain, ash—you already had the basic black; you're not worrying about your mom losing her house.

My rack time was fruitful in one respect, though. I discovered that merchandise in certain pockets of the store, sections out of the line of sight of "management"—defined as employees who were not students at nearby Georgetown University—were less likely to have a security device. One Sunday morning, I was alone, waiting to meet James for brunch, hyperaware of the tissue stuffed in the toes of a too-big pair of shoes I'd taken from Mom, when I happened upon the most perfect, luscious, three-quarter length, aren't-I-rich-and-happy, white cashmere coat ever created. I *had* to have it. I snuck into an open dressing room—the attendant was busy analyzing an underage-drinking exposé in the *Hoya*—and tried it on. I shoved it in my bag, assuming the "these rooms are monitored" signs alluded to human eyes. No such luck; all the rooms were rigged with video cameras.

I had one foot on the cobblestone walk when I felt a firm hand on my arm. In a matter of minutes, I was in the back of a D.C. cop's car, *handcuffed*. Like a common criminal. Which I was. We drove to the local police station and parked in a spot reserved for "prisoner drop-off," and I briefly considered going insane. *This can't be happening*, I thought. I will explain; it was a mistake. I can get out of it. I must. But there was no time; I was processed immediately. The address on my driver's license provoked snickers from the cop assigned to me; my group house was within shouting distance of Pamela Harriman's former estate and a few higher-profile senators' *pieds-à-terres*. Just like that I lost my "I'm one of you" angle; the no, really, I'm broke, it's a lie, just like my weight, can't you let me off with a warning? No. I was told to arrange for restitution—the value of the coat, doubled, plus a fine and an administrative fee to cover the cost of a court-mandated viewing of the movie *No Thanks, Just Looking*—for a grand total of a thousand dollars.

I paid it off, gradually, as was stipulated by the judge, who thoughtfully waived all costs associated with my probation. Moving to Northampton, which is expensive for a small town but certainly cheaper than D.C., was a much-needed fresh start. And since the day I set foot at the Grande, I've worked very hard.

I can't let Eliza run me out of here, I think to myself.

Suddenly, I feel my spine straightening. I'm conscious of my posture, my appearance as a Professional Working Woman, the one who is often profiled in *Living Life* magazine. (Have you noticed that the accompanying photo is always pure male fantasy? If the model's pose and attire— she is perched on the edge of a desk and wearing a miniskirt, legs crossed—were *true* reflections of the modern work force, one would think corporate America dispersed sex swings as frequently as laptops. Then again, if I looked like her, I would not be in need of advice on how to navigate the dim life of the office. I'd be, you know, a model.) I tell Eliza I'd be *happy* to join a management task force of one (myself) to analyze food-and-beverage costs for the past year.

I leave her office and mentally compile a list. I will:

- *Dress more professionally.*
  Divide closet into two sections: work and casual, to eliminate "accidental" wearing of fishnet stockings to the hotel; invest in high quality, lawyerlike maternity wardrobe and learn to wear shells with confidence.

- *Increase business acumen.*
  Subscribe to *Harvard Business Review;* become familiar with notable case studies of hotel industry and cite from memory; read *The Seven Habits of Highly Effective People, The Tipping Point,* and the new Jefferson biography.

- *Take initiative and stay positive.*
  Participate more in weekly staff meetings. Think outside the box and do not repeat phrase "outside the box" in mocking tone in the employee cafeteria.

- *Socialize less.*
  Read during lunch. Desist from command impersonations of Front Desk Bob for engineering department.

There. Looks good. This is my path. Now, I know the conventional wisdom is to stay away from life-altering decisions when pregnant—i.e., don't get bangs or leave your husband because "hormones" are at play. Not me. I will lock myself into a plan, to eliminate postpartum confusion. I will choose to be a Working Mother. I will break glass ceilings! I will be an inspiration to the next generation, women whose career opportunities won't be limited by their piercings, let alone their biological burden!

*   *   *

"Working is O-U-T," Meredith said to me over the phone, after I'd told her of my decision.

"What do you mean?" I ask.

"Sorry, I've got to get better about spelling words. It's driving Alan crazy. What I mean is, working is no longer *en vogue*. Staying at home is in."

"I don't get it."

"I e-mailed you that article from the *New York Times*, about the women at Yale who are planning to stay at home. You didn't read it, did you?" she asks accusingly.

"I did," I lie, "it's just I need you to explain why I care."

"Because women who can *choose* to work are *choosing* not to."

"But they went to Yale, of course they get to decide. Besides, isn't having a choice the whole point of it all?"

"Not if it's only an *illusion* of choice. If societal pressure—"

"I hate when you use those words. Hey, I know, what about a part-time job? That would be perfect—something interesting that pays really well," I suggest.

Meredith laughs so hard she has to hang up.

Fredrik looks confused when I recount this conversation to him. It's nearly one in the morning. The Calvinists were an unruly bunch, with one paranoid notary accusing our wait staff of inappropriately handling his food. Every bone in my body aches and I have never been so happy to see my bed in my life. Fredrik is beside me, reading *French Women Don't Get Fat*.

"Why aren't you saying anything?" I ask.

"You could stay home. We'd have to cut back on expenses and I'd have to take on more clients, work longer hours—but it's not impossible."

"I don't know," I say. "You already work all the time."

"It would be worth it."

"But you'd never see the baby."

"I just want to give you what you want, honey."

I hate choices. If I don't have a choice, then I don't have to worry about the consequences of said choice because, instead, it's Just the Way It Is. And while this is a nice offer, and I love that he is always asking me what I want, Fredrik has never been broke. He is careful with money, but that is because he's smart, and he doesn't care about things, which is likely because he is confident. I don't care about things as much as I used to, but I feel strongly I should give more to my child than my parents gave me, as that is the Natural Order.

"I want to pay for our kids to go to college—no borrowing," I say.

"Seems reasonable. But that's twenty years from now," he says.

Fredrik tosses the book onto the floor. I hear a crinkle as it lands.

"Is that a library book?" I ask.

"Yes. I had it on reserve."

"Reserve?" I ask. "Never mind. I did the math and undergrad will cost a quarter of a million dollars."

"You're kidding. Maybe you could stay home for a few years."

"Yeah, maybe," I say. "We need to look at the numbers."

"Whatever you want, honey."

"Stop saying that," I tease.

I am afraid to say that I am also worried about being home with a baby. After seeing Meredith, I'd say the odds weren't in my favor that I'd be a "natural." I mean, here Meredith was totally capable, totally in touch with motherhood—she studied families for a living, right?—and after she had Ryder, she was all over the place. At first, she kept him in a sling (something about yet another African tribe) and then, mid-maternity leave, reversed her position. He needed to be put down, in the crib, *at the same time every day,* per some book she read. In order to maintain this schedule, she refused to leave the house for three weeks. Or shower. So the idea of returning to the hotel—doing a job I've had forever—where the stakes are *considerably* lower, sounds pretty damn appealing.

Should I tell Fredrik now about the thoughts that have been piercing my brain since I saw the pregnancy test result? My fear that despite being a planner, a Filofax list maker, *there is nothing I can do to prepare for life after the pregnancy because I have no idea, no clue, what we will want or need once we have a baby?*

Nah. Instead, I say this:

"I'm tired, let's talk more about this tomorrow."

And he says:

"Don't worry so much. You will be a great mother."

Chapter 9

"Do your homework. With a plethora of genetic testing options available, it's easy to become confused about what makes sense for you and your partner. Agreeing on a plan of action before you're faced with major decisions can help both of you manage this stressful time."
—From *Ready or Not, An Expectant Mother's Guide*
   (Week 16, page 160)

I open our front door and trip over a box of books. A note card is wedged between two cardboard flaps. "Gretchen—FYI." There must be fifteen books in here. I pull out a few. *The Price of Motherhood, Perfect Madness: Motherhood in the Age of Anxiety,* and *Unbending Gender Why Family and Work Conflict and What to Do About It.* My guess is these are *not* week-by-week guides that helpfully compare the size of the baby to produce ("Your baby is about the size of a lima bean."). I push the stack into the hallway, close the front door, and hesitate for a moment out on the stoop to look for Louisa or her car. Nope. She's not there. I saw her, for just a minute, four days ago and I've called her like a million times in the past two months, but she hasn't called me back. So a few days ago, I just stopped.

After nursing some resentment against Meredith, I decided that although I preferred two best friends, I'd take just the one. And it isn't Meredith's fault that Louisa is giving me the silent treatment. I asked Meredith about it and she claimed that Louisa was "too busy." I laughed. I realized that whatever Louisa had told Meredith, Meredith had decided to keep it to herself and I don't want to make her uncomfortable. Though it's unspoken between us, we all know: I am the odd man out on a three-man team.

Fredrik honks; we're late for our third appointment with Dr. Mitchell. Fredrik skipped the last one but last night his client rescheduled their meeting for this morning, so, here we are, going together. Despite being late, I walk to the truck. I don't want to sweat, especially after all the time I took with my hair. I don't know why but I am excited to see Dr. Mitchell. "He's perceptive and kind," Meredith had said after her last visit, "and he *cares* about how I'm feeling." "I so totally agree," I'd said.

Fredrik tries not to ask me how I'm feeling. He already knows the answer. *Like crap.* I have had to devise other, nonverbal, ways to keep him informed.

I get in the truck and put my legs on the dash.

"Don't put your feet there," Fredrik barks. "You're getting it dirty."

"I have a muscle cramp. I need to stretch my leg."

He groans, "Right."

"What does that mean?"

"Just another complaint."

"It's not a complaint, Fredrik, it's a symptom—a symptom of pregnancy."

"What I want to know is how many symptoms are there?"

"A LOT!" I scream.

Fredrik and I don't speak for the rest of the drive to Dr. Mitchell's office. Once there, I feel calm—I am among my people—but Fredrik is nervously shifting from side to side. Pregnant women surround him, making follow-up appointments, waiting to be seen. I walk to the dreaded nook. *Clank clank clank*. The bottom weight of the scale is at one hundred and the nurse moves the top slider farther and farther to the right, before giving in to the inevitable: moving the bottom weight to one hundred fifty pounds. This is not good.

"Step down, now. Careful—there you go."

"God, could I have gained any more weight?"

"Dr. Mitchell will see you in Exam 4, right around the corner. Go ahead."

I wait in the room silently with Fredrik for a few minutes. He reminds me that we have dinner with his parents tonight (like I'd forget), during which they are making some kind of announcement (Fredrik won't say what) and then we, I assume, are going to make *our* announcement. Fredrik hovers in the corner; I flip through an old magazine. Silence is definitely preferable. Wow, I think, sucking in my breath. I can't *believe* how much weight this model gained in rehab. I can't wait to analyze this with Louisa (she's been obsessed with this particular celebutante for nearly a year). Wait. *We're not talking*. I remind myself that keeping the list of "what to discuss with Louisa" is a waste of time as there will be no end of the "event" (doctor's appointment, shopping trip, meeting with Eliza) recap. I remind myself not to feel mad or sad. I remind myself to be self-aware enough to realize that said madness and sadness are likely exaggerated by having experienced similar emotions after my father died (now in partnership with raging hormones!). I remind myself that self-awareness is not one of my strong suits, so it is good that I can focus on it now, as I am about to jump into the precipice that is parenthood. I remind myself that this is a good day, as I will be *seeing my doctor*.

Dr. Mitchell enters, sits on a rolling stool, chart in hand. How am I feeling? Any unusual symptoms—cramping, bleeding, vomiting? Do I have any questions? Yes, I answer, why am I gaining, gaining, gaining? Fredrik glares at me; he said I should think of the baby and not the weight. Intellectually I agree, but it is difficult to feel utterly out of control of my body.

"For a woman your size, a healthy weight gain is between twenty and thirty pounds. In the first trimester, weight gain should be minimal—a few pounds. You're a bit ahead; you've gained about nine pounds. In the coming weeks, you can expect to gain between half a pound and a pound a week."

"What does the baby weigh?" Fredrik asked.

Why hadn't I thought of that?

"The baby is about the size of your fist."

That's it? Fredrik has a large hand, true, but is it NINE POUNDS?

"What's important to remember is not how much you're eating, but what. Are you still experiencing morning sickness?" Dr. Mitchell flips open my chart.

"It's improving, but I'm not one hundred percent. I can't stop eating peanut butter and jelly sandwiches; it's the only meal I can stand. Except pasta. And bagels. Bagels are tasting really, really good right now."

"I know you're trying your best," Dr. Mitchell says, putting his hand on my shoulder, "but try to incorporate more into your diet. Eat small, nutritious meals throughout the day. That should help you feel better and keep your weight in check."

I lie down on the exam table. Dr. Mitchell takes his hands and gently presses my stomach. He announces that I'm filled with gas. I sit back up.

"Thanks, Dr. Mitchell. We'll see you in a month," I say.

"Come see me in my office after you're dressed," he replies.

I look at Fredrik.

"Is everything OK?" I ask.

"Yes, yes; I just want to discuss some testing options."

Uh-oh. We are woefully unprepared for this discussion. I'm sure this is addressed in one of the many books I've accumulated on pregnancy but I've only scanned them, by looking up certain things in the index. I can't face reading them chapter by chapter because I get too distracted by the authors' tone. They are either too earnest ("delight in every moment") or too cheeky ("use a vibrator to make the most of this orgasmic time") for my taste.

As a result, I don't have a pregnancy "philosophy."

Fredrik and I take our seats in the two maroon cloth-covered chairs that face Dr. Mitchell's desk. He sits behind piles of paper, glamour shot of his wife, school pictures of his children, patient files, and doctor-related clutter.

"First, I need to understand your expectations concerning the pregnancy and the baby; that is, what is your comfort level with testing versus not testing?" Dr. Mitchell asks.

"Like amnio?" I ask.

"Amniocentesis is usually not a first step, given your age."

"What do you recommend?" Fredrik asks.

Rather unlike him to ask for someone else's opinion. But he doesn't make eye contact with Dr. Mitchell; he's looking above his head and reading the diplomas that line the wall behind his desk.

"Every patient is different. Why don't you read this—" Dr. Mitchell pulls a pamphlet from a drawer—"and give us a call with your decision? In the meantime, if you have any questions, don't hesitate to ask."

I tell Dr. Mitchell we'll be back in touch by the end of the week. Fredrik and I shuffle out of his office and my face burns with shame. Shouldn't I have already had a *plan*? If I were Fredrik I'd be so annoyed with me. When he complained about the two hundred dollars I spent at the bookstore ("Did you really need *What to Expect to Read When Expecting*?"), I assured him, repeatedly, that I needed to have *all* of them in order to have a healthy pregnancy. And here I am, exposed for the ignorant fraud I am. We leave the office and wait for the elevator in silence. It arrives and Fredrik is careful to place his hand on the door, lest it shut on me. We board and I push L three times.

"We've got some reading to do," he says.

"Yeah. I'm sorry, there's so much information. It's overwhelming."

We exit the elevator, walk across the lobby and through the parking lot. Once we're in the truck, Fredrik turns on his Steely Dan CD, loud enough so that we can't talk. Doesn't he realize we're too old to be *cranking* rock music? I'm giving things up left and right—drinking, all my clothes, and peace of mind—can't he at least *fake* an interest in classical music? According to the magazines in Dr. Mitchell's office, playing Mozart will practically guarantee our kid becomes a math genius and/or professional ice skater. I shout this to Fredrik but he ignores me and after a few minutes, drops me off at our front door.

I let myself in the house, remove my coat, and look longingly at the couch, where I can easily envision myself napping with Boo for the entire day, as I'm not scheduled to work. But instead, I head for the kitchen. I am going to make an appetizer for the Stirlings: Moroccan Chicken and Lentils. But once I'm in the kitchen, I am distracted by the computer. Maybe I can get some genetic testing answers there? Right. I type in a few phrases in a search box and I proceed to have a heart attack. It's not the tests—

those seem straightforward enough—but the *results*, that is, screening for neural disorders, chromosomal abnormalities. The question then becomes, what do you do with the information? If the baby has a problem, do you terminate? Do you continue with the pregnancy, knowing you may miscarry, deliver a stillborn, or one that will die within hours of birth?

Truth time: I don't have what it takes to make this kind of decision.

Since I need a break and promised to call Mom after my appointments, I pick up the phone. Takes me thirty seconds to regret it. *No, I haven't spoken to Peyton. Yes, it's amazing the work she's doing for our president. No, I haven't thought about what I'll wear to Cathy's wedding.*

I mention the tests.

"Honey, in my day, you took what you were given. And you were grateful."

"From what I've read, the tests can be helpful. If you decide to keep the baby, the right specialists can begin advising you now, maybe treat in utero and be present for the delivery."

"*If* you?"

"Yes . . . if you, you know, don't terminate."

"ARE YOU CONSIDERING THAT?"

"Mother, I'm just saying it's an option. It's one of the reasons the tests are performed. I'm not sure I'd do it or not. It depends on what the results were."

"Like what, you'd keep a child with Down but not one with spina bifida? That's rather Naziish, Gretchen, don't you think?"

"I wish they'd screen for something more useful, like self-righteousness," I say as I study my nails; they are growing so fast. "Please be supportive."

"I *am* supportive," Mom says as though she is stating the obvious. "It's no different from what I said to you

when you were younger: if you have an unplanned pregnancy, I would be happy to raise the baby. And I will be
happy with this baby, no matter what—birth defects or
no."

It is true, she told me many, many times that she'd "support" my decision to "bear" an out-of-wedlock child but
the offer was rooted in absurdity. She could barely care for
Peyton and me during those critical reproductive yet not
responsible years. I'm so irritated I can't speak. But I say
nothing to her about it. Instead, I beg off; I need to get
ready for dinner at the Stirlings. Luckily, this announcement annoys her. "Oh, yes, I wouldn't want you to be late
for your nightly dinner with your in-laws," she says. "Not
every night," I explain. "Just every third Friday." *Buh-bye.*

I leave the kitchen and go upstairs, to my room. I need
something else to wear. The clothes I put on this morning
are (a) uncomfortable, and (b) splattered with lentil residue.
What can I wear? Shit. My pre-pregnancy clothes are out
of the question; my thighs are tree trunks, my ass is wide
and my belly is just *blah*. I look awful. By the time Fredrik
arrives home, I'm on the floor of my closet, crying.

"What's going on?" he asks.

"I have nothing to wear. NOTHING."

"We're just going to my parents' house."

"I'm sorry . . . It's just, what if there's something wrong
with the baby? I know I didn't plan for this, but that doesn't
mean I don't want it."

"Honey, I *promise*. There is no connection between the
two," he says.

Sigh. Of course there is. I start to cry again.

"I just want the baby to be OK."

"We will know soon enough. That is what the test is
for."

I stand up to walk away from him. As I look out the

window, toward the street, I say, "I was so naive! I thought I was done."

"Done what?"

I don't turn around. "Done the hard part."

"You haven't even had the baby," he teased. "I hear that's really hard."

I turn around to face him. I smile.

"I meant done with my bad luck." I look down.

"Ah," he says.

"This is my chance to start over. And I want everything to be perfect."

"Oh, honey," he says as he walks toward me, "there is no reason to think *anything* will be wrong with the baby. It's just a test. You are assuming the worst."

"You think so?"

"You do not have bad luck."

"OK—maybe not now. But I did before."

"But then you married me."

"Right," I say.

"An excellent decision, if you ask me."

"It must be so much fun to be you!" I laugh. "No worries."

"Not exactly."

"I knew it! You are scared, too."

"Of course I am. I worry about you, and the baby, the delivery."

"We'll be fine," I say.

"But I also—I also want to be a good provider," he says.

I snicker but stop when I realize that Fredrik isn't joking.

"You support me and I like working. That's how *we* provide," I say.

"I don't know. I wish—I never thought I'd say this—I wish we had more money, like millions, so you could stay home and just not think about it."

"Oh, Fredrik—I just want the baby to be healthy. I don't care about anything else. Not even about if it's a boy or girl," I joke.

"I never thought I'd hear you say that," he says.

"Yeah, well, me neither," I say.

Two hours later, we're at the Stirlings. My cover-up does a fair job of hiding my crying jag–induced blotchiness, and my outfit, a transitional pre-pregnancy combination (went big on the bottom, smaller on top, hoping this would make my pregnancy obvious to all) isn't my best, but isn't my worst, either. I'm nervous. Fredrik abandons me as soon as we get there to cook dinner, so I'm left to chat with the Stirlings. I've never spent that much time solo with Elaine and Karl; I prefer to be an appendage to Fredrik, an outsider. Is this the cause or the effect of Elaine's ambivalence about the presence of a wife/daughter-in-law? Hard to say. I twitch with anticipation as Elaine and I sit together on the hunter green corduroy couch beneath a shelf of antique cuckoo clocks. Karl is in an overstuffed wing chair, watching a golf tournament on TV. I want to inquire about a match set or some such, but his eyes are half-closed. Elaine and I discuss towels. Finally, Fredrik and Andrew join us; Fredrik serves the lentils with slices of white bread.

"It's all they have," he whispers to me.

"That's fine," I say, wishing like hell I'd made some crustini.

"This is delicious," Andrew says.

"It's very *ethnic*," Elaine adds.

"Dad, are you awake?" Fredrik asks.

"You boys have done a solid job these past few years," Karl begins, suddenly roused from his slumber. *Solid?* Jeez, Fredrik has worked nonstop as long as I've known him. "And the time has come to make some changes. As you know, I inherited this company from my father, and he from his." *Yawn.* "I want to pass the company on now, to the two of you. But I want to be sure that *this* is what you want to do." Karl locks eyes with Fredrik. "It's a serious commitment."

The clocks are ticking. I wish someone would say something. I won't. I'm just an in-law. I don't want to interfere.

"I'm pregnant," I say. Nature abhors a vacuum.

"Yes, dear, we know," Elaine says.

"I'd like to retire September first—" Karl continues.

"You already know?" I ask.

"I told them," Andrew says, leaning over to me.

"So you have a few months to think about it," Karl says.

"Wow, OK—" I stammer. Wait, September first?

"I don't need time to think, Dad. This is what I want to do," Fredrik says.

"Me, too," Andrew says.

"It's settled then," Karl says.

"I'm *due* September first," I interrupt again. *Is no one interested?*

"Yes, dear," Elaine says. "Shall we eat?"

As we walk into the dining room, I purposely step on Fredrik's foot.

"Excuse me," I say.

Fredrik ignores it.

The room is painted a bright robin's-egg blue. The table is one of the first pieces of furniture Fredrik built with his father; the walls are decorated with Andrew's sketches of the house. The chairs are narrow, Colonial-looking and not very sturdy. There is a loud creaking noise as I take my seat. The roast leg of lamb, grilled vegetables, spinach salad, and hot dinner rolls smell delicious.

"Gretchen, I'm not sure if having choices is better or worse, but I think you are making the right one by staying home," Elaine says apropos of nothing.

"I'm not sure what I'm doing yet," I answer. "Pass the butter, please."

"You would go back to work?" Elaine asks.

"This meat looks expensive; where did you buy it?" Karl asks.

"You're looking a bit thick, Gretch, maybe you should watch what you eat," Andrew says.

"That chair can't stand much more of you," Fredrik adds, chuckling.

"Fredrik, you didn't mention Gretchen was going back to work after the baby," Elaine says. *Wait—Fredrik knew Andrew had told his parents? They've discussed it?* "We'd like to buy the crib for the nursery."

"Thank you, but we haven't even gotten that far yet," I reply.

"Whatever you want, you decide, but we want to do this," Elaine continues.

"That's kind of you, but no, thank you, money is—" I say.

"Gretchen doesn't mean to sound ungrateful; Mom, Dad, that would be great," Fredrik says as he shoots me a look. I send him one back that says, *What you gonna do about it, Momma's boy?*

"Ready for seconds, G?" Andrew asks, raising his eyebrows.

"The financial burden of having a child can seem overwhelming, but we didn't have much—no one did—and we did just fine. Why, I read an infant can be *totally* entertained by his mother's face and hands. No need for fancy play mats," Elaine says.

"We haven't decided what we'll do about my job—my career, that is."

Karl coughs. I sit there, like a jerk. The last thing I want is a scene, so I look down at my plate. It's empty. How many servings have I had? I'm so angry I could scream. I *knew* I shouldn't have trusted Fredrik to keep a secret from his parents. He's too loyal to them. But why? They are utterly unenlightened. As soon as I get home, I'm calling my mother; she'll agree *for sure* that they're a bunch of provincial whacks. The rest of the dinner is a blur. I start to yawn loudly and frequently to signal to Fredrik that we need to leave, *now*. We say our good-byes and climb into the truck. Before the key is even in the ignition, I lose it.

"What is wrong with you?" I shriek.

"What?"

"Why in God's name didn't you tell me your parents knew I was pregnant?"

"Andrew told them," he says.

"That's not an answer to my question."

"They were excited, so I confirmed it. What's the big deal? Oh, that's right—I forgot, you don't do *happy family*."

"Taking things up a notch kind of fast, aren't you? Well, how is this: is happy a new euphemism for 'overbearing, highly judgmental, not-at-all-appreciative of the work you do'?"

"I knew you wouldn't understand. That's why I didn't mention it."

"Oh, it's my fault, then! That's rich. At least my mom respects our privacy."

"Only because you refuse to take her calls."

The rest of the ride home passes in silence. When we come home, Fredrik leaves immediately to take Boo out for a walk. I rush over to the phone to call my mother, while I have the time, as I'm sure she'll be up for a Stirling-family bashing session.

"But how will you nurse if you go back to work?" Mom asks.

"Were you even listening to me?"

"Yes. And now I'm asking you a question."

"The answer is: I don't know. Maybe I will supplement with formula?"

"I breast-fed you exclusively for nine months."

"Awesome. Appreciate it."

"The American Academy of Pediatrics recommends it for a year. In fact, the surgeon general is going to put warnings on formula."

"Warning about what?" I ask, somewhat skeptical.

"Warning mothers it's not as good for babies as breast milk."

"How *helpful*. Perhaps the surgeon general could also put a big fat label on the Family Leave and Medical Act, warning the public that it's a *useless provision* because it doesn't guarantee that you get paid while you're off."

"I think that's a different department. I'll ask Peyton about it."

"Yes, please do. Please ask Peyton about it. She is in with the president, after all," I say, snorting.

"Honey, I pray you don't take this the wrong way, but in this case, maybe the entry-level nature of your job works in your favor. It might be easier to leave it. It's not as if you are out there, you know, curing cancer or flying into outer space."

"Right. I shouldn't work because I don't have a PhD. Oh, *wait,* but you *do* and you don't work, either."

"I didn't have the opportunities you do."

"But that makes *no* sense. You're telling me to stay home despite my opportunities? What about my career?" My AWESOME career!!

Mom ignores this comment and asks, "Is it a financial issue?"

"Yes and no."

"Is it a matter of pride?"

"Yes and no."

"Is it the intellectual stimulation?"

"Yes and no."

"I don't know how to help you."

"Tell me I'm doing the right thing."

"I can't do that."

"Can't you just be a mom every once in a while?"

"I see you are not in the mood for an honest conversation. Good-bye."

Forget it! I think as I hang up. I don't want to get involved in some damn national debate. I don't have the confidence to choose sides. Besides, I don't know if anyone has noticed this but I AM NOT EVEN A MOTHER YET!

I don't need this. I need support! I need *blanket validation*. I need a friend.

I call Meredith.

"Wow," she says when I give her a run-down on the dinner.

"Is it me or is everyone an idiot?" I say.

"I think what Fredrik is feeling is a conflict between his family of origin, versus you, his family of choice."

"In English? Please?" I ask.

"His loyalties. He feels torn. Between his parents and you."

"But it's not like we just started dating. We've been married for three years!"

"Yes, but unlike many adult children in Western societies, he sees his family every day. But you've said that's one of the reasons you love him," she teases. "You always describe him as family-oriented."

"Too bad it's to the wrong family. They don't even appreciate him."

"Once the baby comes you will be your own—a separate—Stirling family. And that part of it *is* new, even though you've been married for a few years. You will have to renegotiate some things. Trust me, everyone does it."

"And my mom? What's *that* about?"

"That's called *meddling*."

I laugh. "I feel better. I wish I had an anthropology degree."

"You have a sociology degree—it's not that different."

"Yeah, the semester I spent studying the Asian-American experience in post-World War II United States, specifically in Northern California, is making a *huge* difference right now," I say.

Meredith laughs. "It's not the degree—it's just living through it."

"That you survived gives me great hope. Thanks for listening."

"My pleasure."

As I hang up, I make a note in my Filofax: *Google "family of origin."*

Chapter 10

"Easy does it. You're carrying more weight, your center of gravity has changed and your fingers, toes, and other joints are loosening. Put away your high heels and stick with stable, flat shoes; that way, you'll be more comfortable and safer, too."
—From *Ready or Not, An Expectant Mother's Guide* (Week 17, page 175)

"Watch it!" a deliveryman shouts, balancing a dolly on its back wheels.

"Are you OK?" a mother with two small children asks.

"Yes, I'm fine, thank you. *Excuse me,*" I say as I get off the elevator at Dr. Mitchell's office. I'm teetering about on my one semicool pair of shoes, low-heeled slingbacks that I chose in anticipation of my appointment and tonight's happy hour with Louisa. She called me two days ago and we had a strange, midconversation conversation, as though the past two months hadn't happened. She did not mention her miscarriage, my phone calls, or my pregnancy. When I asked her how she was feeling, she brushed it off with a "crazy at work, the usual." She was late for a meeting, she explained, but could Fredrik and I join her at Mt. Tom's Bar & Grill? We'd catch up then, she assured me, though it seems unlikely. I wish she'd suggested we meet for coffee today instead; after all, no one *really* works on Good Friday. Plus, tomorrow is Passover and the public schools, Smith, and Mass State are on break (Front Desk Bob is in South Padre Island). My phone barely rang all day.

Since I don't have any events planned for this weekend and I wasn't interested in "cold calling" law firms' event planners to solicit holiday office party business, as Eliza suggested, I decided to go to Dr. Mitchell's office, to get my blood taken for the genetic testing. "I have an appointment, for a medical procedure," I say to Eliza in a serious tone as I start to leave. "I'll try to come back to the office if I can. *We'll see.*" I've already worked close to sixty hours this week. I need a break.

The nurse prepares for the blood drawing by placing a rubber band, a needle, and two vials on a plastic tray. She puts on rubber gloves, ties the band on my upper arm and pokes the needle into my vein, filling the two vials with my blood. I shouldn't look. But I can't help myself. "Cute shoes," she remarks. This isn't so bad. My blood appears top of the line. I have a *good* feeling about this test, despite Mom's gloom-and-doom predictions ("You're taking the test on Good Friday? *The very day Christ was on the cross?* That's horrible," she'd said). I should learn to trust my instincts. Like, I'm certain Dr. Mitchell will see me in my not-quite-showing-yet-pregnant outfit and want to chat with me in the hallway, maybe near the scale nook, so he can get to know me better.

"Is Dr. Mitchell in?" I ask.

"No," the nurse replies. "He is out of the office today."

Huh. Not "at the hospital" or "on vacation." Just "out of the office." How vague. He didn't mention being out when we spoke last week. I called him to ask a few more questions about the test (you know, margin of error, that kind of thing) and he was *really* helpful. It's a test of my blood, he explained, and it's measured against a statistical mean of well, I don't exactly remember, but this test, with a sensitive sonogram, can pretty much rule out anything. Since I'm not of "advanced maternal age," which I will be in approximately ten minutes, and amnio has a risk of miscarriage, the blood test is the best option. I asked Dr. Mitchell a few questions about miscarriage, but I still don't *really* understand what happened to Louisa who, *shit*, I'm supposed to meet in fifteen minutes.

My plan was to arrive at the bar early, so I could re-adjust my outfit and check out the scene. But my feet are throbbing so I have to walk slowly. I nearly fall, twice: once in front of Lucky Lucy's take-out—I considered re-covering over some steamed dumplings—and a second time in front of the courthouse. By the time I arrive at the bar, I'm in severe pain and sweating.

"Look who's here!" Louisa shouts as I walk in.

She's tipsy. Before I'm through the door, she's pulled me to the bar. I'm stunned by how good she looks—dark straight-leg jeans (she's apparently lost the pregnancy weight in a matter of minutes) and lingerie-like tank top with black bra straps clearly evident. Her boots are bone-colored, high, the same pair I'd rejected during our last shopping trip. I am as wide as she is tall, my diminished stature exaggerated by her footwear.

"I can't stop boozing," she declares.

Her glass is filled to the brim with a brown, viscous liquid. She guzzles it.

"What is that?" It smells like pancakes. And dirt.

"A mud pie. Tracy told the bartender how to make it. TRY IT!" she shouts.

Who? "No, I can't—well, just a taste."

Cough, cough, cough. God, this is horrible. A few people at the bar stare.

"Back in ten for a sigh-garette." She's gone.

A minute or two standing alone by the bar feels like a

lifetime. Fredrik arrives and orders a drink; he does not ask me about the blood test. My eyes drift to the front door—Jason is arriving. I give him a smile and turn back to Fredrik, scowling.

"The test went fine," I say.

"They just took your blood, right?"

"Yes, but it would have been nice if you'd—"

"FREDRIK!" Louisa shouts. "Jason, look who's here! Fredrik!"

Fredrik and Louisa hug. She offers him a mud pie, which he accepts. They then order shots. I sip my ginger ale slowly and wish I'd asked for a maraschino cherry. I excuse myself for the bathroom, where I take the opportunity to remove my shoes. My feet are swollen. How will I get them back into the eights? They were already too tight this morning but I *can't* go higher; a large shoe on a person my height is unseemly, clownish. I shove my left foot back in but the right one is more difficult. I loosen the strap. It still doesn't fit. I finally just unfasten it and pretend it is a mule. I return to the bar, my shoe straps dragging, to find Fredrik next to several women dressed identically to Louisa. I walk over, smiling a huge fake smile, and join the group.

". . . it's *the* drink at Stasis," one says.

"That's assuming we're sober enough to know what we're drinking,"

Laughter all around. No one acknowledges me. Louisa grabs me in a possessive fashion, and begins introducing me to the women gathered around Fredrik.

"Does everyone remember Gretchen, my best friend?" The words sound forced. She continues, "This is Tracy—you guys met at the company picnic—Hillary and Laura are from the New York office."

"This town is soooo cute and I love this country-fresh air," Laura says.

Isn't the "Apple" lucky to rid itself of these two? I jump

in to correct the mischaracterization of Northampton as "the country." "Northampton, NoHo, is actually a largish city. There's loads to do here—jazz clubs, the improv, the renovated Brayden Theatre,"—not that I've actually been to any of these places.

"NoHo," one exclaims, "like SoHo!"

"Yes, exactly," I nod. We're making a connection. Cool.

Everyone bursts into laughter. Fredrik's draped his arms around Louisa and Tracy, all smiles and good times. I can't be sure, but I suspect one of the New York chicks is checking Fredrik out. I take a look too. He is explaining his predilection for wearing shorts year-round; he's a contractor, whatever. Another round of drinks appears, compliments of Jason. He is about to hand me one and then, remembering, stops.

"You can't drink."

"No, but thanks."

"GRETCHEN IS PREGNANT!" Louisa screams.

"Fun," one says.

"Not for me," Fredrik says, and they all hoo-hah at my expense.

"Fredrik," I whisper.

"WHO WANTS ANOTHER ROUND?" he shouts.

"FREDRIK!"

"What?"

"I'm sorry to yell but I'm tired."

"LOUISA, ANOTHER MUD PIE?" He turns to me and says, "Do you want to go home? Take the truck—you're *not* walking."

"Come with me," I plead.

"But I'm having a good time."

"But I don't want to be alone."

"Then stay here."

"But I want to go home."

There is an awkward pause and the bar instinctively

falls silent as everyone waits to see who will win this argument.

Louisa looks at me and says, "Gretchen, don't be a party pooper like Ryder's Mommy." *Ouch*. That was uncalled for. Why is she trashing Meredith? I want to go home but not without Fredrik, who is clearly up for a night of boozing. I look to Fredrik and hold up one finger and mouth "one hour," to which he replies, "OK." To everyone at the bar he winks and then declares, "We better get drinking then."

I sigh. I suddenly feel silly for *insisting* to Meredith just last night that I could still have fun in a bar. She *insisted* right back that it would not be fun. But as I was not about to completely give up on the idea of a social life—however limited—she recommended I prepare myself. "How?" I asked. "Bring a book," she suggested. I laughed. I realize, now, that it was actually a good idea. As I have nothing to do (I wish I'd stolen this month's *American Baby* from Dr. Mitchell.) I spend the next hour doing the following:

I read closed-captioning on CNN;

I survey the other patrons (Who is the most attractive male/female? Who has the best outfit? Who most resembles a celebrity?);

I silently celebrate my successful spotting of a two of a kind (Meredith finally e-mailed me the rules to pregnancy poker.)—two girls—not a great hand but a clear winner, given the circumstances;

I silently wish someone else would suggest we move to a table;

I silently wish someone else would suggest we order food;

I review the bar menu;

I debate (with myself) the merits of the deluxe nachos versus potato skins;

I attempt to get the bartender's attention to order both;

I tap my fingers on the bar;
I steal two cherries;
I remove the straps from my left shoe;
I resort to shouting at the bartender;
I order.

Finally, my food arrives. Before I know it, the plates are empty. Drunken people are pigs.

"You know what we need?" Fredrik asks, licking his fingers. *Gross.*

"What?" Tracy answers.

"A diner."

"French fries! I want French fries!" Louisa says. Tracy circle snaps.

"Fredrik," I say, attempting to pull him aside via his ordered-twice-a-year-in-bulk Carhartt shirt, "I need to go home."

"YOU CAN'T GO!" Louisa shouts. "*Jesus,* what happened to your feet?"

Not once has anyone paid me any mind until now; they stare. They are grotesquely swollen.

"I just need a Band-Aid, that's all."

"I have some in my purse," Louisa says. "Take one and then let's go! You'll need those feet to drive us to Greenfield!"

I open Louisa's bag. Here's her "oral fixation kit" (cigarettes, mints, candy, gum, etc.), a copy of *Living Life* magazine, her BlackBerry/crackberry thingy, an empty Starbucks to-go mug, and *her* Filofax (again, thank you, Bethany). I move the Filo to get to the side pockets and a small, black-and-white photograph drops to the cold cement floor. I look closely; it's a sonogram with LOUISA MCCARTNEY typed on the top, and the date, February 1. I try to retrieve it by bending over at the waist, but I can't seem to get beyond my stomach; I squat down instead.

"What are you doing down there?" Fredrik hisses.

"Nothing."

I put the photo back in her purse and tears come to my eyes. This is horrible. I will never know this child, the son or daughter of my best friend. I can only imagine how Louisa must feel. I will do whatever it takes to support her; we can talk when she's ready. I want to cry, tell her I'm sorry for her loss, and hug her.

I look up to find her nearly tripping on her walk back from the bathroom.

"SHOTGUN!" Louisa yells as she throws me her car keys.

I resist getting into the car; I'm worried we'll be pulled over—can seven of us fit in Louisa's Volvo? Isn't it illegal to drive in bare feet? The ensuing ride to the Greenfield Diner is marred by the fact that I am dead sober and thus—according to Fredrik, Jason, Tracy, Laura in the backseat, and Louisa and Hillary in the front with me—a "downer." I do not sing when Louisa turns her CD of Madonna's *Immaculate Collection* to *top volume* (Louisa and I stopped keeping up with popular music like ten years ago); instead, I turn it down. She turns it back up, louder. I do not chime in when Fredrik and Jason begin chanting, "G-Dog, G-Dog, G-Dog," as a way of acknowledging my "cool driving." In fact, I nearly crash as Hillary waves her hands in the air—she is sitting next to the window—and the ash from her cigarette goes flying across the car. I do not acknowledge the talk of road-tripping to the Cape for a swim (God, the delusions). Forget support. I hate these people.

At the restaurant, we crowd into a circular booth. There is a raucous debate over whether to order dinner or breakfast. The other diners stare. I'm so *embarrassed*. Is this how I am when I'm drunk? I check my watch. It's one in the morning—breakfast is the obvious choice—and attempt to organize the group's orders. The only moment of silence comes when the food arrives. Shortly thereafter, Hillary runs to the bathroom with her hand over her mouth. Once it's clear no one notices and/or cares, I go to check on her.

"Hillary? You OK?"

She heaves into the toilet. I begin to gag myself. I take a deep breath and push myself into the stall. I hold her hair back and pat her on the back. "Yes, yes, you'll be fine," I say, "let's get you home." I steer her back to the table—announcing we are leaving, the night is over—and arrange everyone in the car. I instruct all passengers to be quiet unless they a) see a deer on the road, or b) feel sick. There will be no music or smoking. *There will be no swimming on the Cape.* Despite some murmurs of protest ("I don't think the water would be too cold, do you? We could swim in blankets," Tracy suggests.), they agree, and within minutes after I pull the car onto Interstate 91, every single one of them passes out.

Whoosh. A car passes. I remember being on a trip when I was little. My parents are in the front bench seat of our twinkley blue Custom Cruiser; Peyton and I lie in the back (The seat had been folded over to accommodate our *Little House on the Prairie* sleeping bags.). I awake to find Mom and Dad playing games and giggling to keep each other awake during the all-night drive. *Whoosh, whoosh.* "A slug bug!" Dad says and Mom laughs. I felt so *safe*; I didn't even mind that Peyton was drifting over to my side of the car. Weird. I hadn't thought about that trip in a long time.

Sigh. I want so desperately to talk to Louisa. A real talk. But she's in mourning (and asleep). I need to be respectful, but I miss her so much. Fredrik doesn't make a good best friend. My mom is crazy; I can't make sense of her—should I trust her interest in the pregnancy? What if she disappoints me again? And Peyton, well, we're destined just *not to be close*. The car is stuffy; I roll down a window. I breathe the fresh air and welcome in a rush of emotions. Come on in! Sadness! Anger! Empathy! Embarrassment! Frustration! Join the party.

Chapter 11

"Timber! There are a number of factors that can contribute to dizziness and lightheadedness while pregnant: standing up too fast, hunger, dehydration, anxiety, anemia, or becoming overheated. The best thing to do is avoid these circumstances."
—From *Ready or Not, An Expectant Mother's Guide* (Week 18, page 188)

Easter
It's as it's always been.

Priest: The Lord be with you
All: And also with you.
Priest: A reading from the Holy Gospel according to John.
All: Glory to you, Lord.

Easter Mass at St. Thomas Aquinas, Main Street. I sit in a pew with Fredrik, his parents, Andrew, Fredrik's cousin Karl and his wife, and Karl's parents, a second set of Mr. and Mrs. Stirlings. I stand and absentmindedly make the sign of the cross on my forehead, my lips, and my chest as I've done one hundred times before. I shift my weight from one foot to the other, awaiting the intermission, the homily.

The priest, a middle-aged man with a bright white mane of hair, is brilliant in Liberace-esque ivory and gold vestments. He completes the scripture reading, dons a lapel microphone, and begins pacing on the altar, Oprah-style. We sit.

I admit I have a love-hate relationship with the Holy Roman Catholic Church. That is, I love to hate it. I have a whole rant. The church is anti-intellectual, patriarchal, and *criminal* even (I literally quote my parents); as flawed as the men who run it, I say. But it's more basic than that: I lack faith. It eroded over time, beginning on a cold November morning, during my junior year of high school. The director of students appeared at my chemistry class door; could Gretchen Fox come to the office? I walked along with her to the headmistress's office, wrinkling my nose at my sulfur-soaked polo shirt, chit-chatting. I wasn't nervous; I expected another discussion with Sister Helen, the nun/CFO, regarding "nonpayment of tuition." That it would take place in the school chapel, where I was deposited, and in the presence of my mother, a priest, and three other nuns, was a new twist. Mom stood.

"Your father, honey—there was an accident. On the Beltway," Mom said.

Within minutes, a priest offered a quiet prayer and communion. I took the wafer on my tongue instead of in my hands; a submissive gesture to indicate I had wholly accepted God's will, defined as He *Will* Take Care of Everything From Now On. And why not? I'd gone to church every Sunday my entire life, attended Catholic school, volunteered at a nursing home (OK, it was required by the school.), abided by the commandments (OK, I was in eleventh grade, so I had little opportunity to covet or forsake.), *and* I was a virgin.

For the days immediately after the accident, we were well cared for—meals prepared, compliments of our parish's Loaves and Fishes Program. At the wake, I was

startled to see friends of my parents, neighbors, class-
mates; so many people. *Everything would be fine—not the
same,* they said, *but fine.* I believed it. My Uncle Frank,
Dad's older brother, in for the day of the funeral from
Chicago, was not as reassuring. Death is bad luck, he said,
and most possess an irrational but pervasive fear that it is
contagious. Within a few months, after Death Valley, when
Mom was busy working the phones to demand the closing
of the Beltway and bill collectors were calling, we had no
one to turn to. My parents' friends, our neighbors, even the
Loaves people, had moved on. You were right, I'd joked to
Uncle Frank's answering machine, *everything is a mess,
and could you give us a call?* But my pleas went unheeded;
he never visited again. We were alone.

> *Priest:* Let us now profess our faith.
> *All:* I believe in God, the Father almighty, creator
> of heaven and earth. I believe in Jesus Christ, His
> only Son, our Lord, the communion of saints,
> the forgiveness of sins, the resurrection of the
> body, and the life everlasting. Amen.

Life everlasting. I take issue with that, too. While I was
subject to earthly despair, Dad was—and this is a loose interpretation of church doctrine and I am assuming he
passed his judgment at the Pearly Gates—in Heaven,
happy. Is this not at odds with what was happening, you
know, *down below?* During one of my lost Christmases, I
spent the day at an Irish pub. When Alexis Newhouse
walked in—I'd not seen her since our high school graduation three years before—I waved her over. Alexis had
spent Christmas Eve at an aunt's; her mother had died of
cancer nine months prior.
"Why didn't you stay?" I asked.
"I worried I'd wake up Christmas morning and forget,

for a second or two, that Mom had died. I'd have to remember that she's, our family, was—is—*gone*. Dad's in
Bora Bora with his new wife and I'm on a pull-out couch
in my aunt's library."

"Interesting," I said. "Why'd he remarry? I wish Mom
would."

"She helps him, he says—she can match his shirts and
ties."

"Lazy bastard."

"The worst is—Mom was devoted to Dad, worshipped
him. What would she think?"

After more Guinness, but before we sang the second verse
of "The Unicorn Song," we experienced an Alcohol-Induced
Divine Revelation, which we scrawled on a bar napkin. It
is this: there is no such thing as Heaven. If Heaven is complete contentment, then we must assume the deceased cannot see the survivors who suffer their loss. If the deceased
cannot see his or her loved ones, how can he or she experience complete contentment? For two years, I kept the
napkin in a plastic-covered insert in my Filo. I don't feel
like a hypocrite, attending Mass today. I'm happy to be
proven wrong. A three person–documented miracle isn't
required, but a rereading of *When Bad Things Happen to
Good People* isn't going to cut it, either. I know there are
faithful who've suffered worse, remain in the flock, and
are less demanding sign-wise; I can only say I admire their
courage.

> *Lector:* For those who've lost loved ones, let us
> pray to the Lord.
> *All:* Lord, hear our prayer.

I have a selfish prayer: *please, let this baby be healthy*.
My stomach grumbles; it's empty. I awoke at five this
morning (the third time this week) and began preparing

for Easter dinner, which we're hosting. I ironed the napkins, arranged flowers, finalized my choices of serving trays and polished the banister. Four hours later, I had a paint roller in one hand and a can of "Marsh Grass" from the Duron Carolina Lowcountry Collection in the other when Fredrik yelled, "TIME'S UP, get dressed." He touched up the powder room while I fought with control tops. I resolved to buy some maternity clothes.

> *All:* Lamb of God, you take away the sins of the
> world; have mercy on us.
> Lamb of God, you take away the sins of the
> world; have mercy on us.
> Lamb of God, you take away the sins of the
> world; grant us peace.

I lean my butt back on the pew, a cheat, as the others kneel straight-backed in solemnity, their hands folded. I look at my fingers and my consciousness shifts; I'm no longer in the moment, with my husband, at Mass, but watching it. The pace of my heart quickens and nausea strikes; the saliva is toxic. A flash of heat and sweat followed by a chill, a feeling I've not had in ten years—no, no—it *cannot* happen here, not now. I focus on the priest. What is he saying? My thoughts rush to an unbalanced point of obsession: am I having an anxiety attack? Please, no. I cannot breathe. If I don't breathe, I will harm the baby. I will go mad with guilt; I will be institutionalized. I will die. I grab Fredrik's arm and he looks at me, smiling, then his brow lowers. My ears are ringing.

"I don't feel well," I say as I bury my head in my hands.

"What is it?"

Deep breaths, in, out, in, out. I sit back in the pew. I must get out of this church, *right now*. I tip my head back and stare at the fresco on the ceiling. Madonna and the

Christ child's golden halos are riddled with veiny cracks. It looks like the calendar that hung in the kitchen of my grandparents' house. Each month featured a reproduction of a Renaissance-era painting, alongside coupons to a local religious bookstore and funeral homes. I clutch the back of the pew ahead of us, just as Elaine notices I'm out of form, and pull myself up to stand.

"Gretchen, Gretchen!"

I sit back down. I slowly—I'm barely conscious of this—fall to my right, and then to the floor. I am facing a cracked, green leather kneeler. I turn my body and see Fredrik's face; he missed a spot shaving this morning—right there, over his upper lip, and there's Andrew, what's he doing? Why is he touching my legs? I kick him.

"Ouch!" Andrew yells.

"What is going on, Fredrik? Is she conscious?" Elaine asks.

A new face joins the huddle. It's the priest.

"What do we have here?" he asks.

"She is expecting, Father; she fainted."

Great, now even this guy knows I've had sex.

"We should call an ambulance," Andrew says as he and Fredrik lift me up to the pew.

An ambulance? Am I dead? Dead on Arrival. D.O.A. That's what Dad was. Dead on Arrival.

"Gretchen? Can you hear me? Say something," Fredrik pleads.

"Jesus, it's hot in here," I reply. Sweat drips down my back.

"I'm sure she didn't mean to say that, Father," Elaine says.

Say what? *Oh, the Jesus.* Jesus, I can't do anything right.

"Can you get up? Let's get you outside; I'll call Dr. Mitchell," Fredrik says.

Fredrik carefully picks me up and walks with me out of the pew. We take the side aisle, I guess in an effort to be inconspicuous, but the entire congregation is staring at us. The priest is back up at the altar; his hands are raised to bring the focus back to the Mass. Wow, it's crowded today. I hadn't realized so many people were standing in the back. I smile and nod as I walk pass—*Oh, hey, hi, yes, just passing through, never mind me, I'm just pregnant and going crazy.* Look, a family with five children—five! Is that a straight or a royal flush? I should have known my fellow Catholics would give me my best pregnancy poker hand yet.

Once outside, I sit down on a cement step and try to put my head between my knees but I have to spread my legs farther apart than a polite woman should. I'm sure my control tops are visible. Someone in a car driving by whistles at me.

"Have him call me back at this number," Fredrik says into the phone. He walks over to me. "That was Dr. Mitchell's service; they're going to page him. But I think we should go to the hospital."

"Is that necessary?" Elaine asks.

"Yes, Mother, I think it is," Fredrik responds.

"Let's go home. I want to lie down." I yawn. "I'm so tired."

Fredrik's cell rings. I take the phone.

"Hi, Dr. Mitchell. Yes, I fainted, I think. No, I'm not nauseous. No, no cramping. OK, I will. Thanks for calling back so fast."

"What did he say?"

"That I should go home, drink water, and rest. But to call him if anything changes."

"I knew we didn't need to go to the hospital," Elaine mutters.

"I'm going to take her home, then."

I look up at his mother as I get into the truck. Fredrik rolls down the window.

"Happy Easter!" he shouts as he pulls away.

Exactly twelve hours from the time I awoke, I'm back in bed. The wind is howling outside. Boo is napping at my feet. Fredrik is downstairs on the phone; I strain to hear his version of events.

"Faye, she's fine. No, no—no need to come up. Dr. Mitchell said just to take it easy for a day or two," he says. A silence and Fredrik continues, "She's sleeping. Of course, I'll tell her."

The phone rings again seconds later.

"Peyton, how are you? Did your mom just call you? Looking for the real story, right, right." Fredrik chuckles. "Why don't you speak with her yourself?"

I pick up. Fredrik stays on the line and for a second or two, we all breathe at each other. "I've got it, thank you." Another moment passes before *click,* he hangs up.

"What happened?" Peyton asks.

I put the phone in my lap and notice the cradle is dirty. Where are the disinfectant wipes? I rummage through my bedside table drawer. What's this out-of-date *Shape* magazine doing here? I flip to the marked page: "Improve Your Abs While Driving." I pitch it toward the trash can but miss and hit the window. Boo barks.

"What are you doing?" she asks.

"Looking for my wipes—this phone is filthy."

"Mrs. Clean," she laughs. "You OK?"

"Yes, I was at Mass and I felt like I was spinning and I collapsed."

"But the doctor said you and the baby are fine?"

"Yeah, we paged him and he called me right away," I sigh. "I'm so embarrassed."

"You fainted, G. No big deal."

"It is. You don't understand. You think I'm a . . . a . . . a poor planner."

Peyton changes the subject. "Did Mom tell you she's joined Curves? She wants to be, and I quote, 'in perfect health' for her grandchildren."

"She *just* told me gyms kill you. Something she saw on *Nightline*. Or *Frontline*. Whatever. Does she even have exercise clothes?"

"A leotard and tights, with leg warmers. Very Jane Fonda. Twenty years old, from when she started the modern singing and dance troupe."

"I remember now. There was some controversy over her interpretation of *Man of La Mancha;* wasn't there a rape scene?"

"Yes, *exactly*."

The next forty minutes fly by. I joke with Peyton as I used to with Louisa. We conduct some armchair analysis of Mom (Is her lack of judgment pathological or circumstantial?); her boyfriend, Alexander (They'd exchanged ILY's—"I love you's"—for the first time Saturday night.); and her job. I was laughing so loudly at her insistence it was my idea, not hers, to make trace drawings of the hippies in flagrante delicto depicted in Mom and Dad's copy of *Joy of Sex* that I didn't hear Fredrik enter the room with Louisa. I wipe the tears from the corners of my eyes and say good-bye. Fredrik winks at me and closes the door behind him. Louisa sits on the edge of the bed. She smells like cigarette smoke.

"How do you feel?"

"Good, just did too much."

Louisa stands and walks to the window, where she looks through the curtains to her house. Her pants are baggy on her butt. She keeps her back to me.

"I can't stay. Tracy's picking me up. I've got to work in the city tomorrow."

"Right," I respond.

"Fredrik told me what happened," Louisa says.

"I hope he isn't mad at me."

"It was stupid to paint at four o'clock in the morning."

I laugh. Louisa does not. In fact, she glares at me.

"Look, you're obviously mad at me," I say. "You don't return any of my phone calls, and then, the one time you do, it's to invite me to a bar. I'm sorry about your miscarriage. I wanted to be there for you, still want to—because you have been there for me—but I can't change the fact I'm pregnant."

"I am not asking you to!" she snapped.

"No, but you're mad nonetheless. I know how it feels to be jealous," I say.

"Don't patronize me, Gretchen. I'm over it."

"Then why blow me off?"

"God, you are so *self-righteous*. You think you deserve this pregnancy? It doesn't take any talent or skill to conceive a child, but it takes a real asshole to screw it up for a platter of Honey-Baked Ham."

"Jesus, Louisa. I understand you're upset but—"

"*Do not tell me you understand*. Because you don't, you just don't."

Louisa turns on her heels. She's down the stairs, through the hall, out the front door. I walk to the window. Louisa is running to her house. I watch her cross her lawn, open the door to her house, and disappear.

Chapter 12

*"Let it all out. With hormones come feelings of in-
tense emotion. Talk to your partner, your mother,
your friends or your doctor about your joys and sor-
rows; keeping your feelings hidden isn't healthy for
you or the baby."*
—From *Ready or Not, An Expectant Mother's Guide*
   (Week 19, page 164)

When Dr. Mitchell called Monday with the news that
the prenatal screening test indicated a chromosomal
disorder, I was, for once, prepared. I'd just caught up on
four months of pregnancy-related information by reading
six pregnancy books. I learned that a good percentage of
positive test results are false. "The same thing happened with
Meredith," I explained to Fredrik over a dinner of spinach
salad and peanut butter and jelly sandwiches, "when she
was pregnant with Ryder. And of course, he's fine." ("The
test measures maternal blood levels against an average
gestational age," Meredith counseled. "If you ovulate
early or late, the test can't account for it. I'd ask for a second blood test. Mine came back fine." "Where is the science in medical science, exactly?" I'd asked her.)

Fredrik was noticeably relieved that I'd done some forward thinking and had "a plan." I proudly showed him

my new Filofax pregnancy section, which contained a reduced photocopy of a week-by-week developmental calendar. I was not going to regress to panic. Panic. I researched
that, too. From what I've read—and no one seems to have
a definitive answer on this, or anything about pregnancy—
you may experience more, the same, or less. Helpful.

Stay calm, I thought when Dr. Mitchell told me the second set of test results were identical to the first.

Stay calm, I thought when I read a description of the
amniocentesis "procedure" wherein "a long, hollow needle will be pushed to the amniotic sac to extract fluid,
which is then cultured and tested."

Stay calm, I thought, before I picked up the phone to
make the appointment.

I had to remind myself that this is one of those occa-
sions wherein I had to be on my absolute *best* telephone
behavior, as I was convinced that if I gave the receptionist
even a hint of trouble, I'd end up with the "bad" doctor
("She was falling apart on the phone; let's give her to Dr.
Barrett. That'll give her something to *really* worry about.").
As I am often on the other end of panicked phone calls
myself—some reasonable, some not ("What do you mean
you cannot release live butterflies in your ballroom?")—I
can say with confidence that how you treat the voice on the
other end of the phone can and will impact your service.

I did not protest when the receptionist scheduled my appointment for April Fool's Day. I listened patiently as she
explained how Fredrik and I were to enter the facility; we
were *not* to go through the Main doors but rather, through
the "South" entrance—located at the back of the building.
After I hung up, I got on my computer and went to the
clinic's Web site. I quickly realized that the testing of
women who were *already* pregnant was a distant second,
business-wise, to helping women *become* pregnant. Their
entrance was called, aptly, "Main."

*   *   *

On the morning of the appointment, I wake up early, only to find that Fredrik had already left the bed. When I go downstairs in search of him, I find him drinking coffee at the kitchen table, in the dark.

"Fredrik? Honey?"

"What time is it?" he asks.

"Five thirty. Why are you sitting in the dark?"

"Is it dark?"

"Um, yeah."

"Are you hungry? Let me make you breakfast."

"No, thanks, I can't eat," I say, taking a seat at the table.

"It's terrifying, isn't it?"

"Yes," I say.

"I don't know if I could do it." He looks down at his coffee mug.

In my mind, there is very little Fredrik can't do but I don't protest. Instead, I say, "Me neither. I can barely care for myself."

"That's not true, and you know it."

"But if given the choice, I'd rather um, not. I'd rather *not* do it."

"Yeah—I hear you," he laughs.

"We are good, selfish people," I say.

"They were a *great* couple, unless you needed something," he adds.

I take Fredrik's hands, and we spend the next hour or so poking fun at ourselves, and then, finally, it is time to go.

Once Fredrik and I are seated in the waiting room, I take a good look around. The facility is, overall, by far the nicest medical building I've ever been in. The leather chairs, big-screen televisions, and complimentary water, coffee, and prepackaged snacks in the waiting room are a far cry from the homey atmosphere of Dr. Mitchell's office, where there is usually a child on the floor, reading a book or licking a lollipop, waiting with Mom to see the doctor.

After a few minutes, we are called into the office of one of the genetic counselors on staff. He reviews our collective medical histories and determines that we're not at risk for anything, beyond what's calculated for the general population, no dominant or recessive genes that carry Tay-Sachs, dwarfism, or cystic fibrosis, and no evidence of X-Linking. I get flustered when I have to explain why my father is "deceased"—I give him a little too much information ("*USA Today* did a story on my mom," I offer, as evidence of the scope of the tragedy.) When our condensed genetic lesson ends the counselor hands us brand-new Onyx Roller Ball pens to sign the waiver:

I hereby understand the risks of miscarriage, of dismemberment, I hereby sign, I hereby beg, please let me be an exception.

We sign, and then Fredrik and I are brought to a large room, in the center of which is an exam table—a size more suited to a hospital than to a doctor's office—and someone tells me to make myself comfortable; I do not, for once, need to remove my clothes. Fredrik helps me onto the table and for a second, I fight the urge to walk out, just not take the test, which is what a lot of people do. But I can't. I have to know. That sound comes out of my mouth again, but I don't laugh to cover it up. I lie down and look to my right. There is a large, flat-screen monitor. Fredrik examines it.

"We are not getting a flat screen TV," I say.

"No, probably not," he says.

A few seconds later, a tall, beautiful, dark-haired woman

dressed in a lab coat enters the room. With her is a nurse who smiles at both Fredrik and me.

"Any problems with the pregnancy?" she asks, after introducing herself.

"No," I say. *None, other than this mind-boggling, nerve-wracking experience.* I roll my eyes at Fredrik, who smiles. I know he knows exactly what I am thinking.

The doctor then explains that they will locate the baby via a sonogram machine—that is what the nurse is there for (Oh, she is a technician, I'm told.)—so the needle wouldn't be inserted anywhere near the baby. OK, I think I say, wondering if she'd paid her way through medical school by modeling, like the doctor on the show starring the guy from that old movie about the pizza delivery boy who sleeps with lonely older women. I then convince myself that this doctor must be *very good* because you'd have to work really hard to convince people you were serious (This is my guess, as I am not usually faced with this obstacle.) and not just a pretty face.

I decide I will start watching the show, so I can get a handle on it.

Am I going crazy?

Once we are done talking, I push my pants, which are underneath my belly anyway, down under my stomach. The technician slathers it with jelly. *Warm* jelly. Fancy. She has to move Fredrik to the side a bit, so she can rub a roller-ball thing—looked like a square mouse for the computer—back and forth over my stomach. Fredrik and I turn to the screen. The baby is crouched on my left side but moving like *crazy*. I see two arms, two legs, and a head, in shades of fuzzy gray.

"Wow," I say, looking at the screen.

"Do you want to know the sex?" the doctor asks.

"Um . . ." I look at Fredrik and shake my head.

"No, but thank you, doctor," he answers.

"Then you may not want to look too carefully. This is a sensitive sonogram."

With nothing left to look at, I decide to focus on Fredrik. His tight, double handed hold on my left hand is pushing my wedding ring into my skin. His blue pullover, worn on top of an original Stirling & Sons T-shirt, is wet under the arms. His stance is unnatural; feet planted hip-width apart, bent at the waist toward me. Fredrik's eyes do not leave my face. He's afraid, I realize, and so am I. And that's not crazy or irrational panic, that's just—that's a normal reaction.

Out of the corner of my eye, I can see the doctor taking the needle off a tray, and removing the plastic cover. I wince. The doctor remarks that I will feel pressure, not pain, but I don't have time to accuse her of being a horrible liar (which is probably bad patient form, anyway), because before I know it, I am looking down, and I am watching this needle push through the side of my stomach. After a few minutes, she removes it. "We will call you in two weeks," she says, handing the needle to yet another technician and then, they are gone.

"I guess that's it," I say as I slither off the table.

"Let's get the HELL out of here!" Fredrik shouts.

When we get to the truck, we're quiet for a minute.

"It's going to be a long two weeks," Fredrik says.

"Yes, and all my usual coping strategies are out. No drinking, no smoking, no triple-shot lattes, *nothing*. Just the hideousness of total consciousness," I joke.

"There is one thing left," he says.

"What?"

"Food."

"God, *you are the smartest man in America*."

On the way home, Fredrik stops at the store—I wait in the truck—and when we get home he unpacks all kinds of tricks and treats for me. At home, Peyton, who'd arrived last night, was putting the finishing touches on dusting our bookshelves. After much discussion with Mom—who wanted to fly up but who would not have been an altogether *calming* presence given she broke down in tears each time the subject came up—we brokered an arrangement to have Petyon come in her place. I was ambivalent about that as well. I wasn't sure I wanted her here, during what I've come to think is a very private time for Fredrik and me. Plus, Peyton and I haven't spent a weekend together under the same roof in I don't know how many years. I wasn't sure we'd get along, or have anything to talk about, anything pleasant, that is. But when Peyton arrived last night with eleven movies, four books, and cross word puzzles, babbling as only we Fox women can do ("Did you know that you actually fly farther West than you need to? It's so the plane doesn't have to get caught up in New York's air traffic."), I realized she was nervous about her "suddenly a sister again" role, too.

She does her best to distract me. We are now on our second viewing of *Coal Miner's Daughter*. The TV is partially obstructed by the trash on the coffee table left over from the first viewing: a tray of Fudge Stripes, empty Kraft White American Cheese wrappers, sleeves of crumbly Saltines, and stacks of trashy magazines. A fingerprinted-riddled glass of ginger ale with a blue Crazy Straw has left a water ring. Oh, well. My feet are up. I'm not moving, per the "Knowing the Risks of Amniocentesis" pamphlet.

"Are you liking your new job?" I ask.

"It's the same job, just a different area."

"Mom was *very* excited about the possibility of her accepting some kind of award from the president, in recognition of all the work she's done, raising you."

"Really? Because when I first told her about it she lectured me for fifteen minutes. She said, 'I can't remember if it was Rachel on *Friends* or an article I'd read in *Mother Jones,* but today's women are overwhelmed by their choices.' "

"Why is that she cannot distinguish between *Mother Jones* and the Turner Broadcasting System?"

"I don't think she cares what the source is, as long as she can drive home the point that I'm not married or pregnant with her grandchild," Peyton says.

"Yikes," I respond.

The doorbell rings.

It's Mrs. Torrez. She is holding a large Pyrex casserole, covered in tin foil. It's funny to see her out of uniform. But then, I'm in my pajamas (What is it about seeing people out of context that is so disconcerting? To celebrate the Singletons' retirement, Eliza planned a pool party. It's Massachusetts, so I'd not been swimming in about four years. The idea I'd wear a bathing suit was inconceivable, but I wondered if I would have to see my coworkers half-naked. I survived, but barely—Front Desk Bob nearly lost his Hawaiian-print board shorts doing a cannonball, giving us all a view of an alarmingly hairy ass, which prompted Mr. Edwards—gay, in the Finance department—to declare, "Oh, the humanity.").

"You must be Gretchen's sister," Señora says to Peyton.

"Yes," she answers.

"I can't stay. Practice is at four." Señora turns to Peyton. "This is her favorite, Sula Simmered Beef. Reheat at 250 degrees, for twenty minutes."

"Of course, thank you," Peyton says, taking the dish to the kitchen.

I stay seated on the couch. Mrs. Torrez gets down on her knees so she's at eye level with me. This gesture, so obviously uncomfortable, is so unlike something my mother would do.

"*Estoy rogando para usted, el pequeño.* I will pray for you," she whispers.

"Thank you. Thank you," I say. I need all the help I can get.

Peyton returns from the kitchen and sits back down next to me.

"Why can't Mom be like that?" I ask as Mrs. Torrez lets herself out.

We're quiet for a minute.

"I don't know. She just loves to be the center of attention," Peyton says.

"Don't we all," I joke as I hand her my empty glass.

When she returns with my refill (water, as Fredrik is regulating all soda / sugar intake by buying only single-serving-sized bottles of ginger-ale despite it being completely uneconomical), I suggest we go upstairs to my room to watch *Steel Magnolias*. We approach the stairs and have an awkward moment—she's not sure if I can do it myself—I tell her I'm fine, I'm not in any pain, and we head up to my bedroom. We walk into my room and over to the bed. Each of us goes to a side and carefully folds down the bedding. We can hear Fredrik on the phone in his office.

"Andrew wants to come over," he shouts.

"Why should today be different than any other day?" I shout back.

"He has something for you—a video game or something," he continues.

"For me? How thoughtful," I tease.

Peyton and I climb into the bed and prop ourselves up on an assortment of pillows. I have two new body pillows, which I grip between my legs when I sleep, on my left side. It's harder to get comfortable, not because I'm huge or anything—I'm still faking it clothes-wise—but because I'm growing. The skin on my stomach is dry and by the end of the day, my joints and muscles ache. (Fredrik wasn't happy about putting even more crap on our bed and he can be careless with the off-white-bordered French squares. "Use the bench. I don't want Boo making a bed on my imported pillowcases," I pleaded. "My mom says there is nothing more impractical than a white bed," Fredrik countered. "Go sleep at your mom's house, then," I said.) Peyton, on the other hand, appreciates my indulgence in all things down; she even checked under the fitted sheet for the brand and content type of the feather bed.

We watch the movie without speaking, until the scene of the night before Sally Field donates her kidney to her daughter, Julia Roberts. The family is playing a game of Go Fish and making transplant jokes. Shortly thereafter, Julia is in ICU, brain dead.

"Is the message here that laughter kills?" Peyton asks.

"No, the message is that *laughter through tears*—" I answer, quoting Dolly Parton who says something to this effect in the movie.

"God, what is it with you and the country singers. Oh, I almost forgot. I brought you some books," Peyton says.

Peyton leaves the room and returns with a "W.A.T.B" (Widows Against the Beltway) tote.

"Mom was on a twice-a-decade cleaning binge," Peyton explains, as she hands me the bulging canvas sack. "I was told to bring this to you, for the nursery."

I pick up some books and begin reading from a page. "I'm sure a newborn will enjoy *The Endless Steppe: Growing Up in Siberia,* or this comforting passage from *Go Ask Alice,* 'I wonder if sex without acid can be as exciting, wonderful, or indescribable!' "

We sort through the remaining books together—the *Little House on the Prairie* series, keep. *Winnie the Pooh* (classic, pre-Disney acquisition): keep. Dad's Boy Scout Manual, keep. *Jellybeans for Breakfast,* keep. *Rosencrantz*

& Guildenstern Are Dead, Slaughterhouse Five—paperbacks with lots of highlighted passages (the thinking being if I use my highlighter, it's as though I understand the text)—are back in the bag. Can Mom not part with anything? A cassette of *Free to Be You and Me,* the *Muppet Movie* soundtrack (Do we even have a tape player?) and a new item, a CD entitled *Philadelphia Chickens,* with a Post-it note attached: "The best, according to early childhood development experts!! XOXO, Mom": keep. I unfold the pieces of paper stuck to the bottom of the tote, ten-year-old receipts, a permission-slip notice, unsigned, and a blank postcard from the Poconos. I pitch those toward the trash can and lean back on a pillow. Peyton is thumbing through one of my pregnancy books; the corner of the page on anxiety is folded over.

"I get those—panic attacks," she says.

"You do?"

"I wasn't sure if you did. We've never talked about it."

"I blame Mom," I say, half-kidding.

"Is it a problem? With pregnancy?"

"I'm fine. Considering this is the most stressful day of my pregnancy thus far, so far, so good. What's happening with Alexander?" I ask.

"Nothing—I was just curious."

"Don't be scared; if I can be pregnant, anyone can."

We're silent. Peyton is the first person, not on professional retainer, with whom I've spoken about my panic problem. I'm surprised—she, the multilingual one, with the Georgetown graduate degree and top-flight job, not to mention the looks, wow. I wonder if my getting them makes her feel better, or worse, comparatively speaking. I am reassured, but then, I'm not the one holding up the bar of achievement for our family.

"What's next? *Terms of Endearment* or *Fried Green Tomatoes?*" Peyton asks.

Fredrik walks into the room and kisses me on the forehead. "Andrew is on his way." He looks over the movie selection. "Hmm. Do you two have any movies with men, made *after* the mideighties? I'm surprised you were able to find these on DVD. Maybe I should get on eBay and buy a Betamax."

"Please, the last thing you need is an excuse to get on eBay."

Peyton laughs. "You know Gretchen, Fredrik, she loves a good cry."

"That she does," he says.

"I do not," I insist as I realize my eyes are watering.

Chapter 13

"It's a bird; it's a plane; it's your baby! Since about your fourth month, you may have felt the baby kicking. Some women describe the movement as similar to butterfly wings flapping gently. Don't worry if you haven't felt anything yet; first-time moms may not notice it until the twenty-fourth week."
—From *Ready or Not, An Expectant Mother's Guide*
(Week 20, page 188)

Who are these women quoted in pregnancy books? And where do they live? I, for one, have yet to meet a single person who'd use the butterfly as a reference for anything, let alone something that occurs in your body. When I asked Meredith this same question, she shuddered. She is deathly afraid of butterflies. Regardless, *it is not a good description because unless you've already felt it, it does not make sense.* Why don't these authors use a more universal experience like the stomach dropper—the feeling you get when you see the guy you'd be willing to give up your sleep for? I had one just the other day, in the Higgers parking lot when I thought I saw Dr. Mitchell. What could he possibly need here? I wondered. Only one way to find out, I thought, as I prepared to follow him to the ends of the Earth and back, just to know what kind of toothpaste he preferred.

But it wasn't him. I wept with disappointment.

The truth is it doesn't take much to get me crying. I'm halfway done with my pregnancy, only I can't think about what's next because I'm waiting for the amnio results. The last week has dragged. I've stayed busy at work, booking dinners and parties for Mother's Day and Smith's graduation. At lunch, I eat with the housekeeping staff, a violation of the unspoken union/nonunion segregation—we have a cafeteria, they have a room with vending machines—happy to be under the watchful eye of Mrs. Torrez. Eliza has kept her distance. I hadn't wanted to tell her about the test because I feel like such a *failure*. But I wanted to cut back on event setups and tear-downs, so I came right out with it.

"Eliza, do you have a minute?" I ask.

"Thirty seconds," she answered.

"I had a test, to see if the baby is OK and," I mumbled.

"Uh-huh."

"I can't lift anything," I said.

"Fine," she said.

"Thank you," I squeaked, pushing back a sob.

Now most of the staff knows I'm expecting, and somehow, word got out about my amnio, too. Lisa from Purchasing slid a right-to-life pamphlet into my locker; I retched when I saw it. Distractions would be nice, but they're increasingly hard to come by. Shopping, the old standby, is out; I won't, or can't, buy maternity clothes. I've reached a truce of sorts with myself; if I can't see it (i.e., my widening butt) in the full-length mirror, I can pretend not to know if it is sufficiently covered by Fredrik's shirts and/or one of my two pairs of black pants, both of which have morphed into off-black as the result of too-frequent washings (I can't wear clothes more than once without washing them. Fredrik, on the other hand, has a rank-and-rotate system that takes more energy, I've noted, than doing the wash and dropping off the dry-cleaning combined.). Second, my days used to include at least one hour of Louisa time—in person or on the phone. But no more. And there is little I want to watch on TV. Even all my old standby shows are irritating me—*ER* is out of the question—so for the past six nights, I've watched *Coal Miner's Daughter* (One of the rarely discussed perks of pregnancy is the sudden acquisition of the TV remote).

Luckily, today is Saturday so I have a few more viewing choices.

"You take the good, something something, you're at a boarding school, on roller skates . . . and there you have, the facts of life, the facts of life," I sing along with TV Land. And then, more loudly, "When the world never seems to be living up to your dreams . . ."

I sniffle.

"G," Fredrik says, "it's just a theme song."

"I feel so badly for Natalie," I explain.

"She's not a real person," he responds.

"You've never been overweight. *You don't know how hard it is.*"

"I'm sure it's difficult, but is that really why you're crying?"

"I'm *not* crying," I say as I blow my nose. "I wish Dr. Mitchell would call."

"Me, too. It's maddening," he says.

"It's all my fault," I say. "I didn't take folic acid."

"We've been over this. You drank orange juice."

"What about the spermicidal jelly? Or my highlights? Or the wine I had at Christmas? I had a lot. And I didn't want to tell you this, but at your aunt and uncle's house over Thanksgiving, I snuck a cigarette with Karl."

"You confessed that last night, remember? And then we decided you weren't even pregnant then?"

"Oh, right."

I sigh. We turn our attention back to the TV. Fredrik's eyes start to droop.

"Fredrik?"

"What? What?"

"I'm going to take a walk."

"That sounds like a good idea," he says, reaching for the remote.

"Feel free to change the channel," I say.

"Thank you," he replies.

Having walked Boo twice today already, we reach a standstill once out the front door. I see Louisa and Jason's cars are parked in the driveway. I'd thought they'd be out doing something fun and nonpregnant, but they're home, so I head that way. I am sick of being in a fight. I need resolution. So I will get it today. And I know just what to say—I wrote it out, longhand, on a yellow legal pad. As a supplement to the speech, I've also kept a running list in my Filofax of things to discuss with her (despite my best efforts not to do so). These include:

- The "Girls of the Seven Sisters" pictorial in the latest issue of *Playboy,* which features not one but two current Smith students. Meredith wants to start an alumnae petition and has been pestering me for weeks to sign—something about how the point of a women's college is to liberate women from these kinds of demeaning, objectifying stereotypes—and when I'd mentioned the "but isn't it their choice" thing again she'd nearly cut my head off.

- Andrew's new girlfriend. Louisa is somewhat obsessed with Andrew, in that he is the complete opposite of her husband, Jason, who is a brilliant lawyer, but who struggles to complete basic household tasks

("He had to get five stitches," she'd complained after he'd tried, and failed, to change a bathroom lightbulb.). I'm not crazy about Andrew's girlfriend, either—nothing she's done—it's just *this is not a good time for me to be meeting other women*. Especially women who've never been pregnant. I'm always crying and I look like complete shit. But I won't mention that part to Louisa.

Boo and I are now at Louisa's front door. I ring the bell. Jason answers.

"Gretchen. How are you? Are you—did Louisa ask you over?"

"I was on a walk and thought I'd stop by."

Neither of us moves.

I hear Louisa yell from upstairs, "Who is it?"

"Gretchen," he answers.

"Who?"

"GRETCHEN. Come down."

I stand on the stoop like a door-to-door salesman, knowing these few seconds of banter are crucial to the sale of my rustproof knives or Pecans for Peace. I say nothing. Neither does Jason. Finally, *a clop, clop, clop,* Louisa is on the stairs and I guess, correctly, before I see her, that she is wearing her red patent leather Dansko clogs. She stands directly behind Jason and leans to the right, giving me a partial view of her head and shoulders.

"I didn't know if you'd be home, but—" I start.

"Our cars are here," Louisa interrupts.

Jason turns around to face Louisa. He moves to the side and steps out of the way, leaving Louisa and me face-to-face. He walks to the living room without saying good-bye. Boo barks, lies down and whines at the doorway, begging entrée.

"I wanted to talk. I'm not sure what to say other than I miss you."

"Oh," she replies.

"Is this not a good time?" I ask.

"For Christ's sake, Louisa, let her in," Jason shouts from the couch.

"We're not going out for an hour or so. You can come in."

"Thanks." Big of her.

Louisa and I sit on the couch. Boo heads to the kitchen; it would take more than a hostile greeting to thwart Boo from his pursuit of fallen food. I fold my hands in my lap as I realize I'm in my "am I awake or am I asleep?" ensemble: the knit pants, Fredrik's shirt, and a long sweater. I've not washed my face or brushed my teeth, though it's nearly four o'clock. I wish I was wearing a better outfit. Or had a tan. I look better with a tan. This would be an acceptable lounge-by-the-pool getup, with a tan and some cute flip-flops. But I need a pedicure.

I'm rambling before I've said a word.

"Do you want something to drink?" Louisa asks.

"No, thanks."

"I see the Saturday Shopping Uniform hasn't changed," I remark.

"What? Yeah, right: sweater, jeans, and clogs, for—" Louisa stops.

"Maximum shopping pleasure," I finish for her, smiling. "How are you?"

"Good. Busy at work. You?"

"Good. Busy at work, too."

This is worse than running into a one-night stand at Mass.

"How are you—how are you feeling?" Louisa asks.

"Good." I pause. I need to change the subject. "Did you see the article in last month's *Living Life* about coriander—how it's the unsung hero of spices?"

"No, I didn't," she says, taking a sip of her wine.

"When did you stop reading *Living Life?*" I ask.

"When they started putting pregnant women on the cover," Louisa answers.

Shit. Which issue was that?

"Right," I say. "I'm sorry."

"Don't be."

"How is Jason?" I ask.

"*He'll* be fine," she snorts. "But I've made it clear *this* baby-making machine is closed for business." She downs the last of her wine.

I'm quiet. I can't seem to remember any of my speech. Or anything on my list. My stomach rumbles. Louisa looks at her watch.

"I should go," I say, "but anytime you want to—"

"Thanks for stopping by," she interrupts, standing up.

I stand up, too. We walk to the door but then I remember Boo.

"Here Boo!" I shout.

We stand in silence. Jason comes down the stairs, with Boo.

"We were upstairs," Jason explains.

"Please don't tell me he was in bed with you," I say.

"Don't worry about it," he says, patting Boo on the head.

"Better Boo than me," Louisa whispers in a voice I've not heard before.

I look at her and lean forward for a hug. But when she doesn't return the gesture, I lean toward the front door instead. I stay that way, tilted toward my left, to make it look like I did it on purpose.

"See you later," she says.

I straighten up.

"Yeah . . ." I say, waiting for the "I'll call," or the "How about lunch?" that never comes. "Let's go, Boo—heel, boy, heel," I say for my own sake more than for Boo's.

During the walk home, I berate myself for not saying something—I'm not sure what—more *forthright*. But of course, I blanked. I tend to think of the right thing to say later—as in when no one is listening. In my own defense, I've never heard her be so mean (OK, other than the yelling at me), so my prepared talking points would have been useless, anyway.

Once I'm home and inside the door, I take off Boo's collar and head to the TV room, so I can recount every detail of my visit to Fredrik. He is quiet, engrossed in the history channel.

"Earhart placed third at the Cleveland Women's Air Derby and was later nicknamed the 'Powder Puff Derby' by Will Rogers," the narrator intones.

I sit down next to Fredrik and sigh loudly.

"I went to Louisa's," I say.

"Uh-huh," he replies.

"We talked—nothing major, but it's better than nothing, right?"

"Sure."

Fredrik is looking very cute today, despite not having showered. I love when he doesn't shave. *Nothing like a dirty man.*

"Fredrik," I say, walking my fingers up his thighs.

"G, please? This is the first decent TV I've watched in two weeks."

"Aren't you even curious about Louisa?"

"You can tell me when this is over," he says.

"Hmmph," I say in return.

I start stroking his arm. He does not move. How odd. This guy never turns down my advances. *Never.* I get up, slowly, take my ponytail out and shake my head, in an attempt to entice him. I head for the bathroom and look in the mirror. My hair, which is dirty, has taken the shape of a large, frizzy triangle. I quickly put it back up, pulling a few come-hither strands out, to frame my face. I make my way back to the couch.

I straddle Fredrik again and sit on his lap. His breath is terrible; he hasn't brushed his teeth. It's all right; I *know* I'm not attractive in this getup. But when you feel real passion for a person, something as stupid as hygiene shouldn't matter.

I kiss Fredrik's neck.

"Fredrik—"

"Gretchen."

"Don't you want me?"

He pushes me to the side.

"I thought we weren't supposed to have sex," he says, scowling at me.

"It's fine any time after forty-eight hours post the amnio."

"That's not what you told me last night."

Was that last night?

I climb back on his lap.

"What if I touch you here? You can call me Amelia."

"No, honey, I'm sorry. I'm not in the mood."

"Fine, FINE," I say, a little too loudly.

I climb down and I run up the stairs to the bedroom to think of a new approach to overcome Fredrik's reluctance. Maybe I should shower. But why? Why are dirty men hot but dirty women just, um, dirty? Except Angelina Jolie. Forget the shower. I will review my lingerie collection instead. Maybe the right bra and underwear combo (not Jockey XXXLs and an old sports bra) is just what I need to get Fredrik going. And despite what you think, pregnant women *can* turn men on. I know this from (a) some Internet surfing ("Oh. My. God."), and (b) following the exploits of various pregnant celebrities who date celebrities, while pregnant with *other* celebrities' children.

I stand in front of my dresser and open the drawer. I survey the contents. But there is no lingerie in here. The truth is, I don't believe in it. I consider dressing up for sex to be far, far too contrived (like "date night," which Meredith is always going on about, really, we get it, *you are having sex next Friday*) to be authentic, unlike my spontaneous, passion-filled advance of only moments ago.

My eyes rest on the jumble of underwear. When did I stop folding? This is a totally unacceptable mess. I dump out the drawer onto the bed and start to organize, forgetting all about Fredrik. Once I start, I can't stop. I pull out all the drawers and then try everything on. I am in a pair of hospital scrub pants, which I hadn't realized had an elastic waistband and therefore could be incorporated into my nonmaternity maternity clothing repertoire (maybe not to work, but certainly around the house), when Fredrik jumps onto the bed. I scream.

"My piles!" I shout.

"You're *hot*—those pants, did you cut the bottoms with scissors? Those are hot," he says, winking at me.

"Oh, no—my offer has expired," I say.

"Doesn't matter. The pope says I can have you, whenever I want," he teases.

"Wow, you *are* enlightened—quoting Paris Hilton *and* the pope," I say.

"Whatever it takes to close the deal," he says.

As I start to untie my drawstring, I laugh and say, "Doesn't take much."

"Never has," he says.

Chapter 14

"Live la dolce vita, but only in moderation. Cravings are a natural part of pregnancy, but there's nothing to be gained by filling up on empty calories. Allow yourself an occasional treat but stock up on plenty of tasty, healthy snacks so you can resist when the tooth fairy strikes."
—From *Ready or Not, An Expectant Mother's Guide* (Week 21, page 199)

I'm in the hotel's walk-in refrigerator, looking for a place to store my "glucola" drink, an orange sodaish thing that is used to test for gestational diabetes, when I spot the leftover wedding cake. It's my favorite flavor—a simple vanilla cake with butter cream frosting, none of that fondant crap (a layer of sugar that gives wedding cakes a smooth texture, which has to be removed before the cake can be eaten). *Oh well.* As tempted as I am—I can almost taste the butter on my tongue—I resist; no need to fail another prenatal test.

OK, OK, I haven't failed the amnio. But I don't know I've passed, either. I'm still waiting for those results and I'm praying Dr. Mitchell will have them by the time I see him this afternoon. Unfortunately, before I can take solace in the loving support of Dr. Mitchell, I must endure a *mandatory* staff meeting, which starts in five minutes.

I enter the ballroom and head for an empty seat, next to Mr. Edwards, who is eating a cookie in the shape of an Irish setter. "Birthday party for a dog," he explains. "Referral from the photographer." "Thank God I didn't have to handle that event," I reply. *Crunch, crunch, crunch.* I want to ask for a bite but I shouldn't—my butt is already sloping down both sides of my chair.

No one knows what this meeting is about. I certainly don't, despite sitting directly outside Eliza's office. It was scheduled weeks ago to ensure the night staff could attend (initially, Eliza didn't want to pay them)—but *everyone* has a theory (and discussing said theories has taken place at the expense of assisting our guests). For example, Mr. Edwards is sure we're here to discuss the impact of Canada's recent legalization of same-sex marriages (no one took this seriously). Front Desk Bob theorized that an informal crime ring is operating out of the hotel, wherein employees with all-access pass keys steal pay-per-view porn from unused rooms as a *community service;* former fraternity brothers watch free of charge (not one person believed this was, as Bob put it, "shot in the dark"); Esperinza and Carlotta are confident we're here for an update on the Local 652 Hotel Workers Union. (The treasurer resigned last month after being charged with misappropriation of funds. A few of the housekeepers bore witness to the collection of state's evidence from the treasurer's home; by all accounts he had an extensive, maybe even a one-of-a-kind, bulldog-inspired art collection. Everyone agreed: money doesn't buy taste.)

We'll know soon enough

The room is loud with exaggerated whispering as we wait for Eliza. Everyone is squirming—most noticeably Front Desk Bob, whose jeans jacket is cluttered with buttons. I can read only two (Is it possible my vision is worse?

My eyes are *so* dry.): I AM A YOUNG WOMAN and TAKE ME DRUNK, I'M HOME. A nerve in my butt is pinching, clamping down. *Sciatica.* I arch my back and I am about to stand up when Eliza enters the room with two men, one fortyish, one fiftyish, both in dark blue suits. The room is quiet. Lisa from Purchasing coughs on my right. I glare at her for the infraction. Perhaps she is guilty of something horrible; I'd happily slip a scarlet letter in her locker.

The older man clears his throat. He has salt-and-pepper slicked-back hair. "Greed is good," Mr. Edwards whispers to me, quoting Michael Douglas in *Wall Street*. It's my turn to cough, pushing back a chuckle. Why is it that you want to giggle the minute, the second, you *know* it's totally inappropriate? Put a clown in front of me and I feel creepy. And mimes? I get outright angry. But put me in a situation, work or social, wherein I should be serious or circumspect and all I can do is laugh. And I'm not alone. Mr. Ali, the head of Engineering, leans in and says to me, "You want the truth? You can't handle the truth," and Mr. Edwards retorts with "You talkin' to me? You talkin' to *me?*" By the time Front Desk Bob chimes in with "I am an agent of the FBI!" (I believe this line is spoken by Keanu Reeves in *Point Break*.), we are ready to stand on our chairs and cry out, "O Captain! My Captain!" Eliza walks to a microphone.

"Thank you for coming today. I'd like to introduce Mr. Matheson and Mr. Link."

Mr. Link is the older one; he moves ahead of Eliza and smiles broadly. "Last night, after some tough negotiations with Ms. Singleton, the Hotel Alliance Corporation completed the acquisition of the Northampton Grande, effective September 1. At this time, we do not plan to announce changes in personnel or staffing levels. Those won't be finalized until the team from Concorde Consulting finishes evaluating the property. As unexpected as this news may be, we ask that you simply go about doing your jobs and let us work out the details. Any questions?"

Huh? How about, *why is the universe converging on September first?*

I can't ask, so I look at my hands and catch the time on my watch—oh, no. If I don't leave right now, I'll be late for my appointment with Dr. Mitchell. No one is saying anything, so I stand up to leave, picking up my purse from the floor and taking my raincoat off the back of my chair.

"Gretchen, do you have a question?" Eliza asks.

Everyone looks at me.

"I have an appointment. I apologize, but I should leave."

"Take a cookie," Mr. Edwards whispers.

"Gretchen Stirling, catering department," Eliza says by way of introduction to my new bosses, "is pregnant."

"Congratulations, Ms. Stirling. Don't let us keep you," Mr. Link says with a half-smile.

Stupidly, I sat in the center of the aisle. At least ten people have to stand to let me pass, so I waddle away leaving a trail of "excuse me, pardon me's," and "I'm so sorrys" in my wake. I run out of the hotel, putting on my coat as I walk up the hill toward Dr. Mitchell's office. I tie the belt of my coat at the top of my belly, to accentuate the pregnancy, glancing periodically at my profile in store windows. It's finals week at the college and there are Smithies *everywhere,* hovering over laptops at the Java Joint, sitting on the stairs of the courthouse, smoking, and practicing the age-old art of procrastination by retail (You can't study without new pens/paper/shoes.). I make it to the office two minutes early; the trip to the bathroom gives me the time I need to quickly wipe the sweat from my upper lip and under my arms with a paper towel. I don't want to look frazzled.

Before I get on the scale, I lay my coat on my purse and

remove my shoes and my cardigan. My new lightweight Timex stays on. One hundred fifty, one hundred fifty-five, *Oh, my Lord*, one hundred fifty-seven pounds. Five more since my last visit a month ago, sixteen pounds total. I've surpassed minimum weight gain requirements, which might explain why even Fredrik's clothes are starting to look ridiculous. What does it matter? I look like shit anyway. ("For your convenience, I have *posted* the revised grooming guidelines on the bulletin board," Eliza said yesterday, noting that my hair, which was flying in a million directions, was in violation of Guideline #6: "Women should keep hair in a close-cropped cut or pulled back in a tasteful ponytail.")

I leave the nook and follow the nurse to the exam room. I lift and lower my legs repeatedly, hoping to burn some calories while I wait for Dr. Mitchell. He knocks; I sit up straight and smile.

"How are you feeling?" Dr. Mitchell asks, his eyes darting from me to the chart.

"Fine, I guess," I answer.

I lie down on my back and lift up my shirt. Dr. Mitchell takes out a tape measure and stretches it out across my stomach. You know, I'm curious, is it really necessary to go to medical school to learn how to use this "instrument?" Between that and the due-date wheel (and the inability of the medical establishment to correct the popular misconception that a pregnancy is nine months when, in fact it is ten, TEN MONTHS), I'm wondering if we even *need* doctors?

The exam is over. Dr. Mitchell has his hand on the doorknob and is about to leave when he asks me if there is anything else. I look at him. He does *seem* genuinely concerned. Oh, why the hell not. I launch in.

"I haven't felt the baby kick. I might lose my job."

"Ah, yes. Well, the baby kicking—not unheard of for a

first-time mom, but if you're still worried in a week or so, why don't we schedule a sonogram?"

"That sounds good."

"Call me and I'll set it up. What's happening at work? You are at the hotel?"

"Yes, and Eliza, my boss, sold it yesterday."

"Layoffs?"

"We won't know until September."

"That can be tough, but with some forethought, we can manage it together. Any anxiety or depression?"

"Nothing out of the ordinary." My idea of ordinary, that is.

"Just know that if your worry becomes a distraction or all-consuming, I can recommend therapists and psychiatrists who work with pregnant women."

"I don't need that." Christ, do I?

Dr. Mitchell continues, "Anything else?"

"Why am I gaining so much weight?"

"Hmm. How are your eating habits?"

"Great. Well, not all that great. Waiting for the amnio results has been awful. I've been eating a bit more than I usually do. Do you think age is a factor?"

"You're."

"Thirty-two."

"That's still on the young side. Let's just keep an eye on it. The baby is growing rapidly now, so you should gain *up* to a pound per week. Every woman experiences pregnancy differently, but too much weight gain can lead to complications—gestational diabetes, for one. You are scheduled to take your screening test today."

"OH, MY GOD. I forgot the drink. I put it in the walk-in and then we had this meeting and I meant to go back and drink it but, but I never did." I'm about to cry.

"You can come in another day and take it."

"When do you think I'll hear about the amnio? I'm not

sure I can take another day of waiting." I take a tissue and blow my nose. It makes a honking sound. *Sexy.*

"Let me make a call; we should have the results by now."

"Great."

"Be right back, then."

Dr. Mitchell leaves the room for real this time. I breathe in and out. I examine a water stain on the far-right corner of the ceiling. I study the blinking lights on the wall phone. I touch a plastic model of a woman's uterus; what on earth is a "fornix?" I should savor this moment. I can still have hope.

"Good news, Gretchen," Dr. Mitchell says as he comes back. "The baby is fine."

"Thank you. Thank you so much, Dr. Mitchell."

I jump off the exam table and move to hug him. Wait a minute—I can't do that. It's a total violation of GYN/patient protocol. *And what if he doesn't like me back?* For a few seconds we stand only inches apart. I do not, as I'd wanted, break into song ("I love you, I honestly love you."). Instead, I back away from him slowly, mumbling something about my everlasting gratitude.

I leave Dr. Mitchell's office elated and decide to score a celebratory post-weigh-in decaf latte at the Java Joint. I try Fredrik's cell, no service. I leave a message. I do *not* mention that soon I will be a) jobless, and b) his equal, pound for pound. The other good news is I will be a young mother, relatively speaking. I like that. I'm young. I sit alone, in a purple velvet chair, half-reading the local *Gazette,* half-listening to the students, three of whom are at a table right next to me. They are in pajamas and T-shirts and order soy, no-water, extra-hot chai teas without flinching. They look like freshmen. One *might* be a boy.

"When I was a junior in high school," the one in the plaid pajamas says, "I cowrote *and* produced an original play, which was loosely based on *No Exit,* which I read, bien sûr, en Française, to get to the real heart of Sartre and the nature of existentialism. I bring this up because it's complete bullshit that we're expected to prove our understanding of nihilism in two hours and forty minutes."

"It's all so fucking pointless," adds the one in sweat-pants with *Pink* scrawled across the front of her sweat-shirt. "Completely irrelevant, knowing what we do about the West Bank. My trip there junior year with Operation Smile opened my eyes to the challenges the citizens of the world face every single day."

I no longer feel young. I feel old, horribly old. Ancient. As in, kids today are so driven and accomplished; I have nothing in common with them. The only thing I achieved in high school was graduating without killing myself, or my mother. No Operation Whatever It Was. No playwriting. No chai tea. And we didn't dress younger, in pajamas— what's that about? The whole idea was to look older, more mature, to offset otherwise highly juvenile but perfectly normal behavior. This would be a great Louisa convo. I have all these thoughts and no one to share them with. I try them out occasionally on Fredrik, but confiding in your hus-band is just not the same as confiding in a friend. To wit:

> *Me:* Eliza is a bitch. She said I need to be better about my time sheets.
> *Fredrik:* Was it late? You should get those in on time.

Contrast this, if you will, with the following:

> *Me:* Eliza is a bitch. She said I need to be better about my time sheets.
> *Louisa:* I hate her. Your boobs look awesome in that sweater.

The *ding-dong* of the Java Joint door startles me. I hear a familiar voice. Who's that? My ears perk up; it's Dr. Mitchell. Ordering coffee. *Good God,* he's here. In the Joint. I crumble up a greasy cookie bag and shove it between the chair cushions.

"A small cup of coffee. Honey? For you?"

My back is to the register. Who is he with? A patient? A nurse? *His wife?* I love that he ordered a plain coffee. I take out my compact mirror to "check my makeup" and I see him with his hand on a woman's back. They turn around and he catches my eye in the mirror. Shit. I stand and turn around as crumbs fall to the floor.

"Dr. Mitchell! HI!"

I give the woman a once-over. Unfortunately, she is very attractive.

"This is my wife, Lisa."

"Pleased to meet you. I'm a patient of your husband's. He's the best."

"I'm glad you think so; I certainly do. Nice to meet you," Mrs. Mitchell says.

They take a table near the back and I sit down, basking in my elation. What a totally unexpected celebrity sighting; what a *stomach dropper.* The pajama party is laughing at me. I don't care. This is the best stomach dropper I've ever had. Little flips, like a tiny—OH, MY GOD. A TINY BUTTERFLY. It's my baby. My healthy baby. I hop out of the chair. I rush over to Dr. Mitchell.

"Sorry to interrupt, but I felt the baby move. I wanted to tell you."

"That's wonderful news," he says. He's looking at me like I'm a sociopath. In fact, I am a sociopath; it's called "first-time mother feels the baby move."

"I just couldn't keep it to myself," I explain.

"It's OK, it's been a big day for you," he says.

I nod and smile at his wife. *She's so lucky.* I leave them

to grab my things, nearly tripping over multiple extension cords. The Smithies stare at me and I send them a mental note: you wait, sister, someday this will be you. And then I turn to them and shout, "I felt the baby move!" I bounce out of the Joint and speed dial Fredrik. He answers on the third ring. "Honey? Honey? Can you hear me? Guess what? The baby is fine. Perfect! *And* I felt the baby move! I just saw Dr. Mitchell at the Joint with his wife who is very cute and—oh! Eliza sold the hotel to some Michael Douglas lookalike and I could be out of a job come September. Are you having a good time? Hello? Fredrik? Can you hear me?"

Chapter 15

"Save the date! If you haven't called your hospital yet to register for childbirth preparation classes, add it to your to-do list. Classes can fill up early."
—From *Ready or Not, An Expectant Mother's Guide* (Week 24, page 210)

Fredrik is asleep.

I lie next to him, trying not to move. What if he wants to bring me breakfast in bed? It is my first Mother's Day. He *must* have planned something. Fredrik snorts in his sleep; his boxers are twisted up at his waist. I wish he would wake up. We need to discuss our "birth plan." I'm worried about asking Fredrik to take a birthing class. He is an antijoiner. He does not do what others do. He does the opposite, sometimes on purpose, sometimes not. He isn't one of those "we're pregnant" types (And I thank God for that, because if he even, for *one minute,* attempted to take credit for the work my body is doing right now, what with the stretching, scarring, and gum bleeding, I'd have to kill him.) and he isn't one for gratuitous touching. Meredith told me that Alan *massaged* her. She took a Bradley class. The Bradley Method, I learned, relies upon heavy in-and-out breathing, no drugs. How is that a method, exactly? She also used a mirror to look at her vagina, an experience she described as "miraculous." I seriously doubt I will think the same thing. Isn't the very placement of my vagina a clue that I'm not supposed to see it?

Is Fredrik ever going to wake up? I'm out of bed a few times a night and he sleeps right through it. If my bladder's not exploding, I still wake up because of nightmares. They are realistic, harrowing. And not about the baby, exactly— more like every unresolved issue in my life plays out in a weird kaleidoscope. Shit—the phone, who's calling at this hour?

I answer.

A loud voice yells: "Happy Mother's Day! It's your first—how exciting, honey. Have you talked to your sister? Any more thoughts on names? How do you feel? I remember the last Mother's Day we celebrated as a family—"

"Happy Mother's Day, Mom," I interrupt.

"Did you get my e-mail? I have a new address, Mother-Fox111."

"Yes, right, I did."

"I wish you would have responded, honey. I don't ask much, Gretchen, but when I send something, if you would just hit the REPLY button."

"I should have e-mailed you back; I'm sorry."

"I beg your pardon?"

"You're right, that was rude."

"I thought so, too, but thank you, honey, for saying so."

Fredrik is stirring. I hang up, promising to call her later with the details of my day.

"Mmm. What'd your mom say?"

"She wanted to wish me a happy Mother's Day."

"That's funny." Fredrik turns away from me.

"Huh?"

"You're pregnant, not a mom."

He hasn't fixed his underwear. He is going back to sleep.

"Fredrik, honey, did you plan anything for today?"

"I told my mom that we'd go there; Andrew and I are cooking."

He turns back around.

"FYI, I will *be* a mother. Shortly, like in a matter of months," I announce.

"All the more reason to sleep while we can."

"We need to sign up for birthing classes—education classes."

"Go ahead."

"You'll go, then?"

"Why? I'm not having the baby, am I?"

"No, but couples go together."

"Can we talk about this later?"

I don't respond. I slip out of bed, go downstairs and begin to cook, muttering under my breath as I crack the eggs, smashing so hard that tiny bits of shell infiltrate the yolk, forcing me to retrieve them with a fork. The nerve. Here I am, on Mother's Day, making *him* breakfast. That we will eat before we go to *his mother's house*. I take out the cloth napkins, set the table, and pour the juice. I step out the back door and grab a few wildflowers and arrange them in a vase, à la *Cottage Living* (which I read at four in the morning last Thursday). I drain the roasted tomatoes that garnished last night's steak. Fredrik comes into the kitchen in his underwear.

"I couldn't go back to sleep. Smells delicious," he says as he kisses me.

We sit down. We split up the sections of the *New York Times*. It is the picture of domestic bliss and Fredrik moans in delight over his breakfast. A little tune from *Sesame Street* pops into my head, the song about noticing different things: "One of these things is not like the other, one of these things doesn't belong"—only I change the lyrics to: "One of these people is angry with the other, one of these people hasn't a clue, one of these people is re-

venge, one of these people—" Crap, what rhymes with revenge? Fredrik has some tomato stuck to his chin. I take
my napkin and lovingly wipe it away from his mouth. He
takes my hand and kisses it.

The phone rings.

"I'll get it," I say, leaping from the table. "Hey, Peyton."

She's yawning. "Mom told me to call. What time is it?"

"Eight forty-five."

"Happy Mother's Day. Can I call you later?"

"Of course. You didn't have to call at all," I answer.

"I was going to anyway, just later. Is there an aunt's
day?"

"Every day."

"OK, talk to you later," Peyton says.

The phone rings again. Who could that be?

"Hello? Hey, Meredith."

"Happy pre-Mother's Day. Quiet, Ryder, Mommy is on
the phone."

I laugh. "Thanks. Happy Mother's Day to you."

"What are you doing today?" she asks.

I take the phone and walk into the living room, out of
Fredrik's earshot and answer, "Nothing. Apparently this
day is about the *other* Mrs. Stirling." I sigh. "Is that normal?"

"Oh, my God, *yes*. Alan completely blew me off for
Mother's Day last year. But I take solace in the fact that I
have Ryder. Perhaps he will remain devoted to me even
after he's gotten married and had kids of his own."

"Phew. I was worried."

"Remember what I said—it takes time. Now, I have to
go—Ryder, please do not color on Mommy's wall. Alan,
are you watching him? Do you not see that I'm on the
phone here?" She pauses again. "Let's have coffee this
week."

"Definitely."

"Enjoy your day." She snickers.

"Thanks. And Meredith—thanks, thanks for everything."

"It's my pleasure," she says, and I can see her smiling.

I walk slowly back to the kitchen.

"Fredrik? Do you think we could get ready a little early? To stop by the hotel? I want to check on brunch."

"I didn't know you had to work today."

"I don't, but I told the guys I'd stop by. Why don't you come with me?"

Fredrik puts down his paper. "Why?"

"Because maybe after, you and I could do something fun," I suggest.

"I'm happy here. You go ahead; take the truck. Come back and pick me up."

"We could go on a walk through town."

"What's in town?" he asks.

"Never mind!" I answer.

The hotel kitchen is crowded and hot. I take a break from arranging muffins to wipe the grease from a few stolen home fries off the front of my shirt. Such a weird pregnancy side effect, the constant dropping of food on myself. The executive chef is yelling in my ear, "GOD-DAMMIT, WHERE ARE THOSE POTATOES?" Everyone is nervous and on edge; we're still being observed by Concorde Consulting. Ugh, here comes Eliza. She corners me in the pantry.

"I'd like to speak with you, Gretchen."

"Do you know where the scallions are?" I ask.

"Never mind that. I was reviewing the banquet event order for"—she flips through a stack of papers on her clipboard—"HART. Yes, the HART organization. The net profit for the event is unacceptably low. Have you read my memo regarding quotas?"

Memo? Oh, right. I spilled a latte on it. "Not yet."

Jeremy the consultant joins us. It's not a large pantry, so we're elbow to elbow.

"Why didn't you up-sell to wine service?" Eliza asks.

"HART—that's an acronym for Helping Adolescents through Reality Therapy," I say, deciding the best approach is to bore her with details. "They encourage teenagers to monologue about their lives. The kids get on a stage and they can scream, cry, or talk. It's *very* successful."

"Ah," Jeremy says.

He is looking at my stomach. He puts his hand out, then pulls away. Was he going to touch it? That is so utterly inappropriate. Maybe I could sue. I continue.

"It was started by a graduate of Smith's Master of Social Work program." To Jeremy I add, "Which is one of the best in the country."

"Gretchen—" Eliza starts.

"The point is, Eliza, they work with addicts. *Alcoholics.* I didn't want to be insensitive."

Eliza frowns and says, "I think Chef needs you back in the kitchen."

Ha. After Eliza and Jeremy leave us worker bees to do our jobs, we have a good laugh. The tension has lifted. Despite the meal being a culinary joke, Mother's Day brunch *is* kind of fun, because as a hotel worker, you blend into the background. This means the guests forget we're here. And because they've forgotten us (that's the impetus behind the dress code of dark, solid colors), we get an up-close-and-personal view into their lives.

Think real-time reality TV show.

Think family dysfunction on parade.

"We have a crier at table nine," a waiter reports.

"What happened?" I ask.

"Too many mimosas. Something about how the kids only visit on holidays."

Right.

I end up staying at work longer than I should. By the time I get home, we're close to being late for dinner. Fredrik is seething; he *hates* to be late so to make matters worse, I purposely dawdle. I change my clothes several times, brush my teeth, wash my face, and apply some makeup. I can hear Fredrik pacing down by the front door. Once I'm done, I walk very slowly down the stairs, while I yawn.

"I'm exhausted," I say—I know he is dying to rush me.

On the drive to his parents' house, I fake sleep.

As soon as we arrive, Andrew ushers us into the dining room. Everyone wants to be critical of our late arrival; I can sense it. I feel invincible! Once we're seated, I use this newfound power to memorize the tone of Mrs. Stirling's feigned surprise. "I hadn't expected all this," she said, even though the night was a carbon copy of last year. Since Fredrik is unlikely to be receptive to my mimicking his mother on "her day," I pin my hopes on Kim, Andrew's girlfriend. Unfortunately, as she is new to the relationship and is also likely a decent person, she seems unable—or unwilling—to make eye contact with me.

On the way home in the truck, I make small talk with Fredrik.

"Kim seems very nice. Does Andrew like her?" I ask.

"Sure. They had sex in the basement," he replies.

"What?"

"Between dinner and dessert," Fredrik explains.

"No."

"Yep."

"God, I can only imagine what you tell Andrew about us," I say.

"Not much to tell," Fredrik says.

Poor Fredrik. We are so beyond sex in the basement. I feel kind of sorry for him.

"It's just—I feel like crap. And I *look* like crap. Did you see Kim's pants? I didn't even know the military look was back in," I offer by way of explanation.

"Why don't you buy some maternity clothes, then?"

"I guess I could."

"You might feel better," he suggests.

"One thing that would make me feel better is if we started taking these family holidays more seriously."

"By we, you mean me?"

"Yes *and* we need to take the classes," I say.

"Sign me up," he say as he helps me out of the truck.

We walk into the house and I announce I'm going to go shop, now. I head for the computer in the kitchen. I guess I had this thing, this need to make it as far as I could into the pregnancy without buying so much as a maternity T-shirt. I *hate* shopping for clothes—not shoes or purses—but real, will-this-make-it-over-my-ass? pants. Nothing ever looks like I *imagine* it should. What's worse, I was hoping that pregnancy would give me a fashion "pass," but instead, I discovered that the models who mocked me from the pages of *Vogue* have relocated to *Child* magazine . . . "Tania is pictured wearing a pashmina wrap skirt (her own)." *I am so sick of those pashminas!*

After a few minutes of surfing, I realize that the dueling pregnancy philosophies are reflected in maternity clothing. The earnest people are wearing nursing shirts (Are we not supposed to notice that the top is divided into two parts, by a wide band of Velcro, to facilitate a feeding?) and the cheeky people—models who live in Los Angeles, like Tania—are wearing belly-revealing tank tops. I finally find a site with seminormal clothes and enter in my pre-pregnancy size. I then build an online "model" of my proportions, to "try" on clothes, giving myself an Afro for an extra inch or two of height. I'm still as wide as can be. Hmm.

I pick up a few pairs of pants and some shirts. Do I need

a maternity trench? Oh, why the hell not. There, three hundred dollars. Twelve minutes. New record.

Problem solved.

I decide to check my e-mail. Perhaps I will have a missive from MotherFox111. (She has discovered the ability to forward articles, so each day I sort through five or six e-mailed links. At least one of these pieces is typically about car seat safety, which I can tell is an issue that will be near and dear to her.) But I skim down the Inbox and see that I have an e-mail from Fredrik, which he apparently sent from his laptop upstairs (a new purchase, something about digital photos of the baby and architectural drawings). The subject line is HOLD ME. The body of the message, all caps, as he doesn't unlock the CAPS key, reads: I THINK YOU LOOK GREAT BUT BUY WHATEVER YOU WANT. I laugh. I have never, not in our one hundred years together, heard him say "buy whatever you want!" I e-mail him a response, "For that you may 'meet me in the basement.' " I wait a minute, and then, I hear *him* laughing. Which is good because I have no real intention of having sex in the basement. I turn off the computer and as I head toward the stairs, I start shouting at him.

"All talk and no action," I say.

"I can't—I ate too much," he responds.

"It was a joke," I say as I walk into our bedroom.

"Too bad for you," he says as he lies on the bed, rubbing his stomach.

He says nothing as I turn off the light and climb into bed.

"You are dying to ask me how much I spent," I say.

"Am not."

" 'K—then, good night," I say.

A minute passes.

"DAMMIT! Just tell me!" he shouts.

"I win, I win, I win!" I shout back.

"Just this once—you win—but just this once."
I smile in the dark.
"For 'the once' crack—I have changed my mind."
"I hate you," he says.
"I hate you, too, honey."
"Happy Mother's Day," he says.
"Thank you."
"This time next year—" he continues.
"I know. I know," I say as I clutch him tighter.

Chapter 16

"Shhhh. Amniotic fluid, your uterine wall, muscles, and skin all protect your baby's eardrums while in utero. However, your baby can hear, and she doesn't like loud noises. Play soothing classical music or have your partner murmur quietly to your tummy to reassure her."
—From *Ready or Not, An Expectant Mother's Guide* (Week 26, page 214)

"Happy Birthday to you. Happy Birthday, dear Gretchen, Happy Birthday to you!!"

The staff sings off-key loudly in order to drown out the sounds of the hotel's washers and dryers. An industrial-sized iron is pressing tablecloths. The result is a lot of extra moisture, which gives the room a sweatshoplike feel. My forehead is sweaty and I imagine that my nose is awash in shine in the photograph that was just snapped. Doesn't matter. I'm touched by the effort and happy that the celebration, in a part of the hotel that Eliza would never frequent, is well attended; I was completely surprised.

"Thank you so much," I say to the housekeepers as they load up their carts. "Here—take some cake upstairs," I say as I wrap up a few extra pieces for the employees who aren't free to leave their desks. "Señora, *gracias, gracia*s. I really appreciate it."

"I know how you love cake, *el pequeño.*"

I hadn't expected an at-work celebration for my birthday, but a small sheet cake goes a long, long way to making me feel special. The day is going well. By eight thirty this morning I'd heard from Mom and from Peyton, who left a message. But I have not heard from Louisa. I guess the good news here is that I have rediscovered my "real" sister. We talk nearly every day now. In fact, I think I'll call her now, so I can tell her about my little party. I go back to my desk, pick up the phone, and dial her number.

Peyton answers with her standard, important-sounding "Peyton Fox, State." (I answer my phone with the following service economy song, "Good morning/afternoon/ evening, Northampton Grande Sales and Catering department, this is Gretchen, how may I help you?")

Shit, here's Eliza and Jeremy. I hang up on Peyton with an abrupt, "See you on the eighth! I look forward to meeting you and your daughter!"

"Gretchen, we have an emergency," Eliza announces.

"Oh?" *Has a down-market person been spotted entering the lobby?*

"We have a 502 violation in progress."

Hmm, 502, which one was that? Why is Jeremy's face so red?

"Security has knocked on the couple's door several times," she continues.

Right. A 502 is loud, guest-disturbing sex. What is it about hotels that makes everyone so, so—OK, I will quote Bob here, no never mind, I can't—worked up? If anyone out there is deluding him/herself and thinking we staff don't know what's going on, I have news for you. We do. We laugh about it. And guess what? You're not superspecial sex gods/goddesses *because all guests do it.*

"Can you take my two o'clock appointment?" Eliza asks. "It's in the Burton Boardroom. Jeremy, you go with Gretchen. It's best I handle this other situation myself." Eliza starts speaking into her headset as she leaves the office, walking briskly ahead of us, "I am now making my way to the room. *I repeat.* I am now making my way to the room. All posts on standby. I repeat. Standby. OVER."

I open the door to the boardroom and recognize a smell. It is the smell of socks, and not clean socks, either (thank you "pregnancy nose"). I look at the executive-style-seats-twelve-faux-mahogany table and do a double take. Seated at it are Front Desk Bob and four young, wet-haired guys. They are all wearing navy blue blazers that have not seen the light of day since approximately their high school graduations. They are fidgeting.

What is going on here? Are these guys the clients?

One of the kids throws a Northampton Grande pencil at Front Desk Bob but he misses. The pencil hits a wall with such force that the tip remains wedged in the wood paneling. The boys screech with delight at this "accomplishment" and begin to high-five each other.

"Hey, no more throwing—someone could lose an eye," I interrupt. Oh, my God, I used Ryder's Mommy's voice without even thinking! "Bob, did you have a meeting with Eliza?" I ask.

"Ya," he says as the other boys chime in, "Ya, ya, ya."

I sit down at the table, as does Jeremy. I have to push the faux Queen Anne chair back a bit, to accommodate my stomach.

"How can I help you?" I ask.

"These are my Pau Pau's." Bob high-fives one of them. "My brothers."

"Nice to meet you," I say.

The boys look to Jeremy, who says nothing.

"What were you meeting with Eliza about?" I ask.

"We want to have a party here at the Grande for our fraternity, Sigma Pau Pau," the one with the hair in his eyes, says. Come to think of it that could be any of them.

"But don't worry, Gretchen. You won't have to do anything. We have the menu planned out," Bob says.

"Great! What would you like to serve?"

"Kegs and eggs," Bob answers.

I pause.

"It's a breakfast?" I ask.

"Nah, dinner," Bob replies.

"Here at the hotel," I venture, "we usually serve eggs for *breakfast.*"

"Yes, but this menu rhymes," Bob adds, helpfully.

"You are right about that. May I ask what the purpose of the party is? Is it social, a get-to-know-you? Is it a fundraiser? Is it to recruit pledges?"

"It's social, to improve our image," Bob answers.

"And adults, um, parents will be there?" I ask.

There are nods around the table.

"Is there a tone, or a theme?" I continue.

"No, but should we have one?" Bob asks.

"It's up to you," I say, "I just want to understand—"

"I've got it!" Bob says, rising to his feet. "Let's do one of those parties with the big meat legs, the jousting and wenches and shit—the what's-it-called festival."

"Renaissance?" Jeremy asks.

"YES!" Bob shouts, nodding toward the lobby. "Can we get horses in there?"

I jot down "horses, ASPCA??" on my legal pad.

"That's an interesting idea," I say, hating it. "Maybe we should start off the discussion by going over your budget."

One of the boys hands me a piece of paper. Somewhere to the left of a ketchup stain I find the total for food and beverage. *Whoa.*

"You've got plenty," I say.

Jeremy is taking notes. I wonder, what could he *possibly* be writing down that would capture the spirit of this meeting? This does not bode well for anyone. I want to somehow communicate to him that even though we look crazy, we are all doing our best, and that we really, really, really want to keep our jobs.

But I'm so tired of being "observed."

"Wenches it is!" I shout.

"Awesome! More cowbell!" Bob says, high-fiving me.

"More cowbell," I reply, slapping his hand. "Whatever the hell that means."

I spend a few more minutes with the boys and clarify that I am not, in fact, the coworker with whom Front Desk Bob has been cavorting with, well, behind the Front Desk. No, it's Susan, the "hot chick" from Accounting, the one who saw me at Dr. Mitchell's. Geez, I think, as the boys shuffle out of the room mumbling their thanks, I hope *she* doesn't get pregnant. I don't need the competition. I make another note on my legal pad, "Bob birth control?" as a reminder to myself that I must reinforce the *importance* of protection to Bob. *After all, he's got his whole life ahead of him!*

Jeremy sets off to find Eliza and I head for my secret little bathroom, off the lobby. Technically, we are not supposed to use any area the guests might use, but I like this bathroom; it's very quiet and semiprivate (two stalls, but floor to ceiling doors). I'm too embarrassed to use the staff bathroom because I mostly just go in to take a break. I store a *Buying for Baby* under the sink.

I take it out, sit down, and open to Chapter 3. Strollers. The Travel System. Hmm. Am I an "urban dweller" or "mall crawler"? I'm not sure.

Wait, I hear voices. Are they coming in here? A door is closing. Is that Eliza? It sounds like they are in here. But they're not. Oh, I get it—the bathroom shares a wall with

Mr. Singleton's old office, which is usually empty. I recognize Jeremy's voice. Who else is in there? Must be a meeting.

"We're recommending that the Hotel Alliance Group move up the acquisition date. With the local union leadership under investigation and the chapter in receivership, the staff will be in a weakened negotiating position," a woman says.

This must be the lead consultant; Eliza mentioned she was arriving later today. Apparently they were rivals.

"It'll lower our initial operating cost estimates," she explains.

"You want to cut pay?" Eliza asks.

"Yes. Jeremy did some research; the national union isn't likely to squawk. Too small a constituency. The Grande is hardly General Motors, Eliza."

Jeremy nervously laughs at the joke and the boss continues.

"Administrative functions—HR, finance—can be moved to corporate. The Hotel Alliance Group has a single back-office system for all ninety-four of their properties. Much cheaper. The remaining nonexempt employees should be converted to contractors to eliminate as much overhead as we can. Discontinue health insurance, 401(k), and the like. The sooner the better."

"Some of the staff have been here twenty years. I'm not sure I—" Eliza says.

"*You* won't be. You will be with your parents—in Florida, is it?"

"We have a pregnant woman on staff. We can't cut off her insurance."

GOOD GOD. Eliza is standing up for me. To this *bitch*. I finish up in the bathroom and furiously rewrap the book, while wondering what I should do with this information. Should I call a secret staff meeting at my house? Do I have enough chairs? Is Dr. Mitchell on Fredrik's insurance? I will call Mom; she'll know what to do. From now on, I'm bringing my phone in here. I open the bathroom door. Uh-oh. I'm face-to-face with all three of them.

"Gretchen," Eliza says.

"A client asked about our handicapped facilities," I lie. "This is Rebecca Morgan, of Concorde Consulting."

A pregnant woman offers her hand. "Please, call me Becca. I'm in charge of the project, so any questions, just let me know."

This pregnant Becca, *she* is axing my insurance?

"Pleased to meet you," I lie again as I grip her hand in mine, hard.

I dial Fredrik as I head up Main, toward home. Voice mail. I terror-phone. Redial. Call me. Redial. Call me. What kind of name is Becca, anyway? She's a grown woman, for Christ's sake. Redial. The sidewalk is so crowded; the entire town is out tonight. Move out of my way. This happens every year—the postgraduation reclamation of the bars, restaurants, and the PVTA buses. The week of the ceremony is always harrowing for us "townies." The college hosts the big-year reunions at the same time, and you can't walk a foot without running into an alum. I didn't have a single celebrity sighting this year; last May I saw Gloria Steinem at the Joint and watched her order a decaf. Now I'm panting, nearly running toward the house. I flip open my phone; yes, it's working. Louisa has (almost) officially forgotten my birthday. Where's Fredrik, that bastard? I almost trip, look up. Look, there's Char. Wave. Keep walking. My phone rings. Caller ID: Unavailable.

"Hello?"

"This is my new cell phone, honey," Mom says. "Please memorize the number."

"What do you know about labor unions?"

"Are you starting a chapter? How marvelous!"

I am briefly distracted by a vision of myself atop my desk holding a large UNION sign, á la Norma Rae, followed by a vision of myself on the ground, askew, next to the desk, which had collapsed under my weight.

"No, I just need you to research some bylaws for me," I say.

"By-laws, yes." She pauses. "What are you wearing?"

This is Mom's new favorite question.

"The blue linen with the tie in front and white pants," I answer.

"You must look lovely," Mom replies.

If emphasizing one's belly and breasts in an attempt to diminish size and appearance of other parts of your body is lovely, then, yes, I am. I'm a big fan of long jackets. I only fasten the button that rests on top of my stomach; even better if it ties. Ditto with sweaters, now of light-weight variety, which I have worn on some not-quite-but-almost-hot days. There needs to be a lot of fabric, a lot of *draping*, around the rest of my body. Walking quickly, it creates a capelike effect. Andrew now calls me "Stevie Nicks," and when I Googled her and remembered the *Rumors* album cover, I laughed out loud. Now, when he calls out "Stevie" I sing, "Stand back, stand back" and flap my arms up and down.

"Gotta go, Mom, I'm home now. Talk to you later."

"Love you."

I walk in the front door, shouting, "FREDRIK?"

THANK GOD for air-conditioning. I'm *damp*. Under my arms. Between my legs. I look through the mail: a birthday card, a real estate mailer, a nursing-bra coupon with a picture of a woman's breast on it. Dear Lord, I'm dealing with *breast* models now, too?

"FREDRIK!" I yell again.

"I want to show you something," he says.

"DID YOU GET MY MESSAGES? YOU WILL NOT BELIEVE WHAT HAPPENED AT WORK!"

"Come up."

"WHY? I NEED TO EAT. I'M STARVING."

"Get up here!"

He's so impatient. Doesn't he understand that if I don't eat right now I will die? Probably not; he's never even glanced at *Ready or Not, A Father's Guide* that Mom sent him a few months ago. Fredrik walks down the stairs, takes my arm, and brings me back up.

"OUCH! WHY ARE YOU ON MY ARM? WHY HAVEN'T YOU SHOWERED? WHERE IS YOUR PHONE? ARE WE HAVING ANY KIND OF A BIRTH-DAY MEAL? NEVER MIND, I WOULDN'T WANT YOU TO KEEL OVER FROM CELEBRATING A HOLIDAY." Yelling has exhausted me. "Anyway, I overheard Eliza"—I take another breath—"and I heard the plan for the hotel. It's bad for me. I'll keep my job but lose my health insurance. We need to call Dr. Mitchell right now. Mom says there is some kind of law; *no one* can make me change doctors. ARE YOU EVEN LISTENING?"

We stand in front of the guest room door. It's going to be the nursery. I keep meaning to empty it out but I haven't. Can't. Too fraught with meaning. If I throw out my size 8 clothes, am I not giving up entirely? Never mind that most were purchased at least six years ago—the peasant look was in—and are today totally out of style. And surely stowing away the sewing machine—that is, putting the un-opened box somewhere else, like in the attic where it can't be immediately accessed, is an admission of my failure in the arena of "home arts." What if I need to whip up a beaded shawl? Lastly, I can't think of a better place for the gifts from Fredrik that I will never, not in a million years, use: a snowboard, a GPS locator, a boogie board, and a fly rod.

"Close your eyes," he whispers into my ear, and he opens the door.

"Why? Was *Trading Spaces* here? Or was it *Extreme Makeover? Celebrity Makeover? Starting Over? Oprah?*" I ask, laughing, and open my eyes.

The room has been cleared out. The walls have been painted—light green and white stripes. An old dresser, salvaged from the house in Takoma Park, has been refinished and painted bright orange; the knobs are letters of the alphabet. A white rocking chair, like the one the Stirlings have on their porch, is in the corner, next to a little green and white polka-dotted footstool. A bookshelf made of twigs is on the opposite wall. The window shades, Fredrik pulls one down to demonstrate, are orange. I look closely; the pattern is whimsically drawn circus animals.

"Fredrik—how did you do this?"

"Andrew and Mom helped. I wanted to surprise you. Do you like it?"

"Like it? It's everything I wanted!" He'd been looking over my shoulder, it seemed, as I was browsing decorating magazines.

"I'm glad. Happy Birthday!"

I walk over to the dresser and open the drawers. It's empty except for the little HOLD ME onesie, and I imagine that soon it will be filled with tiny, white things with snaps (Meredith tried to teach me how to put these on Ryder, but I kept getting the inner and outer snaps confused) and all kinds of clothes—clothes for a *person*—who will be living *here* with us, in this room, in our house! OUR PERSON.

"Wow," I say.

"I know," Fredrik says.

I take a seat in the rocker, my feet on the stool.

"The stool—this is good. For some reason, it's much more comfortable."

"Because your feet can't reach the floor?" he teases. "Actually, Meredith told me to get it. It's called a nursing stool. I went to look at a few at the baby store and I didn't like the designs, so I made one instead. It's basically to force your knees up, to create a little shelf for the baby on your lap—also, easier to rock with it."

"I guess I have a lot to learn."

"God, no kidding," he says.

"What if the baby cries?" I ask. "Mom keeps saying new parents have no idea how much babies cry. And the parenting magazines seem to confirm this."

"Then we will do what every other parent in the world does," he says.

"Panic?"

"I was going to say sing—see, I put some mixes up here, in the CD player."

I hadn't noticed the stereo, as it is tucked away on a shelf and the cord has been hidden from view. When my eyes do find the outlet, I see Fredrik has already put plastic safety covers over the openings.

I love this man. He is the ultimate planner.

"This is by far the best birthday present I have ever received," I say, as I let him open the closet, show off the shelves (He even has bought matching child-sized hangers—I am a stickler for that kind of detail.), pull out the tins for storing diapers and wipes *and* demonstrate the newly installed dimmer.

"How did you hide this from me? All this stuff?"

"It was easier than I thought, actually."

"What else are you hiding?" I tease.

"I wanted to do this for you," Fredrik says, his voice one notch deeper than usual. "I know how hard you are working trying to keep your job. And that being pregnant—with the amnio and everything—it's a lot. But you've taken it all in stride. I'm so impressed on the one hand, but not at all surprised on the other."

My eyes tear up. "Thank you," I squeak.

He leans down toward the chair and kisses me, gently, on the lips. We are still for a moment, and move only when the phone rings.

"*My* mother," he says. "She was desperate for you to come home."

Fredrik brings me the phone and we speak for a few minutes and then the other line rings. "I'll let you get that, dear, it might be long distance," she said.

"Thanks again," I say. *Click.* "Hello?"

"I've put together a FedEx for you with some information," Mom says.

My hand rests on my stomach. I'm still in the rocking chair.

"The baby is kicking," I say.

"A nighttime baby. You had your days and nights confused for weeks. I was a zombie. Your father was wonderful, though—he walked a mile in the apartment, singing to you while I slept."

"I thought you lived in married student housing?"

"It was really just a one-bedroom apartment. Pat and Bill lived right next door. Pat and I would sleep in one apartment while Daddy and Bill took care of you and Cathy in the other."

Weird. I haven't heard her refer to my father as "Daddy" in, well, forever. It was as though the sixteen years of life we'd had together had never existed.

"About the wedding, Mom. I'm not sure I can go. I have a party, a Renaissance festival."

"A Renaissance festival?" Mom pronounced this reNAY-sance.

I wait for her diatribe—the "I cannot be alone. This is important to me, Gretchen. I'm disappointed you're not taking my feelings into consideration." Mom is a master of emotional extortion; she can conjure tears in *seconds.* She used to resist my leaving her, for even a minute. "It's a silly movie, Ma, with my friends. I won't be long," I'd explain. "Why don't I come along with you?" she'd ask. "Or why don't you and I go see something else? Just the two of us? There's a documentary playing at the Outer Circle, *Onward We March.*"

"Mom?" Here it comes.

"It's late, honey. Get some rest. Let's cross that bridge when we come to it."

"What?"

"Don't forget to call me when you get the package. Nighty-night!"

Who was that woman? I look at the digital clock above the stove, ten thirty at night. Is it too late to call Peyton to debrief her on this Latest Mom Development? Is it too early to admit the obvious: that my best friend in the whole wide world, well until quite recently, blew me off on my birthday? Yes and no. *There is still time.*

An hour and a half, to be exact.

Chapter 17

"Hair today, gone tomorrow. Hair growth is affected during pregnancy by progesterone, estrogen and increased cortisone. You may notice hair where you hadn't before: on your chin, upper lip, and even on your breasts. After about six months postdelivery, growth rates will return to normal."
—From *Ready or Not, An Expectant Mother's Guide*
   (Week 27, page 219)

We're in Fredrik's truck and I have the visor down, mirror open. Oh, my—what are those? Whiskers? I guess I shouldn't be surprised. I have the worst pregnancy-symptom luck. If hair is going to grow more, of course, it will do so here, on my chin, versus somewhere potentially looks-enhancing, like my *head*. And, oh, my God, look at my eyebrows! They are very untraditional beautylike, a look only *beautiful* people can pull off. I sneak a glance at Fredrik, who is driving us to Pioneer Valley Maternity Center for a tour (only a tour—there weren't any spots available in a birthing class for another two months), to make sure he didn't witness my discovery. What should I do? Arriving at the Center sporting the female equivalent of the five o'clock shadow is simply *not* an option, so I've got to pluck. Now. But I can't do this in front of Fredrik. I need to get rid of him. Wait, I know.

"Can we stop at the Joint?" I ask Fredrik.

"What for?"

"For coffee."

"We're already late—"

I look at my watch. "At this rate, we'll be thirty minutes early."

"But you drink decaf, why do you need it?"

"I don't know, Fredrik, why do YOU need to be a man and not get to experience the joy and exhilaration that is pregnancy? It's one of life's greatest goddamn mysteries, I will tell you that."

"Um. OK, G. Let me pull over."

Once Fredrik is out of the truck, I begin my work. I've got to get a stronger lightbulb in the bathroom. I've also got to make an appointment for a bikini wax. Can't even IMAGINE what's happening down there because, of course, cannot *see* it. I run my fingers across my chin—yep, all gone—and reapply my lipstick. What is taking him so long? I pray he doesn't forget I want my skim decaf latte *iced*. It's barely eight thirty in the morning and I'm so hot I could die. I crank the AC. I'm pointing the vents at my armpits to prevent staining when I hear a rap on the window. It's Louisa. Fredrik is standing next to her. I roll down the window.

"Look who I found," Fredrik says.

"Which is mine?" I ask.

"Here."

Fredrik starts to hand me a cardboard cup, with a brown corrugated cardboard strip, to prevent burning.

"I wanted it iced."

Fredrik pulls his hand back. Louisa is quiet.

"Shit, I forgot sugar. Be right back," Fredrik says. He shrugs at Louisa as if to say, *she is clearly crazy, so tread lightly*. I decide I will address that later, after I have my ICED coffee.

"I'm glad I ran into you," she says.

"Yep," I reply.

"I hadn't heard from you."

"Yep," I reply again.

She sighs. "Can you meet me for lunch?"

"We have a tour this morning, at nine. I don't know how long it will take."

"What about Friday? At the diner? Noon?"

Fredrik is back, climbing into the cab. He has a new coffee for me.

Louisa asks again, "Twelve then, on Friday?"

"We'd better get going," Fredrik says.

"See you then," she says, waving.

"I guess so," I reply.

"You're going, right?" Fredrik asks as he puts on his seat belt.

"I don't know—"

"You should."

I don't say anything. I look in the rearview mirror. I see Louisa walking down the hill, toward her office. I wonder if it's too late for us. So much has happened since we last spoke. You know how when you first break up with someone and you hear "your" song on the radio? Well, this entire town is about Louisa and me. At first, I couldn't walk a foot without thinking about her—oh, Lucky Lucy's lunchtime special went up a dollar, I should call her; wow, this starlet's Broadway debut bombed, who'd have guessed? Let's discuss and get a latte . . . But can we get back *there*? What in her life have *I* missed?

My phone rings.

"Let me guess. Your mother," Fredrik jokes.

"Hello?"

"Your visit to the hospital got me thinking about my living will," Mom says.

"OK."

"I don't want to linger," she continues ominously. "I want to go quickly, like your father. If I ever fall into a coma or a vegetative state, you and your sister are to pull the plug, *no matter how hard it might be.*"

I want to say, *wouldn't be as hard as you might think,* but instead say, "OK."

"I would like to know of your plans as well."

"My plans?"

"Should you lose consciousness during labor," Mom explains.

"Are you kidding me? I don't even have a *birth* plan and you want me to tell you my *death* plans?"

"There are risks associated with childbirth, honey, you know that."

"Don't you think I'm scared enough as it is? I'm terrified—"

Mom cuts me off. "But why? It's a perfectly natural process."

"YOU ARE TOO MUCH," I shout. "I have to hang up. We're here."

I flip my phone shut and pretend to throw it out the window.

Fredrik looks over at me and says, "If she just didn't make it so easy."

"I know, I know, she's crazy."

Fredrik parks the truck and I climb out of my seat but I misjudge the distance between my feet and the parking lot and I spill my latte all over my shirt and skirt. I start to cry. Fredrik rushes over.

"It's fine, you look fine, please, I'm begging you, do not lose it."

I laugh. "OK, OK, not much I can do about it anyway."

I use the time it takes for us to walk to the Center and into the lobby to reset my annoyance levels. Must. Relax. I'm calm. As soon as we get to the Information Desk, Sarah, the "outreach coordinator"—who looks to be approximately two hundred years old—greets us. I do a quick mental check (Will this detail cause me to explode? No, great, then I am not guilty of ageism and should proceed as normal.) and take stock of the other couples who are on the tour with us. I observe the following:

Couple No. 1: *It's Never Too Late to Start a Second Family*
    Pregnant woman
    Cream-colored maternity skirt, matching blazer over arm. White silk shell, pearls. HUGE engagement ring. *Hose.* Medium build. Early thirties.
    Father-to-be
    Dark blue banker suit. Light blue shirt. Phone clipped to belt. Tall, thin. Nearly bald. Rimless glasses. Midfifties.

Couple No. 2: *Attractive People Prefer the Company of Other Attractive People*
    Pregnant woman
    Levi's. White oxford, over a white maternity tank top. TINY. Flip-flops, toe ring, but no wedding ring. Long, wavy light brown hair. Late twenties.
    Father-to-be
    Madras shorts. White oxford over WILLIAMS T-shirt. Baseball hat. Reef flip-flops. Short, wavy light brown hair. Midtwenties.

Couple No. 3: *Two Mommies Are Better Than One*
    Pregnant woman
    Drawstring linen pants. White maternity T-shirt. Understated silver jewelry—beaded necklace, matching bracelet. Plain wedding band. Early-forties.

Other woman, not pregnant
A-line floral skirt, Ann Taylor circa 1994. Pink linen blouse. No-nonsense haircut, graying. Wedge espadrilles. Plain wedding band. Early-forties.

I smile at everyone and mumble something about my coffee, my shirt.

"Let's get started, shall we? I'm Sarah," the coordinator says. "Here to my right is Admissions. You can preregister, file your birthing plan, and select your room preference before you're admitted. How many of you will take the childbirth education classes offered here at the center?"

We all nod. I elbow Fredrik. See, everyone takes classes!

"I have a question," the pretty pregnant woman says. (How can she have a question? *We just started the tour.*) "Will all the doctors on staff be advised of our birthing plans? I'm committed to a drug-free delivery."

Really? I think. I'm committed to a lot of things—eating less refined sugar, for one—but you don't see me bringing that up now, in front of total strangers.

"Yes, but all birth plans are subject to the birth. Your husband—" Sarah says.

"We're not married," the pretty boy interjects.

The pregnant lesbian raises her eyebrows. *Not married?*

"Are you the birthing coach?" Sarah asks.

"Yes," he replies.

"Then it is your job to act as your partner's advocate during labor," Sarah says.

The professional-looking woman takes out a BlackBerry and types something.

Her husband says, "This is my fourth child. Never once had a birth plan."

"It's my *first* child, Charles, but thank you," she replies.

The cute pregnant woman raises her eyebrows this time,

as if to say, see? *We're not crazy, fifty percent of all marriages end in divorce.*

"Let's head up to Labor and Delivery," Sarah says, changing the subject.

We shuffle onto the elevator. I've never been in a hospital, so I've no idea what to expect. When we step off onto the third floor, I'm struck by how quiet it is. No screaming women, no doctors yelling STAT. We follow Sarah two-by-two to the nurses' station. There is a whiteboard on the wall to the left, with patient names, attending doctors, time of arrival, special instructions. Monitors are beeping.

"Once admitted, you'll be brought here, to a birthing suite."

We remain in form and follow Sarah to look into an empty room. At the far wall, under a row of windows, is a long leatherette chair, like a lounger. The hospital bed is in the middle, next to a computer monitor. On the inside wall, which is shared with the bathroom, there is a mini nurses' station; red plastic boxes marked HAZARDOUS MATERIALS line the wall. Overall, the décor is not entirely unlike that of the Grande: blend-in-the-background wallpaper, a few paintings selected for size, not subject, and a big-screen TV mounted to the wall. Under the TV there is a large wardrobe.

"You can bring whatever you'd like—music, books, DVDs. Once you move into active labor, the room is easily adapted for delivery."

With the flip of a switch, lights descend from the ceiling. Fredrik whistles, impressed.

"I'm glad you like it," Sarah chuckles.

The professional pregnant woman shakes her head, no doubt thinking, *How immature—this is why I married an older man.*

"Should you and your doctor decide on a Cesarean, the

operating room is located down the hall; I'll take you there now."

We file out to the hallway. A pregnant woman in a hospital gown and huge sweat socks is walking the halls with her husband (partner? brother? partner's brother?), breathing *in, out, in, out.* She doesn't notice us staring. We peek through the window of the empty OR. A lot of shiny metal. I turn away quickly. As I wait for the rest of the group to take their turns looking through the oval window, I notice a nurse taping a drawing of a leaf with a drop of rain on it onto a birthing suite door. There is faint crying from the room. We're waiting to be buzzed into the maternity ward when I ask Sarah about it.

"It's a sign of a baby's death. We use it in Labor & Delivery and in the maternity ward, so the professionals who treat the patient do so in the best way possible," she explains.

All eight of us shudder. *A death?*

"To think you make it that far—" Fredrik whispers.

"God, it's horrible," someone else says.

The lesbians clasp hands.

The doors buzz and swing open.

Sarah walks backward down the hallway as she speaks "This is a restricted area. Every mother, baby, and father or partner is issued a band with a nine-digit number that is checked each time a baby is taken from and brought to the nursery and his or her mother. There are single-, double-, and triple-occupancy rooms. Overnight guests are permitted in single rooms only."

I make a mental note: will bribe anyone/everyone to get a single room.

"Here we are at the nursery," Sarah announces.

We line up at the window, faces pressed to the glass, looking at four babies. They lie on their backs in plastic-sided Isolettes that sit atop rolling metal carts. They are wrapped in identical hospital-issue blankets, white with a blue and pink border; they all wear hats. One of the hats is topped with a pink curled ribbon. Toward the back of the room, two nurses are bathing a just-born boy and his penis and testicles are enormous—oddly out of proportion with the rest of his body. The women handle the baby without hesitation, talking to him the entire time.

"Excuse me, sorry, just need to get through," a tired looking man in a T-shirt and pajama bottoms says as he walks by us.

He stops at a table located not far from the nurses' station. On top of it are three coolers. He takes a few single-serve containers of juice out of the cooler and proceeds to drink them loudly. When he's done, he tosses the empty bottles in the trash and awards himself four points. He walks back down the hallway and disappears into a room, only to emerge seconds later, looking sheepish.

"I forgot her juice," he explains. "Must get juice."

The men nod sympathetically. Oh, yes, the *hardship* of remembering juice.

Sarah continues, "Circumcisions can be performed by your surgeon or a doctor on staff."

"I've read that circumcisions are not medically necessary. What do doctors here recommend?" the nonpregnant lesbian asks.

What? Seriously, how is Sarah going to answer that question? I am considering recommending we "table this issue" (a favorite phrase of Eliza's) when Fredrik clears his throat. I look at him, aghast. "I've read a lot about it," he announces. "There are a lot of arguments for the procedure, but not all of them are medical."

"Such as?" the professional woman asks.

"Religious, or, um, gender identification," he answers.

Did he just say gender identification?

"What do you mean, identification?" the preppy guy asks.

"Having it done so the son looks like the father," Fredrik says.

I stand there, staring at the lesbians. I clear my throat. Are we being insensitive? Or not? Is Fredrik running around discussing gender identification behind my back? Or is this even Fredrik at all? Maybe an alien has—

"I'm Jewish," the pregnant lesbian says to her partner, at whom she is scowling. "So it's not even up for debate. We're doing it. *Period.*"

Whoosh. The maternity ward doors swing open (putting an end to our tour banter) and a man walks in with a young towheaded girl in his arms. She is clutching a CON-GRATULATIONS balloon in one hand and a stuffed elephant in another. They smile at us and enter a recovery room, where her mother greets her excitedly.

"Katie, my big girl!" the mommy says. "Come meet your baby brother!"

A tiny voice squeaks back, "No, thank you."

We all laugh.

The tour ends.

We exchange some pleasantries . . . *No,* we don't have a pediatrician yet. *No,* we're not sure if we'll learn to sign with the baby. *No,* we have not put our unborn child's name on the waiting list at the Holyoke Co-op, the best nursery school in a two-hundred-mile radius. And finally, *no,* I have not selected a "push present" whatever the hell that is.

Fredrik and I leave the hospital.

We climb into the cab and Fredrik starts the truck.

"I'm exhausted and out of breath," I choke. "Totally drained."

"Oh, my God, me, too."

"What time is it?" I ask as I fan myself with my "What You Need to Know about Pioneer Valley Maternity Center" booklet.

"Nine thirty-five."

"You are joking," I say.

"Nope," he laughs.

"I don't have to be at work until lunchtime," I offer.

"Let's take a drive," he suggests.

"Sounds fun," I say, even though I suspect tunes will be cranked.

Sure enough, the CD player is on before we've left our space in the parking lot. I want to complain but it feels like complaining for the sake of itself, versus complaining about the pregnancy, which feels justified. I decide I will let this blasting of CAKE—they are singing about sheep going to Heaven, it seems—go on without even groaning. We drive for about twenty minutes—I'm not exactly sure where we are because I never drive—when Fredrik pulls in to a long dirt driveway.

"I want to show you something," he says.

"What is it?"

Before he can answer, the truck stops in front of what appears to be an abandoned farmhouse.

"Oh, no," I say.

"I want you to visualize," he says.

"I cannot visualize. You know that," I say.

"Think about it—I would do the work myself. We'd be in the country!"

"Fredrik—" I say, laughing.

"I don't want to hear about your allergies, or how you are intimidated by the Patagonia catalogue, or how you are afraid of spiders, or how you are clumsy, or not self-confident, or any of your usual rants—because those are excuses to not change anything in your life, even if there are some things that could be better."

"You really do listen to me, don't you?" I tease.

"No, it's just you say the same things over and over," he responds.

I laugh. "OK, I agree to get out of the truck."

"That's a start," he says.

I half-jump out of the truck, and walk beside Fredrik as he points to different parts of the property—a place for his shop and office, here, an area for Boo, over there, the part of the yard he'd fence in for the kids, *there* (kids? Is he insane?). I'm listening but only halfheartedly. It's not that I couldn't get excited about moving—I can get excited about things—it's just I feel like with the baby, everything is already such an unknown. Why add to it? Even if I fall apart postdelivery, at least I'd be able to take solace in knowing that the towels are in the same place they've been forever. That has to count for something, doesn't it? But as Fredrik keeps talking it occurs to me that what he said is true—I *am* afraid to change. And it's not because I have any real reason to be, so it's more that resisting change has become a habit; I'm not even conscious of it most of the time.

Some pretty scary things have happened these past few months and still, I am here, walking on a dirt path with shoes that are entirely inappropriate for the Great Outdoors—Fredrik is talking now about "appreciable assets"—and I'm fine. *Happy* even.

I interrupt Fredrik. "Honey?" I ask.

"Yes?"

"I was thinking—I don't want to be the kind of person who doesn't want to do new things because of something that happened a hundred years ago."

"Ah, right."

"I'm not saying I want to move, mind you."

"Of course not."

"I want to be a good role model."

Fredrik smiles at me and says, "OK."

"Now, this role model needs a bathroom."

Fredrik laughs "You lasted longer than I thought you would. Let's head out—there's a little store down the street; it's less than a mile from the front drive *and,* they have coffee, lattes."

"Enough with the hard sell! I can't think anymore—I won't have any brain power left to work on my birth *slash* death plans."

"OK, OK, bathroom, then the plans."

"If I die, maybe you can pull the plug on my mother."

"Now, *that's* what I call a plan," he says as he helps me up into the truck.

Chapter 18

"As you approach the end of your pregnancy, you may find that many people are offering to help you. Try to start accepting the offers; before you know it baby will be here, and you will need that support network in place."
—From *Ready or Not, An Expectant Mother's Guide*
  (Week 29, page 231)

"Gretchen, are you all right in there?" Mrs. Stirling asks.

"Just a minute," I answer.

I take a look around. This is a nice bathroom.

I'm in no real rush to leave it because when I do, I will have to continue shopping with Mrs. Stirling—I should start calling her Elaine—for maternity and nursing bras. Last week my mother called her, in what I consider to be one of her top boundary-crossing acts, because she is "concerned about my breasts." Elaine agreed that this was an *emergency situation,* which is why I find myself now, here, on the toilet at Mother 2 Mother, a small store on the west side of town.

"When you're ready, I've got a few styles for you to try on," she says.

What's happening to me that I'm bra shopping with my

mother-in-law? Is nothing sacred? I give up, leave the bathroom, and enter the dressing room.

There are two piles of ugly bras.

I hear the saleswoman approach Elaine. "How is she doing?"

I don't know, lady, my breasts are practically lying on top of my stomach; how do you *think* I'm doing? I'm trying to get a bra on (this thing is frickin' HUGE) and I'm all sweaty and, wait, what is that on my nipples? I move closer to the mirror and see a crusty, yellowish substance in the cracks. *What the?* I am examining my breasts in the mirror of the dressing room when Elaine and the saleswoman opens the door to my dressing room. They stare at me. At my breasts. And the half-on, half-off bra. The saleswoman doesn't miss a beat.

"Let me help you. Here, this is a nursing bra. See the flaps in the front? That's to help you move them aside when you need to feed the baby."

"Oh."

"Let's try a maternity next," she suggests.

"Gretchen? I'll wait out here but first—" Elaine stammers.

"Yes?"

"Your mother, well, she wanted me to, um, examine your nipples."

OH. MY. GOD. I will *kill* her.

"You're joking," I say, smiling.

"No. She told me that she will call me this afternoon. For a report."

"A report? Anything specific?"

"Apparently, inverted nipples run in your family," she replies.

"God, 'Mother Fox' is going to drive me *insane*," I snort.

"Mother Fox is your mother?" the saleswoman asks.

"Yes—"

"She called, earlier. I'm so sorry about your father," she says.

"Um, thank you," I reply, trying to avoid eye contact.

"She wanted me to slip some literature into your bag," she explains.

"I'm so sorry," I sigh.

"Don't be," the saleswoman says. "I wish my mother was that interested in what I was doing."

Hmm. That's one way to look at it. After a few minutes, I select a few bras and Mrs. Stirling takes them to the cashier. By the time I'm dressed, Elaine already has her credit card out. Who knew she had one?

"With tax, that'll be one hundred seventy-eight dollars and fifty-seven cents."

Elaine hands her card to the woman.

"No, it's too much," I say.

"Let me do this," she says.

I look up from my purse and Elaine is smiling at me.

"OK," I say, adding, "thank you."

Elaine and I walk outside together.

"Thanks, again, I appreciate it."

She comes toward me for a hug, something she's never done before. I lean in, too, but with my stomach, it's hard to get close. Plus, she's tall like Fredrik, so I have to encircle my arms underneath hers. We look like we're about to slow dance. It's nice just the same. To be honest, I don't mind that the pregnancy is the only thing that's bolstered my standing with my in-laws. I will take attention anywhere I can get it.

We say our good-byes and I start to walk back to work, swinging my shopping bag back and forth. After about thirty seconds, I decide to stop at a coffee shop for a snack. I've (sort of) given up fighting the weight gain: twenty-seven pounds total. I'm healthy and my baby is healthy, what's another muffin? I shouldn't. I won't. But I have to pee and I can't go in without buying something; that would be rude. I stand at the counter, contemplating my order. I check my watch. Is this a snack? Or lunch? A protein would be good. What here is a protein?

Out of the corner of my eye, I see something, someone. It's Louisa. But before I open my mouth to call out her name, I remember. She rescheduled our lunch because of a last-minute work crisis, and I took it personally and never called her back. I turn back around and study the menu. Why has she not noticed me, glorious as I am in my white linen dress, which I'm wearing over pale blue XXL Old Navy pajama bottoms and a smattering of turquoise jewelry, a maternity and/or the Look for Less interpretation of Urban Cowboy style? There are only a few of us here—wait, who is she with? I turn back to her table. She and a guy are sitting on one side of a table; his arm is resting on her leg. They are—and this is a word my mother would use—*canoodling*. I gasp and Louisa looks up.

"Gretchen," Louisa says.

"Hey," I say. I look over at the guy.

Louisa stands up. "What are you doing here?"

"I was just bra shopping with Elaine—can you believe it? Bras. Totally humiliating. But then on my walk to the Grande, I had to go to the bathroom and couldn't wait so I came here instead. I go to the bathroom all the time, even right after I've already gone, and then I thought if I'm in a café, I should get something to eat because if I don't, I will get a headache," I answer, sounding like a complete lunatic.

"Do you want to sit down?"

I look at the guy, the fellow canoodler, and pretend we've already been introduced because *not* introducing us would be awkward. I explain I could not possibly sit down (again, it is a very small café and I would have literally blocked the entrance had I joined them) because I'm in a huge rush, in such a rush that I knock over a travel coffee mug display as I gesture to reinforce my newfound sense of urgency—urgency I've never felt before—to get to work. Louisa helps me rearrange the cups and my necklaces get all in a tangle and the whole time I'm trying to check this guy out, this *nonhusband person,* who, I think, has nice shoes but who has still, awkwardly, not uttered a single word.

"It was great to see you," I shout as I run for the door.

Once on the street, I realize I did not use the bathroom. Now what? I cannot, CANNOT, believe I saw Louisa MAKE OUT—OK, not a complete make out but behaving intimately—with someone who is not Jason. *How random.* As I walk back to the hotel, I take my phone out of my purse and dial Fredrik. I hang up before it even rings, because reschedule or not, speaking or not, I can't betray her to him. He will judge and what I need is *analysis.* I need to talk to someone who can distill a complex situation into an easily digested, one-line assessment. *I will call Peyton.*

"Are you busy?" I ask.

"Nah. Just working on a memo for Homeland Security. How was bra shopping?"

"Never mind that. I just saw Louisa kissing a man. Not her husband."

"One sec—Patrick, put those there." She's back to me. "WHAT?"

Peyton has an assistant. His name is Patrick. He left a small town in Ireland to attend the School of Foreign Service at Georgetown. I imagine he looks like a young Russell Crowe, who is Australian. When I can't remember a person's face, they morph into celebrities. Ann Newhouse is no longer Ann Newhouse, she is that chick from *Dharma and Greg,* but cuter and less weird. And Dad? He is Clint Eastwood. Why? Because of a picture I keep next to my bed of Dad that was taken during a six week hiking trip to the Rocky Mountains. In it, he looks rugged; his graying black hair is longish, wind-swept, and his salt-and-pepper beard was a departure from his usual clean shave. In my mind's eye, Clint and Dad share a face. I have never told anyone I do this. I think it might sound crazy. Peyton is breathing into the phone.

"It was bizarre," I say.

"You haven't talked to her at all?" she asks.

"No. Do you think she and Jason have broken up? I can't believe all this is happening and I don't know anything about it! I mean, we're best friends," I say, not caring how silly that sounds. "Meredith hasn't talked to her, either."

"I'm sure she'll call you," Peyton observes. "When she's ready."

I hang up with Peyton and take a seat on an empty bench. *How is my urgency now?* I place my bag of bras next to me. I push my butt to the back of the bench, but my legs are too short and I cannot bend my knees. I stare at my rigor mortis–like legs. The few inches of flesh visible between the hem of the pj's and my sandals, size 9, have patches of stubble; I missed some spots in the shower. I don't want to leave this bench, ever. I don't want to go to work. I take a bottle of water from the bag, open it, proceed to spill on myself, take a sip, and laugh. My butt hurts.

"Gretchen?"

It's Meredith. She takes a seat. Ryder is asleep in the stroller.

"We're on a walk," Meredith begins, "but we stopped— *I* stopped, when I saw you. Oh, my God, when will this pregnancy end?"

"I don't know how you do it with Ryder."

"In one sense it's better. There is no time to obsess on

the little things that consume you the first time around, like memorizing the calcium content of spinach."

"You are nothing if not thorough," I joke.

"What's in the bag?"

"Bras."

"Did you add disposable underwear to your list?"

"I hate the list."

"You, hate a list? Never," she laughs. "All right, I've got to go. If I don't keep walking, I will fall asleep here."

Meredith starts to stand up.

"Wait," I say. How do I describe what I just saw? And should I? The balance of three friends, well—you have to be careful, you can't be going on and on about the other one. But, I—oh, screw it. "Can I tell you something in confidence?"

"Of course."

Meredith is pushing Ryder's stroller back and forth, back and forth.

"I saw Louisa"—I look around to make sure no one can hear me—"and she was with someone."

"Who?"

"Doesn't matter. Not Jason. They were canoodling."

Meredith bursts out laughing. *"Canoodling?"*

"I am sorry but that is what they were doing."

"You're sure it was her?" she asks.

"I talked to her! And the guy, he never said anything. Just sat there."

"Weird. I don't know what's going on. Louisa's never home. She's always going out with that Tracy, so I never see her. But then, can I *reasonably* expect her to want to spend time with *me,* of all people? If I were her, I'd be the *last* person I'd turn to. You know what I mean?"

"Yeah."

"We're sympathetic, of course but at the same time, we're—" she starts.

"Completely self-absorbed?"

"Yes," she says, laughing, "we are, we are like—I don't know what."

"We are like *brides*," I suggest.

"Like brides, *yes*. Exactly."

I stand up, as does Meredith, and begin to walk back up Main Street with her. I make an "executive decision" (another favorite phrase of Eliza's) and ditch work. I call Eliza to plead illness. She is brusque, per usual, and hangs up with the news that she will be handling Char and Kate's wedding—they've finally set a date; September first. *Of course*. Is there any other day to do anything?

Meredith and I enjoy a wide berth on the sidewalk, as other pedestrians seem to be making great accommodations for us.

"This isn't so bad," I say, between pants. "Tell me again about term."

"It's anything from thirty-seven to forty-two weeks," Meredith says.

"Wait, there is a *five-week* swing?"

"Yep."

"Jesus, I'd like to be a doctor. If I gave Eliza that kind of timeframe—oh, yes, the reception will be ready sometime this *spring*—I'd be fired."

Meredith laughs. We're at the top of the hill under the Gates.

"I'm going to stop at my office. You headed home?"

"Yeah, I'll call you later."

I walk the rest of the way home motivated by a single purpose: to lie down. As soon as I walk in the door, I head for the couch. Within seconds, I'm asleep.

Suddenly, I hear my name. My left cheek is sticky.

"Gretchen? Are you all right? You're not at work."

"No, I am not. I am here," I say, teasing him. "What time is it?"

I sit up so he can take a seat next to me.

"It's after four. I called your cell—I was worried."

"I'm sorry, it was just a weird day."

"The bra shopping?"

"What?" Was that today? "No."

"Eliza?"

"No, no—nothing like that. What's weird about being pregnant—and believe or not this is *not* a complaint—is how much you end up thinking about the past, as much as you do the future; like everything that shaped you up until this point must be reanalyzed."

"Like your dad?"

"Exactly."

"You don't talk about him."

I don't say anything.

"Would he like me?" he asks.

"What's not to like?" I tease.

I lean in next to Fredrik and he holds me close.

I spot my Filofax and reach for it.

"Please, no," he begs.

I open it up.

"Do you think we have enough food for the Grande meeting?"

I'm hosting a meeting of my esteemed coworkers to go over our plan to save the hotel. After Eliza's announcement, everyone wandered around in a state of denial, which manifested itself as near full-on neglect of our jobs. "Why not sit here all day?" Mr. Edwards asked, as we enjoyed a post-window shopping iced coffee at the Joint. "What's the point of rushing back to a job I don't even have?" But after a time, we became bored. "I have officially run out of errands," Mr. Edwards declared on our way home from the Department of Motor Vehicles, where we'd renewed our licenses. Our choices were to simply go back to doing our work or throw ourselves, wholeheartedly, into a dramatic, *We must save the Grande, we must save this town!* plan of attack. It was unanimous. We would continue to neglect our guests in order to galvanize a counterselling effort. Within about three minutes of the staff realizing that someone, at some point, would have to *focus,* we formed smaller committees, which are comprised mostly of my friends. I appointed myself overall organizer, responsible for the final presentation, and no one objected. Mom's FedEx package had come in really handy; it was a step-by-step guide about how to create an employee-owned business.

"We have more than enough," Fredrik says.

"Did you remember the Combos? They're Bob's favorite."

"I got two party packs."

"Pizza flavor?"

"Yes, pizza flavor."

Luckily, the "oh, my God, people from work are going to see where I live" cleaning frenzy coincides nicely, timing wise, with my "the house must be perfect before we bring this baby home" list. I review the list with Fredrik.

- Closets, dressers: mine, Fredrik's, upstairs, linen, downstairs, coats *check*.
  My closet is organized by season and size, with maternity and XXLs in current rotation. For Fredrik, I refolded approximately thirty blue and bluish gray short- and long-sleeved T-shirts, shorts, khakis, and jeans. Those I considered wearable outside of work went into a separate pile.

- Attic, *check*.
  I ordered acid-free storage for Fredrik's artwork—he sketches and paints—and filled clear Rubbermaid containers for our collective crap: report cards, year-

books, stamp collections (mine), scouting badges (his). Each box has a corresponding label created by a hand-held label maker. It took several tries before I settled on an acceptable font.

- Basement, *finish by 6/17*.

That's next week. The basement is Fredrik's territory, except for a single shelf of cardboard boxes that hold hun-dreds—no, thousands, of unsorted Fox family photographs. I rescued them from Mom's laundry baskets when we moved into this house. I've not looked at them since. I've never been to Dad's grave, either. At first, it was because I didn't know what I'd do there (this is the kind of thing a sixteen-year-old girl focuses on—whether or not it is queer to bring your dead father flowers). Then, as time passed, I didn't go because I didn't want another reminder. I had enough re-minders and quite frankly, *they sucked*. I just wanted to put it all behind me and pretend it never happened. In some ways, this kept me from remembering any of the good stuff, too—because if I remembered what I *had*, I then would have to remember what I had *lost* all over again. Fredrik is right. I never talk about him. But I would like to put some pictures of Dad in the baby's room—I think that would be nice, maybe one of the two of us together.

"Come with me to the basement. I want to go through the pictures," I say.

"I'll bring them up. Stay here," Fredrik offers.

"That's it? Two boxes?" I ask once he returns from the basement.

He nods yes. I hesitate before opening one. What's in there? I open the box and quickly pull out a picture. It's Peyton. She looks so young! Here she is with Dad, her arms around his neck, not a care in the world.

"Here's a good one of you," Fredrik says.

I look at it.

"That's not me. It's my mother."

Fredrik is quiet, reflecting, no doubt, on the genetic predictor he held oh-so casually, only moments before. "*Whoa*. You look exactly the same."

"Don't worry—" I soothe.

"I'm not," he interrupts.

"I am!" I add, laughing.

The baby kicks and shifts to the left. There is an ongoing battle for space. I'm losing. I reposition myself. I locate a picture of Ann Newhouse, one of those telescope shots, taken during a weekend at Dewey Beach, in Delaware.

"What do you want me to do with this?" Fredrik asks.

It's a folder of Clint Eastwood magazine clippings and articles.

"Throw them away," I reply, and turn back to the boxes.

We spend the next few minutes pulling pictures out, then Fredrik suggests we organize them chronologically. Suddenly, I have an idea.

"Can you bring me the speakerphone?" I ask.

"Why?"

"To call my mom. She can help us create a timeline of major events—like this trip, here, to Niagara Falls—and then we can figure out where the other ones go."

He brings me the phone and we place it on the coffee table. I dial Mom.

"IS EVERYTHING OK?" she shouts by way of answering.

"Yes, Mother," I say. I look to Fredrik, who nods at me to continue. "Do you have a few minutes? Fredrik and I are going through the pictures—our family pictures—and we want to organize them—"

"Of course you do," Mom teases.

"Anyway, we don't know when some of these were taken. Can you help us?"

"I would love to."

For the next hour or so, we sit on the phone with Mom—Fredrik takes notes on a yellow legal pad—and we start to put the pictures in piles. Mom and I remember a lot of stuff, stuff I had forgotten, and I had more than one moment when I wanted to scream "Enough!" But mostly, it was good. And while Fredrik and Mom argued over the precise year of Elvis Presley's death (Googling proved Mom right), I made a little pact with myself to do this more often after the baby comes. After all, everyone deserves to have a grandfather, and the truth is, I wouldn't mind having a dad—even just a memory here and there—either. It's been too long.

Chapter 19

"The heat is on! A summertime pregnancy can mean you're at higher risk for water retention. Start paring down your days (ask friends for help if you need it), stay off your feet, and drink water. If you have any sudden swelling in your hands or face, call your doctor immediately."
—From *Ready or Not, An Expectant Mother's Guide* (Week 31, page 240)

"I told you, the thermostat cannot go any lower," Fredrik says to me as I readjust all the knobs on our AC unit. "Besides, I'm freezing."

"Then put on pants."

"It's July; I'm *supposed* to wear shorts."

"But *I'm* hot."

"Then sit down, for Christ's sake."

The doorbell rings.

The Save the Grande committee heads arrive en masse: Mrs. Torrez (she brought Carlotta), who are working with the union; Susan and Front Desk Bob (because they're attached at the hip), who are running all the numbers; Mr. Ali and Mr. Andrews, who are looking for cost savings or new sources of revenue. Our goal today is to finish the second draft of the plan.

Bob heads straight for the kitchen and opens the fridge. "Can I have a Chimay Red?"

"Um . . ." I look at Fredrik.

"Of course," Fredrik says.

"Awesome."

He takes two, pops open a bag of Combos, and takes a seat on the couch. He places both beers between his legs. I start to pace the room.

"I hope she doesn't start talking about Thomas Paine's *The Rights of Man* again," Mr. Edwards whispers to Susan. "Or liberation theology. What a bore."

"I heard that," I say. I take a deep breath. "I just thought we could benefit from understanding our situation in a, in a—" I can't think. What had Mom said? "In a *broader* context. But never mind. What's happening with the union?"

"The new union is on standby," Mrs. Torrez reports. "They ratified our vote to join last Thursday. We have money in the bank, a representative available for negotiations, and, best of all, our fallen leader, Señor Rockwood, is cooperating with the district attorney."

"I thought he inherited the money," I say, teasing her.

"*Se sellan mis labios*, don't you worry about it."

"Come on," I plead.

"We went to his house. Señora punched him," Carlotta offers.

I write down "first-time assault?? Penalty?" on my legal pad.

"Moving on, then. Mr. Andrews, how was your meeting with the bank?" I ask.

"Excellent," he replies.

One of the Pau Paus fathers works at the Bank of Boston, and he's helping us with something called the "financials." In the meantime, we're refining our "business model" (less complicated than it sounds—basically how to make more money than we spend). We enlisted the staff's help to identify ways to cut costs and bring in more guests. Then Susan ran all *those* numbers.

"We cut operational costs alone by 15 percent. The most significant impact would come from adjusting the temperature of empty rooms—three degrees up in the summer and three degrees down in the winter," Mr. Ali explains.

"Wow." Winter sounds so appealing right now.

"Don't forget our other plan," Mr. Andrews says to Mr. Ali.

"Why don't you explain, Mr. Andrews?"

Mr. Ali and Mr. Andrews—despite all outward appearances of having nothing in common (Mr. Ali, conservative Muslim, Mr. Andrews, gay Quaker)—are united in their attempts to return an air of formality to corporate America.

"Mr. Ali and I have had a brainstorm."

"A what?" Bob asks, his mouth full of Combos.

"A brainstorm, Bob; a *thought*," Mr. Andrews explains, not bothering with Bob's last name, which I'm not sure any of us knows.

"What is this thought?" Señora asks.

"A real brainstorm," Mr. Andrews adds.

"What is the brainstorm?" I ask impatiently.

"Mr. Ali and I think we should enlist that blind photographer to create an ad campaign," Mr. Andrews says, "on behalf of the Grande. Of course, *we'd* be the models."

Mr. Andrews beams at all of us. I clear my throat.

"Um, the photographer is not blind. The photo in the lobby—that he took—was of a blind *person*," I begin. "And, while I think this idea is totally cool and deserves some serious, um, cowbell, I'm wondering, where were you thinking we'd put these ads?"

"*USA Today*, the *New York Times*—" Mr. Andrews says as though this was obvious.

"Cool. Count me in," Bob says.

Bob jumps up from the couch and starts prancing around as though he was on a catwalk. Susan laughs hysterically.

"Please, let's focus," Carlotta says.

I stand up again and chide Bob. "Bob, sit down."

"You're embarrassing yourself," Carlotta says.

"He wasn't half-bad," Mr. Andrews observes, winking at Bob, who smiles.

"Never mind, people, let's focus. Susan, how do the numbers look?" I ask.

Susan pulls a stack of papers and a scientific calculator from her JanSport backpack.

"I *finally* got the math to work," she says.

Susan has a passion for numbers that rivals her feelings for Bob.

"We can reduce the overhead of our group through one early retirement, one job share, and a collective one-year salary hold."

"Ouch," I say.

"I know." She sighs. "I'm broke enough as it is."

And she is. I can tell. She has that semidesperate, freshman-year-of-life look about her. (She did not go to South Padre with Bob, and fretted the whole week that he would fall in love with the winner of the annual Spring Break wet T-shirt contest.)

"Why don't you move into my house?" Front Desk Bob asks between gulps of beer. "You're there all the time anyway. We could save on rent." *Oh, no.*

"OK," Susan says, grinning.

"No, no, no," I interrupt. "You *just started dating*! Moving in together for financial reasons is—" I am using my Ryder's Mommy voice again. I look to Mr. Andrews as if to say, *Please stop this, we cannot let this happen.*

"How exciting for you two," Mr. Andrews says.

He mouths a "sorry" to me. I mouth back "helpful."

"We are never going to get out of here," Señora observes.

After a few hours of Coke, Diet Coke, Caffeine-Free Coke, Caffeine-Free Diet Coke, and Combos, we're satisfied with the final document. I e-mail it to Peyton.

"Is your sister a spy?" Susan asks.

"No."

"Can we use State Department letterhead?" Front Desk Bob asks.

"No."

"*Dammit to hell,*" Mr. Edwards shouts.

"Calm down. It looks great," I say.

After I push the SEND button, we agree we will, *no question,* outsmart Eliza and wrest control of the hotel. Shortly thereafter, we are wracked with doubt, convinced we'll be thrown out on the street, jobless. Minutes later, we congratulate ourselves on our hard work. *Around and around.* Someone puts the TV on. It's a special, something about pandas on a nature channel. Front Desk Bob remarks that the species is in an "evolutionary cul de sac" and we are all quiet, wondering how he is capable of such a declaration. Mr. Andrews presses him on it and Bob responds with a fairly well-thought-out case (something about the inefficiency of their digestive tracts, the low nutritional value of bamboo, and their inability to copulate without watching pornography). When he says the last bit, several of us nod our heads as if to say, *At last, the connection.* Finally, we grow bored of the conversation and everyone leaves.

I take a Popsicle from the freezer and flop down on the couch next to Fredrik.

"What do you think Eliza will say?" he asks.

"I have no idea."

"Does complicate things."

"Yeah," I say.

I look over at my Filo, on the coffee table. It can no longer clasp shut; it's exploding with articles, spreadsheets, and coupons for flip-flops, my current shoe of choice. I look down at my feet. They're nearly square.

"Do you think I'm retaining water?" I ask.

"What?"

"My feet are huge."

"You have a Popsicle mustache."

"I'm a mess," I say.

"Oh—no, honey—you look great."

Fredrik is seated at my feet but turns to his side, in an attempt to come lie down next to me. But there is no room— I barely fit on the couch myself—so instead, he pulls me up toward him. I think I see him straining. I swing my legs from the couch to the floor. When we are seated side by side, he puts his hand on my knee and begins to stroke it. Wow, it looks grotesquely large; could my *knee* be retaining water? Why is Fredrik still touching me? Surely he realizes that *any* physical activity is awkward at this point, which significantly reduces the enjoyment potential of this moment (a "hey, I'm bored and it's a Saturday afternoon so why not have sex on the couch?" kind of moment) but he does not appear to agree; the stroking is still going on. I continue to sit. I don't feel like doing anything else. Hopefully, he will tire of the knee and we can get back to the television. The problem with the third trimester of pregnancy is that you are not really able to lose yourself in *any* kind of moment, most of all a sexual one. I sigh loudly. Fredrik steps up his efforts. He obviously misinterpreted that as interest. Luckily for me, the phone rings. I lift myself out of the couch so I can reach the portable to answer it, but Fredrik stops me.

He whispers, "Don't." *Oh*.

"Fredrik," I say.

"What?"

He now has his hands on my breasts. He seems to be impressed with their size. "Are these getting bigger?" he asks.

I push his hands aside. "I admire your persistence, I really do, but, um—"

"Come lay down with me," he says, motioning to the floor.

"You're joking," I say.

"I'm not." As he says this, he is throwing blankets and pillows on the floor.

The phone rings again.

"I should get that," I suggest.

"Lay down," he says, pointing to the jumble.

I feel I have the upper hand, so I start to negotiate.

"My feet hurt," I say.

"Oh, yeah," he says. "I am turned on now."

"I am not *trying* to turn you on."

"Just give it a chance," he pleads.

"OK, OK," I say.

I lie down. He rubs my feet, then my legs and my back and I start to giggle. I let him do everything, which is *very* relaxing . . . (You don't have to acknowledge the sexual needs of your partner when you have sex in your eighth month of pregnancy—*because your presence is gift enough!*) For a moment, I entertain the possibility that I'm sexier than I realized—maybe, just maybe, I am irresistible, even though I am starting to waddle when I walk—and that is a very nice feeling. Plus, I've always been crazy attracted to Fredrik (I wish I could use sex as a weapon, but I'd rather just have it.), and before I know it, I am officially suspending my disbelief. Immediately after, we look at each other, embarrassed at what's just taken place. *We are so not sexy.* He gives me a squeeze and a kiss on the forehead.

The phone rings again.

"Definitely your mother," Fredrik says.

"I'm not answering."

After a few minutes, we stand up to arrange ourselves in blankets and retreat back to the couch. Fredrik turns on the TV and lands on HBO. One of our favorite movies, *Die Hard,* is on.

"Turn it up! I love this part!" I say.

There's a knock on the door.

"Don't answer it," Fredrik says, turning the TV up louder.

"Yippee-ki-yay, motherfucker!" Bruce Willis shouts.

There is another knock on the door.

Boo barks.

"Fredrik—answer the door."

"I'm not dressed."

"Neither am I."

"Take the blanket—"

Knock knock knock.

"Fine, I'll get it."

As I stand up, Fredrik turns the TV to top volume.

"AIYEEEEEEEEEEEEEEE!" I scream.

Fredrik laughs.

I open the door in my T-shirt, the blanket wrapped around my waist (if only it was a *Pashmina*), letting in a rush of hot air into the house. Before me stand two firemen. One is holding an axe above his head, in a predestroy position.

"JESUS CHRIST, WHAT ARE YOU DOING?" I shout.

I lift my hands up to keep them from swinging. The blanket falls to the floor.

"Are you Gretchen Stirling?"

"Yes, I am. What is it? Put that away! Please!"

I squat down to get the blanket. Boo is barking like crazy.

"Boo, Boo. *Calm down*," Fredrik says as he turns off the TV, scrambling for something to put on himself. He grabs my maternity sweater and puts it around him. *Gross.*

"Your mother called us over," the older one says.

"Oh, my God."

The younger of the two takes out his walkie-talkie.

"Negative. I repeat, negative—she is not in labor." His eyes glance toward us and then to the floor, where our clothes rest in a heap. "Your mother thought you were having the baby alone. You didn't answer the phone," he says to me.

"No, we did not," Fredrik says.

"We heard screaming," the younger one says.

"It was the movie," I explain.

"She would like you to call her," the older one says.

"I will. I'm so sorry. Thank you so much—"

"Now. Call her now," the older one says as the younger one nods.

"OK, then."

Fredrik invites them in and I hear the *crunch* of a few Combos beneath the firemen's boots. God, what must they think?

"Mom?"

"DID YOU HAVE THE BABY?"

"*No.* I was here. Watching a movie." The younger one raises his eyebrows; I turn away from him. "How did you convince them to come here?" I whisper.

"I told them the same thing I say to you girls: "I'll just keep calling and calling and calling."

I hang up and turn to Fredrik, who has that "I just had

sex with a very pregnant woman" look on his face. It's really a one-of-a-kind expression.

"She told them she'd just keep calling," I explain.

"Promise me you'll never get that bad."

"I promise."

Chapter 20

*"An ounce of prevention . . . Most likely you've fin-
ished with the nursery by now. Take the next few
weeks to stock up on items for the household. Cook
and freeze meals and buy extra supplies to reduce un-
necessary trips to the grocery store once you're home
from the hospital."*
—From *Ready or Not, An Expectant Mother's Guide*
  (Week 33, page 251)

It's two o'clock in the morning. I am crouched inside my
closet, where I've stored the sum total of my baby-related
items. I have two onsesies, a bib from Mom, a copy of Dr.
Spock (from Elaine), and a nightlight. I want to review before I go shopping with Meredith tomorrow. Today, it's
today. A hanger crashes to the ground. My ankles crack as
I squat to the ground to find it, wedged in a metal container
of flip-flops. I wobble a bit and fall back on my wide, fat
ass.

Fredrik grunts. "What are you doing? What time is it?"

"Go back to sleep."

Fredrik rolls from his back to his side and extends an
arm. Two arms.

"I can do it."

He gets out of bed, helps me up. He climbs back into

bed. I return to the bed. Within minutes, Fredrik is back to sleep. Not me, I'm wide-awake. I will be so tired tomorrow. But I'm always tired. I don't know how Meredith functions.

Fredrik is snoring. The sight of him there, sleeping soundly, peacefully, angers me. *I am so jealous of him.* He can sleep. He can actually forget I'm pregnant (something he confessed to me a few days ago and then immediately regretted). But me? I can't think or do anything else except be pregnant. I'm just killing time, and, unfortunately, the age-old time-killer, sleep, eludes me. Which would be fine if I didn't have to listen to someone else do it, *every single night.*

I guess I could go to the couch but why should I? He should. I need the bed, even though I'm not technically sleeping. It's so unfair. I elbow him. He snorts. "Turn over," I say, hoping that this will lower the decibel levels in the room. He does not respond. I push him.

"You want me," he says, half-asleep as he reaches for me.

Someone shoot me.

The next morning, Meredith and Ryder arrive promptly at ten. Once I'm in the car, I make a list of yet *more* baby-related accessories, these for the truck (I crossed "car" off my *Buying for Baby* list shortly after I'd learned the hotel was to be sold): sun shades for windows; two mirrors— one to attach to Mom's visor, one on the backseat for rear-facing baby to admire himself and for Mom to watch; more hanging toys; a special trash bag that attaches to the door handle, little blue bags for emergency diaper disposal.

Meredith pulls into a spot designated for "Expectant Mothers and Mothers of Infants." The lot is like a war zone, hands of pregnancy poker walking about everywhere, minivans backing up and beeping, mothers transferring screaming children from car seats to strollers. Almost every child has a cup and a plastic Baggie filled with brown crumbs. A pregnant woman sits in an air-conditioned car, window down, yelling instructions to her husband as he struggles to fit five or six bulky boxes into the backseat of their hatchback, adding, "Now you know what it feels like to be carrying your baby around." The merchandise pickup line is at a standstill; a woman with two crying children is trying, without luck, to secure a plastic pool to the roof of her car. My phone rings.

"Hello? Yes, OK, great, thanks."

"Who was that?" Meredith asks.

"Mrs. Torrez. She told me they've given Eliza our plan for the hotel."

A discussion on the matter of who should approach Eliza led us to the conclusion that while Eliza may not have any favorites amongst the staff, she definitely hates me. "Are you sure?" I asked. "YES!" everyone said. Mr. Ali finally did it himself.

Once off the phone, I look around the strip mall. I've been here a thousand times before—to the pet store, Smooches for Pooches. But I suppose all the chatting up of other dog owners—"How old is he? Still a puppy, yes, how they do chew." kept me from noticing this whole other world, over *here*. There is similar talk here as we walk in. "How old? Is he a good sleeper? Have you read the *Baby Whisperer?*" But as the electronic doors swing open, I realize that this trip is going to cost me way, *way* more than ten years' worth of top-of-the-line light-reflective collars and Lab-proof chew toys. Directly ahead of us, stocked floor-to-ceiling: *things*. Things I Need. Things I Have to Buy. My leg twitches; I have a mild cramp on my left side, there since this morning.

We push the cart back and forth through the store, with Meredith translating for me. Clothing: onesies, sleeper "bags" that tie at the end, footed things—"for day *and* for night" she says "neither you nor the baby will know or care which it is." Feeding: she grabs two bottles, nipples, and a few pacifiers, and throws them in the cart.

"Forget about nipple confusion," Meredith advised. "Babies like to suck; it's you or this."

"What's nipple confusion?"

"The belief that a baby can't go back and forth between your breast, bottle, and a pacifier but—" Meredith is cut off by a woman standing behind us.

"My Benjamin never took a bottle," she says, nodding toward a toddler.

Meredith and I are silent. A second woman wanders over from a display of plates and cups decorated with cartoon characters. She is pushing a double stroller; twins—one boy, one girl, in matching denim overalls. They are crying for someone named Dora. Meredith continues, "Anyway, if you want to pump, I'd rent one from the hospital. It's cheaper."

"Did you tandem nurse?" Benjamin's mother asks the twins' mom.

"For about ten minutes. They were small babies and they ate every two hours. After a week, I got mastitis and they got thrush."

"I thought nursing was supposed to be easy, natural," I remark to Meredith.

Everyone laughs.

The cart magically fills with a thousand small items (the larger purchases will be made with Fredrik, as they are vaguely "mechanical" and thus of interest to him—like the car seat), diapers, wipes, washcloths, baby soap, shampoo, black-and-white toys that make crinkly noises, crib sheets, waterproof mattress cover, blankets that stretch "for swaddling," infant Tylenol, scent-free wipes—*Oh, my GOD*. I bend over, grab a side of the cart.

"Gretchen, don't freak out—we can put some stuff back."

"I have to go to the bathroom."

I shut the door behind mc. Phew. It's a single-serve. Should I hover over the seat, germs-related? Ugh, no—too much pressure; must sit. I pull down my pants and there, in the *cotton panel comfortable and absorbent enough for all-day wearing,* I see blood. More than a few spots, and dark red. I sit. I want to push but the cramping has turned to pressure. I don't know what to do. I look again. Still there. I pop my head out the door. Meredith is right there, waiting.

"I—" I clear my throat. "I think I need to call Dr. Mitchell."

"What is it?" she asks.

"I have this weird feeling, and there is some blood—"

"Let me call him." Meredith takes out her phone, presses #6 and begins speaking. "Is Dr. Mitchell available? I'm calling for Gretchen Stirling, and—"

"I'm sorry," I cry from the passenger seat of her car. We're going to the hospital. Ryder is crying, too. I turn back and feel the top of his head; his hair is damp. In the mirror I see a red, scrunched-up face, full of rage. I jiggle the elephant at him. He bats at it, annoyed. "He's mad," I say. I turn back in my seat and dial Fredrik's cell phone again. Right to voice mail. I call Andrew; he answers on the first ring. "It's me, Gretchen. Where is your brother?" I yell at him. "What? Right. I forgot!"

Fredrik is chopping wood today. *No cell service.* Andrew's sending someone to get him and will meet me at the hospital. Meredith pulls up to the ER drop-off. Ryder is wailing. I open the door and she points: "Go there, ask for Labor & Delivery; they're waiting for you. I'll be up after I feed Ryder." I walk, alone, and state my name and my case to the woman behind the desk. An orderly appears with a wheelchair and we take a huge steel elevator up to the

third floor. A sign reminds us to RESPECT PATIENT CONFI-
DENTIALITY. Great news. I can cry without worrying that
this very handsome African-American man will talk about
me during his next elevator ride. A nurse, Stephanie, leads
us to a delivery room. She hands me a hospital gown and I
place my clothes in a plastic bag labeled PATIENT'S PER-
SONAL BELONGINGS. It looks a bit like the bag I was given
to put my purse and my watch in at the police station,
after I'd been arrested. I climb in the bed. Stephanie folds
back the sheet.

"Dr. Mitchell called. He wants us to check a few
things."

"OK."

She lifts up my gown and squirts gel on my stomach.
She wraps a large black band around me, tightens it and
moves a little monitor around.

"This is the fetal monitor—let's get that heartbeat. Do
you know what you're having?"

"No."

"There it is."

Thank you. I look at the screen. Heartbeats per minute.
One hundred forty-five. One hundred forty-three. *Thump.*
A kick.

"A kicker," Stephanie says. "Are you still crampy?"

"Not as much."

"You had some spotting?"

"I didn't see any more when I undressed."

I feel a small wave in my uterus and a line on the seis-
mograph thingy rises. *A contraction.* Stephanie walks to
the sink and pulls on plastic gloves. She generously applies
K-Y Jelly to her fingers and lifts my gown.

"You might feel pressure."

"Uh."

Her hand is pushing against me, in me.

"Not dilated at all; your cervix is high and tight."

"That's good?" I ask.

"Yep," she answers and leaves the room.

I'm alone. I'm cold. I rub my stomach and watch the heart monitor. I inhale. I exhale. I want my husband. I want my mother. I want my sister. I want someone, *anyone*. But I can't get out of the bed to get my phone.

The door opens. It's Andrew. He's brought Kim.

"What'd you do, Stevie? Eat too much?"

He takes a seat on the chair, next to the bed. Kim stands there.

"Hey, Kim," I say as though we were meeting for coffee at the Joint, don't mind me in my hospital gown. "No, you ass," I say to Andrew.

"Cool room. Where's the TV?"

Kim perches on the heater, near the window. The door opens again.

"Gretchen? I'm Dr. Taylor, the staff obstetrician. I spoke with Dr. Mitchell and he wants me to do an internal."

I don't even know this man and he's going to do an internal? Should I tell him about my oddly located cervix or let him discover it for himself? Dr. Taylor offers his hand to Andrew; they shake and he keeps speaking. Kim introduces herself and before I can explain everyone's relationships, Dr. Taylor continues.

"The good news is that your contractions are likely nonproductive, meaning you are not in labor. But we want to check out the spotting. A few questions first. Are you with me?"

"Yep," I answer.

"Any problems in the pregnancy so far?

"No."

"Lift anything heavy? Muscular pain?"

"No."

"Any fever?"

"No."

"Any vaginal penetration, stimulation, or orgasms in the last twenty-four hours?"

I look at Andrew, who is playing with the buttons on the side of the bed. Kim is staring at the ceiling, no doubt thinking what a great and unique new relationship experience this must be. *Bloody show, anyone?*

Dr. Taylor is waiting for an answer. I clear my throat.

"Um, Andrew?"

"I think your wife would like you to answer."

"I'm her brother-in-law," Andrew replies.

"And Kim is his girlfriend," I say. "My husband couldn't be reached."

Dr. Taylor suggests that Andrew and Kim relocate to the waiting area.

Once they're gone I say, "I had sex—intercourse—last night."

I look up at the monitor as Dr. Taylor inserts the speculum. I have sex a handful of times during my entire pregnancy and then I have it twice in as many weeks and I end up in the hospital? I will kill myself if I've harmed the baby.

"Whatever it is, it's over. Some dark red blood, old." He snaps off his gloves. He looks at a printout from the computer. "No more contractions. How's the pressure?"

"I feel like I need to go to the bathroom."

"Constipation?"

"Yes."

"We've got some unrelated events, here, Gretchen. I'll prescribe you a stool softener for the constipation. It is likely intercourse caused the spotting. My guess is you had a few Braxton Hicks. To be on the safe side, no sexual activities until you're to term. We'll keep you here for an hour or so, just to be sure, and I'll give Dr. Mitchell an update. But if you have any other problems, give him a call.

He'll probably want to see you in a few days, regardless. Any questions?"

"No. Thank you."

"I'll send your brother-in-law back in if you want."

"OK."

Andrew, Kim, Fredrik, and Meredith walk in together. Fredrik rushes to me, kisses me. He smells of sweat and dirt.

"Did you stop for a mud pie?" I joke.

"What did the doctor say?" Fredrik asks.

"Is cable extra?" Andrew asks.

"Everything is fine, honey."

"Are you in labor?" Meredith asks.

She looks pretty close to labor herself.

"Meredith, *please* sit down. Where is Ryder?"

"What did the doctor say?" Fredrik's voice is rising.

"That I'm not in labor."

"Good news! Right? That's good news?" Kim asks.

"I wonder if they have pay-per-view," Andrew says.

"They have everything here, even massages," Meredith adds. "Ryder's asleep in the stroller in the hall; he's fine."

"You should bring him in," I suggest.

"Do they give the dads massages?" Andrew asks.

"TELL ME WHAT IS GOING ON NOW!" Fredrik yells.

"Just another day in the life of a pregnant woman," I say, laughing. "I'm constipated—that's the pressure. The contractions are "nonproductive," but I need to go home, drink water, and rest. And the spotting was probably caused by sex."

"You've had sex?" Andrew and Kim ask in unison.

"Mystery solved," Meredith declares.

"*Good God,*" Fredrik yells, and we all laugh with relief.

Chapter 21

"Gesundheit! Up until now, you've provided your baby with immunity to mild infections, but now, with delivery imminent, your unborn child is developing some protection of his own."
—From *Ready or Not, An Expectant Mother's Guide*
  (Week 34, page 260)

"I have some bad news," Fredrik says solemnly, taking a seat on the coffee table across from me. I am lying on the couch, surrounded by half-used tissues.

"Is it Meredith? Is she OK? Is the baby OK?"

Meredith was induced this morning.

"Shit, I'm sorry to scare you. No, entirely different subject."

"Fredrik, don't do that."

"I said I was sorry!"

I squint at him. He will never be as sorry as I am right now. *He can breathe!*

"A few weeks ago, Peyton e-mailed me about throwing you a shower," he begins. "I had her call Meredith. She thought she'd have had her baby by now, so it seemed like a good weekend."

Meredith is forty-two weeks. She thought the second baby would arrive on its own, promptly at week thirty-nine, which coincided with her parents' annual trip to Northampton. To say that she's cried a lot these past three weeks is a *serious* understatement. "My mucus plug hasn't even come out," she reported. To which I responded, "Please. There is such a thing as too much information."

"Is there some kind of surprise shower or something?" I ask Fredrik.

"Not exactly. They decided on something low-key. A girls' weekend."

"Is Peyton coming up here?"

"Yes, her flight gets in at six. But there's more."

"*Please, please, please* do not say—"

"Your mother is coming with her. And my mom will be here in an hour."

"*At-choo!*" I sneeze.

"God bless you."

"Why didn't you tell me?"

"I was sworn to secrecy; I'm sorry."

Fredrik leaves me on the couch and starts to prepare dinner. Wow. Mom. *Here.* She's only been to the house once, for my wedding. I glance around the TV room; it's fairly neat, though I could do some last-minute decluttering. *Screw it.* I'm not getting up. I'm too tired. Besides, Peyton is an excellent cleaner. I don't want to leave her with nothing to do. Oh, God. *How will I keep Mom away from Elaine?*

A few hours later, we are all seated around our dining room table. I've purposely steered the conversation toward neutral subjects. Thank God for Peyton, who'd interrupted Mom before she got too far into a description of her latest e-mail writing campaign. (I saw a few drafts; the subject line was "Commuting isn't just a Bitch, it's a *Killer.*") Elaine takes all of this in and says very little, until Mom starts talking about the baby, and my job. Suddenly, they are united. *Against me.*

"Elaine, I agree with you. It seems to me they have everything they need."

"Mom, please," I say.

"What? Elaine and I are mothers, we know—"

Fredrik gets up to clear the table. Elaine pops up as well. Mom keeps talking, as she tends to do whenever manual labor is about to take place. Once she realizes Elaine is in the kitchen, she moves to "help."

"Faye, please, sit down. You're our guest," Fredrik says.

"I'm not a guest, I'm *family*," Mom protests. "I'm happy to do it."

She sits back down at the table, not having done anything. She turns to me and asks, "What is happening with Louisa?"

"Nothing, Mom," Peyton says.

"Did you call her?" I ask.

"I did—she said she'd talk to Meredith," Peyton says.

"Ah," I say.

"It's so sad you girls had a falling out," Mom observes.

"We didn't. We're just taking a break," I explain.

"A break? I just saw a show where the boy and the girl were dating but took a break, I believe it was *Two and a Half Men and a Little Lady*," Mom says, unsure.

"There is no such show," I say.

"Well, there should be," Elaine says, having rejoined us at the table.

Great.

"Why don't you invite her over? I'd love to see her," Mom suggests.

"I don't know . . ."

Mom clinks on her glass. Peyton, Fredrik, and I roll our eyes.

"I have an announcement. A wise man once said, 'To err is human, to forgive divine.' "

"How original," Peyton observes.

"What a wonderful expression," Elaine says.

I get it, you're friends now.

"I think what everyone needs is a glass of wine. Most notably you, my dear daughter." Mom winks at me.

"What?" I ask.

"It's not going to kill you. Fredrik, what do you think?"

"I think it would be fine," he answers.

"It might relax you," Elaine suggests. Wow, even she thinks I'm uptight?

"You know, I think I will call Louisa," I say, desperate for a diversion.

Fredrik hands me the portable phone. Louisa answers. I sneeze.

"Sorry, I'm just very—*At-choo!*"

"God bless you," Louisa says.

"Listen, Mom and Peyton are in town and Elaine is here."

"That's this weekend?"

"Yep. And, um, Mom would love to see you."

"Now?"

"Sure, or later, if you're busy."

There is a long pause. My stomach drops, but in the bad kind of way.

"Be right there," she says.

"Great," I say with a bit more excitement than I intended.

Within about thirty seconds, she's at my front door. Mom hugs her.

"I'm sorry for your loss," Mom says.

Elaine walks up to her and rubs her arm sympathetically.

"OH MY GOD!" Louisa exclaims.

"What?"

"YOU'RE HUGE!"

We all laugh. She is not as thin as the last time I saw her

and looks a lot better. Will I ever have a waist again? I miss *jeans*.

"What's all this?" she asks, nodding toward stacks of baby clothes.

"I brought up some things for Gretchen and the baby," Mom explains.

"So—" I say.

Everyone is silent. Peyton busies herself stacking my pregnancy books in ascending order by size. She looks at me, one eyebrow raised. I nod yes.

"Fredrik, can you show Mom and me the baby's room?" Peyton asks. "Elaine? Gretchen said you did the most amazing things with the curtains."

They all head up the stairs.

Louisa takes a seat at our kitchen table.

"Any word from Meredith?" I begin.

"No, last I heard at four o'clock she was still in labor."

"I wish Alan would call."

"You're getting pretty close, too; just six weeks left."

"I know."

"It's weird to say but—I wonder if I would have had my baby my now." Louisa is looking down at her hands.

"I don't think it's weird."

"At first, the smallest things would set me off. Like, the sonogram place calling to confirm my appointment. I was like, *Check your records; I had a miscarriage!*"

"That's awful."

There's a crash from the baby's room.

Mom shouts, "I'm fine. Nothing broken."

I roll my eyes and Louisa whispers, "I can't believe she's here."

"She's insane."

"Anyway, I just wanted to get through the nine months and be done with it."

She takes a sip of my wine.

"That's how it was with my father: suffering through the first Thanksgiving, then Christmas, his birthday, my parents' anniversary, yada yada yada. It sucked."

"It's not the same; I wasn't even into my second trimester," Louisa protests.

"Sounds sort of the same to me."

Louisa's eyes water. "I was—I've been—horrible. After I miscarried, I got to thinking, maybe I don't *want* to have a baby. Maybe this is a sign. Maybe, instead, I should go out and get FUCKED UP every night. Maybe I need new friends, a new job, a new house, a new husband. A do-over."

"Right," I say.

"That guy—John—who you saw me with? I actually convinced myself I was in love with him. Because if it was about love—passionate, I am willing to destroy myself, my marriage, my entire life kind of love—then it didn't have to be about anything else . . . like my sadness over losing the baby, or my jealousy of you. And it was so weird to be going through all of it—even though some of it was about you—*without you*. Nothing I did felt real. I started confessing things to empty elevators, like 'I am having an affair' or 'I didn't do any work this afternoon because I was too busy surfing the Web looking for the name of the girl who transferred to Dartmouth our senior year.' Do you remember her?"

"Of course—who transfers their *senior* year?"

"The truth is, I was soooo mad at you," she says, speaking like a teenager. "Sorry," she says, resuming her normal voice. "That's what Jason likes to call the "Tracy Hangover." For the record, I am far, far too old to be 'RAGING AGAINST THE MACHINE' with twentysomethings. That is what I did almost every night, before I met John."

"Ah, OK."

"Gretchen, I hope you can forgive me. I know I treated

you horribly, even though you were trying to help me. And I blew off your birthday. That was so low."

"It was tough," I admit.

"I hope we're OK," she says, again. "I'll try and make it up to you, I promise."

"To be honest—though this isn't how I would have chosen it to happen—I probably needed the distance," I say. I am surprised when I hear myself speak these words, but suddenly it's all becoming clear. Confiding in Louisa, keeping *her* as my emotional partner, well, it was the perfect way for me to keep from getting too close to Fredrik. I was hedging my bets with him *not* because I didn't love him— I really, really do—but because, I think, I was afraid he would die.

"We've been friends a long time," Louisa says. "Things do change."

"Yes. They do," I say.

"Honey, may we come down now?" Mom shouts from the top of the steps.

"YES!" I shout back. "How are things with Jason?"

"Getting better. Every day is better."

"Good."

"We have a lot to catch up on," Louisa says, winking at me, as Mom joins us and makes a sweeping gesture with her hands, nearly knocking over Elaine.

"*All* of the baby's things I brought need to be washed. I'll start on the laundry tonight," Mom announces.

"OK," I say.

"Where is your washer?"

"Downstairs."

"On second thought, I'll save that for tomorrow. Plenty of time for chores."

"Oh, yes, plenty of time," Peyton says.

Louisa stands. "I should go."

The phone rings. Fredrik answers.

"Yes? Yes, I will tell her. Great news. Let us know if you need anything."

"Was that Alan? What did he say?" I shout.

"Everyone is fine."

"Is it a boy or girl? TELL ME!"

It *had* to be a boy. A few months ago, when we consulted the Chinese Gender Chart, Meredith had "boy." When I did mine, I saw "girl." Fredrik was skeptical, asking why, if the Chart was so accurate, doesn't Dr. Mitchell use it?

"It's a girl. A healthy baby girl, Hannah." He smiles.

"*A girl?* No. That can't be right," I say.

"We can call the doctor if you'd like, G," Fredrik says, teasing me.

"Let's celebrate," Mom says, reaching for a bottle of champagne I'd purposefully hidden in the back of the fridge. "Where are the glasses?"

"We can use these." Fredrik takes out our wineglasses from the cabinet.

"No champagne glasses?" Mom asks.

"Uh—no," I answer. "Please do NOT start about my wedding."

"*Fine, fine.* But let me say, for the record, that Pat and Cathy were devastated they weren't included. They would have thrown you a lovely shower."

"We offered several times to have a party," Elaine says.

"I know you did, Elaine, and that was very generous of you," Mom replies.

Oh, my Lord.

"Give it a rest," Peyton shouts.

Louisa clears her throat. "Enjoy the rest of your visit."

"I will, as soon as I get some sleep," Mom says. "I'm exhausted."

"From what?" Peyton asks.

"From *travel*," Mom replies.

I whisper to Louisa, "Don't go. Better yet, take me with you."

"No—you seem fine."

"HA!"

"I'll call you tomorrow. Promise."

Louisa half-walks, half-skips down our front path. Before I can shut the door, Mom's shouting.

"ARE YOU FRIENDS AGAIN? WHAT DID SHE SAY, HONEY?"

"MA! COULD I CLOSE THE DOOR FIRST, *PLEASE?*" I shout back.

"KIDS TODAY ARE SO RUDE!" Elaine adds, shouting as loudly as my mother.

As I hear the click of the clock, I smile. It was nice to hear her say that she missed me (I was starting to think I'd seriously overestimated our friendship.), and that her anger had nothing to do with me—even though I'd suspected that already (I can spot that a mile away—it's called projection and Mom used to accuse me of it, constantly.). It feels good to have her back. And as I turn around to face my mother and my mother-in-law, who are now lamenting the lack of a proper baby shower on my behalf, I can *hear* myself describing the scene to Louisa and Meredith, over coffee at the Joint. And unlike during the past few months, this thought is not followed by a reminder to myself that the three of us will never meet for coffee again.

Because we will. I'm sure of it.

Chapter 22

*"Patience is a virtue. At this point in your pregnancy,
you might find yourself feeling tired of the pregnancy.
As much as you may want it to be over, try to trea-
sure these last few weeks. Believe it or not, there are
some things you might even miss (like baby's kicks!)."*
—From *Ready or Not, An Expectant Mother's Guide*
(Week 36, page 270)

Week 36 and 6 days

Fredrik pulls the truck up to the entrance of the Grande.
I no longer walk to work. "LOOK AT ME, FREDRIK,"
I'd said when he'd suggested I keep at it. "LOOK AT ME
AND TELL ME THAT'S A GOOD IDEA." "Let the
dance begin," he'd replied, referring to a Viagra ad; we're
allowed to have sex again starting tomorrow, when I'm
considered "term." Anyway, I *won't* open the truck door,
because if I do, I will (a) have to participate in tonight's
event—the much-anticipated Pau Pau Renaissance Festival—in this godforsaken heat, and (b) see Eliza. Word is
we'll get a decision today about the hotel.

Fredrik comes around to my side and helps me out. I
hear the jugglers before I see them; they are warming up in
the parking lot, which is tented and decorated in a Renais-

sance theme. This required a lot of Google searching and *considerable* convincing of the wait staff, whose uniforms have been replaced with historically inaccurate costumes. A bellman is lighting torches.

"M'lady!" Front Desk Bob shouts as he rushes up to greet us. He offers a beer-filled stein to Fredrik.

"Sure you don't want to stay?" I ask. "Please?"

A juggler cries, "Shit!" as he drops a torch.

"I will pick you up at eleven," Fredrik says as he rushes to get back in the truck. He takes off so quickly I believe he became airborne.

I walk through the tent, to the employee entrance, and waddle to my locker. I remove my blouse and a sweater; the world is just going to have to deal with me and my JUST HAD A BABY T-shirt. I cannot layer. NO! IT IS NOT TOO EARLY TO WEAR THIS, I'd shouted after Fredrik pointed out that I had not, in fact, "just had a baby."

I waddle from my locker to the hotel kitchen and a wave of heat hits me as soon as I open the door. The kitchen staff is placing large legs of meat, referred to in the contract as "brontosaurus-sized," on pewter trays. I take one for myself.

"Any word from Eliza?" I ask Carlos.

"No."

"Christ, I can't take another minute of this."

Mrs. Torrez walks in. "*Es tiempo*. Eliza wants us in her office."

I keep eating as I walk with Señora toward our offices. I can't be expected to go hungry at a time like this. Señora and I join Mr. Ali, Mr. Andrews, and Susan outside Eliza's office. We all walk in and take a seat at her conference table.

The brontosaurus thingy is dripping. I need another napkin.

Eliza clears her throat. "I wanted all of you here because after reading your proposal, I can see how much the hotel means to you. But the sale of the Grande is final."

I look up at the ceiling, hoping gravity keeps the tears in my eyes.

"I have spoken with the Hotel Alliance Group and we agreed that they will take into consideration some—not all—of your recommendations, instead of those made by Concorde. I cannot say, for certain, what will happen after September first, but the new union will be recognized for the purposes of salary negotiations. For nonunion staff, I've been assured that benefits will be offered. As for actual employee responsibility, I don't know. We currently pay about eighty percent. But you know that already." Eliza pauses. "Are there any questions?"

We look around at each other.

"I'm disappointed," I say, waving the leg for emphasis. "It was a good plan."

"It was. It is," Eliza replies.

Can't she say something more or show some modicum of emotion?

I want to scream, *Please do not give up on us, I will try harder to be more upscale,* but I cannot because the lead minstrel in tonight's entertainment, "The Age of Chivalry" has begun his act.

It must be seven o'clock. The Festival has officially begun.

Mr. Ali stands, offers his hand to Eliza. "Thank you, Miss Singleton."

"Thank *you,*" she says.

"Another day, another dollar," I say to no one in particular. Unlike the gracious Mr. Ali, I cannot bring myself to be, well, gracious.

Susan looks devastated. It occurs to me that she is young and has not experienced anything like this. This is her first job. She doesn't know yet that there will be other jobs and that, over time, she will care less. I take her aside and without adopting my Ryder's Mommy voice, try to comfort her. "Susan, you were awesome. You are *so smart;* you'll be fine. Bob, too."

"I don't understand. I thought for sure." Susan lets her thoughts drift.

"We did the best we could," I offer. "And that's what matters."

"Well, if you say so. You're the mother."

Um, not exactly, I think, but if it makes her feel better, so be it. I toss the leg into the trash and walk out of the office, behind Mr. Andrews, who has linked arms with Mr. Ali ("It's a common practice amongst men in the Middle East," he'd said after I'd noticed them strolling arm in arm through the ballroom. "Sorry, I'd forgotten we'd relocated to Pakistan," I'd replied.). Time to break the news to the others.

I walk outside; the entire parking lot reeks of beer and kerosene.

"Where are the horses?" a Pau Pau asks.

It's dark out now, but I can make out sweaty faces—the steins are a hit. Zellos the Torysteller is in the midst of his "tongue-twisting, fast-paced act," as described in his flyer. "O Romeo! O Romeo! A fair whore you need, Romeo!" he cries and the Pau Paus chant in response, "More whores, more whores." I have to laugh. I can't blame Eliza for selling. *This event is definitely ground zero on the war against down-market.* I walk to the side of the tent that faces Ryland, to confer with Mr. Ali and a few other hotel employees.

"I CANNOT believe she's still selling."

"Shit!" Jack, our fire marshal and/or deputy head of Security, cries, as he takes off to chase a lit torch that is headed for a tree.

"That's the last time I hire amateur jugglers," I say. "What a mess."

"It's not all bad. It is a compromise. It is not a perfect world." Mr. Ali smiles.

"You can say that again."

I hear a pop. All the lights in the tent go out.

The Age of Chivalry stops playing. Jack rushes over.

Mr. Ali's walkie-talkie is squawking. "What the hell was that?" Mr. Ali asks.

Jack takes out his walkie-talkie to contact Security.

"Jack here. What's going on? Over."

Everyone mills around helplessly. Zellos and Bob run over.

"Did we blow a fuse?" Mr. Ali asks.

"I'm *so* fired," I moan. "I double-checked all the wiring, the voltage—"

"Jack? You there? Over," a disembodied voice says.

"Yes. Here. Over."

"Everything is out. Over."

"In the hotel?" Jack asks.

"No. Over."

"In Northampton?" Jack asks.

"No. *The entire East Coast. The entire East Coast is without power*. We do not have a code for this um, violation. Over."

So a party—*a party I planned*—with a theme that is supposed to evoke a time in history during which there was no electricity, effectively wiped out power to the entire East Coast? Damn. I'm good. When I fuck up, I fuck up big.

I take Bob's arm, to say good-bye. "In a weird way, I'll miss you."

Zellos eyes Mr. Ali. "Is it a terrorist attack?" he asks.

"I beg your pardon," Mr. Andrews says. "But you are a minstrel! Go—go, minst, or whatever it is that you do!"

Mr. Ali nods a thanks to Mr. Andrews.

Eliza, Carlotta, Esperinza, and the rest of the staff begin filtering out of the building, as do the guests. The hotel is being evacuated. The sidewalks are packed with people.

"What is going on?" Eliza asks.

"My cousin said New York, Philly, D.C.—all dark," Susan says.

Oh, my God. Mom. Have got to get to Mom. And Peyton. Ouch, what the?

Just then, another pop—*from me.* Water splashes to the ground.

"What the fuck was that?" Zellos asks.

"*Please,* there are ladies present," Mr. Ali says.

"My water broke!" I cry. "This is not supposed to happen!"

My legs are drenched.

"Mr. Ali, Mrs. Torrez," Eliza says, "please tell the staff that we are enacting Emergency Plan A; nonessential employees should go home to their families. Jack, please make an announcement to the guests that we are working with the power company but that the problem appears to be affecting most of the East Coast." She turns to me. "Let's get you to the hospital."

"I need to call Fredrik," I say.

Without warning, a strong downward motion grips me. I do the test Dr. Mitchell suggested, after my labor dry run, to see if a change in position stops the pain. It does not. This is an honest-to-God contraction.

"I need to call Dr. Mitchell," I say, loudly.

Mrs. Torrez hugs me and I wait for Eliza to get her car.

"You will be fine, I promise," she says.

All the Pau Paus are gathered around me now. I consider how lucky they are to be facing the blackout *absolutely wasted* and not, as I am, *bone chillingly sober and in preterm labor.* A few of them attempt a high-five with me, but I am hunched over and cannot reach their hands. Mr. Ali and Mr. Andrews each take a side of me and walk me to Eliza's car, which she has brought up Ryland.

I get in her car, which smells faintly of cigarettes—ah ha!—and buckle the waist part of my seat belt underneath my belly. I lean forward, my right arm gripping the door. We drive slowly through town. There are people everywhere, sitting in chairs, drinking, eating, as though everyone in the town had moved their living rooms out onto the sidewalks. We continue on toward the hospital. There are no stoplights. Each intersection is a negotiation, with Eliza inching forward, *gas/break, gas/break*, hoping other cars will give way. "Almost there," she says, for her sake as much as mine. I breathe loudly through my mouth, in and out, like I'd seen in the movies, because they are my only guide—our birthing classes start the day after tomorrow.

As we pull up to the circular driveway of the ER, I'm so relieved I start to cry.

"Do you want me to come in?" she asks.

"GRETCHEN!"

It's Fredrik. He has Andrew and an orderly with him and a wheelchair.

I sit down. I feel totally normal. I notice Andrew and Kim. *Jesus*. They had to come too? Hmm. I'm irritated. Maybe I'm not in labor. I turn to Eliza and try to mouth, "no, thank you," but my mouth takes another shape, more of an "AHHHHHHH" as another downward force grips my body. The orderly pushes me through the ER, up toward Labor and Delivery. Everything is dark, no, dim, as though we'd come here to enjoy a romantic evening. I'm surprised we're able to take an elevator up to Labor and Delivery. Fredrik says something about a generator. Andrew and he briefly discuss brands, voltage, that kind of thing, and I sit there wondering if you need electricity to administer decent pain medication.

The elevator doors open and I see Dr. Mitchell, waiting for us. He is in scrubs. He looks *cute*. Damn, I never got that bikini wax. Or the pedicure. Shit, I didn't even shave my legs. Or pluck my chin. Maybe the dim lighting is a blessing in disguise.

"This the real thing, Gretchen?" He squats down to speak to me. "You're not quite thirty-seven weeks. It is the hospital's policy to treat this as a premature birth."

"Is the baby OK?" I ask. I start to cry, realizing *that's* what's scaring me half to death, not my stupid stubble. "Please, tell me. Is it too early?"

"I think you'll be fine. Let's check you two out."

"How long can the hospital stay on generator power?" Fredrik asks.

I take his hand. *As long as Fredrik is here, I will be fine. I love my husband.*

"We've got plenty of juice, don't worry. The rooms might be a bit darker, but everything we need to get this baby here safely, we have." He pats Fredrik on the back.

I'm wheeled into a birthing suite and I'm left to undress.

"Did you call Mom?" I ask as I take off my T-shirt, throwing it at Fredrik. "Peyton? What about your parents?"

"Your mom and your sister are on their way. Told my parents to stay put until we know more."

"Have them come, Fredrik. They should be here."

"OK," he says, surprised. Fredrik folds the T-shirt. "Good thing you wore it."

A few nurses who come in the room to help me into the bed interrupt us. They move quickly, taking my blood pressure, inserting an IV. As soon as I hear the heartbeat, I relax.

"OW OW OW OW OW!"

"You're having a contraction," the nurse says, standing at the end of the bed, gloves on. I show Fredrik where to look on the screen. "As soon as it's done, we'll check your cervix." Her hand is pushing in me; she takes it out and whips off a glove. "I'd say four centimeters. Is this your first baby?" Her name tag says "Janice."

"Yes. OW OW OW OW OW."

"Do you want an epidural?" she asks.

"YES!" I answer. "Please?"

"I'll tell Dr. Mitchell and get the anesthesiologist. It may be a few minutes; we're backed up."

Another nurse is handing Fredrik a clipboard with forms. He seems to be confused about how to fill them out. He looks up and asks me for the pediatrician's phone number.

"OH, MY GOD. I don't have my Filofax. Write down Northampton Pediatrics. They have privileges here. OUCH!" I grab his hand and squeeze it.

"Jesus!" he yells. "That hurt."

"DOES IT?" *I hate my husband.*

Janice is back; she adjusts the fetal monitor.

"How are we doing?"

"Janice," I say, hoping my use of her name will personalize my plight, "how much longer do you think the doctor will be?"

"Let me check."

She leaves again. I grab on to Fredrik's collar and pull him toward my face.

"The whole POINT of MEDICAL INTERVENTION, Fredrik, is that there BE MEDICAL INTERVENTION. WHERE IS THAT DOCTOR?"

"I don't know. I could use a pillow though."

"SO YOU CAN CATCH SOME SHUT-EYE WHILE I GIVE BIRTH TO OUR CHILD? HOW ABOUT A BEER? MAYBE BOB CAN BRING YOU A STEIN?"

"OK, so, let me get this straight: no jokes," Fredrik teases.

"GO GET THE DOCTOR. DO WHATEVER YOU HAVE TO. GET HIM."

Nurse Janice is back.

"Did you take childbirth classes?" she asks.

"He wouldn't take them. HE IS NOT A JOINER AND HE DOES NOT BELIEVE IN GREETING CARDS!" I shout.

"That's not entirely true—" Fredrik says.

"I'm not getting in the middle of that," Janice says, laughing. "Dad, look at the monitor. When you see a contraction, I want you to work with Mom on breathing through the pain."

"OW. ANOTHER ONE!"

"Breathe, breathe. It's cresting—stay with me, almost done, breathe, breathe, breathe," Janice soothes.

"Good job, honey," Fredrik says, brushing my hair to the side.

Janice leaves the room again. How can they leave us alone? Don't they realize we have no idea what we're doing? We stare at each other.

"Is Kim in love with Andrew?" I ask. "I can think of no other reason that she'd be willing to go to the hospital not once but twice with his freakishly pregnant sister-in-law."

"I don't know if she is. But Andrew says the sex is great."

Before I can say anything, another contraction comes on.

Breathe, breathe—I hate breathing.

Janice is back. No doctor.

"Let's take another look," Janice suggests.

FYI, It is not a look. *It is you putting your entire hand in my vagina!*

"Six centimeters. Good progress." She rubs my leg.

The anesthesiologist arrives. I've never been so happy to see anyone in my entire life. A needle in the back seems like a small price to pay for some decent pain relief. I swing my legs to the edge of the bed. I curve my back around a pillow, as instructed, into a "cat" position. Or "camel." I have no idea what he's talking about, until he asks me if I take yoga. Um. *No.* "Done," he says. "You will feel pressure to push, but the edge should be off the pain. I'll come back to check on you."

Fredrik takes my hand.

"You look nervous, honey," I say.

"It was a long needle."

Another woman walks into the room with my chart. She is wearing a white lab coat. She is tall with short-cropped hair. Spiky almost. Probably not a lot of time for *coiffing,* what with the saving of lives; Mom would definitely approve of her career choice.

"I'm Dr. Wiley, the staff neonatologist. You're thirty-six weeks?"

"Almost thirty-seven." I WANT SO BADLY TO GET TO MYTHICAL "TERM."

"Hospital procedure requires that a member of the neonatology team be present for your child's birth. I didn't want you to be alarmed by the presence of extra medical personnel in the room. We'll be there regardless of the time."

"What do we need to be concerned about?" I ask.

"Lucky for you not much—the baby is so close. But the hospital, we like our policies. Let's see here,"—she consults my chart—"good, Northampton Pediatrics—we know them well. I'll give them a call, though I suspect someone from the practice is here at the hospital now. It's busy because of the power outage."

"Any word on what caused it?" Fredrik asked.

Please, please, please don't say a Renaissance Festival.

"Something went wrong in Vermont; human error. Try and get some rest."

Fredrik lies down in the leather chair.

"Not you, ME. I need to rest," I tease.

He puts his hand out.

"Hold me," he demands.

Over the next six hundred hours (OK, four) I do not rest. I get comfortable and chat up Kim who, again, being new to our collective relationship, is very tolerant of my babbling. But then the epidural wears off, so my dose is adjusted and then my cervix is checked and checked again so Kim leaves with Andrew (to go have sex maybe, in a dark corner of the cafeteria?). Later, my in-laws arrive and there is more discussion of my progress ("My mother clapped when she heard you were close." "Your mother *clapped?*"), and finally, Mom and Peyton arrive.

Mom comes to the bed, kisses me, and leans over to whisper to me. I close my eyes, imagining the words of comfort that she will murmur to me as she strokes my hair, as I am finally about to experience the one thing that will link us together forever. Instead I hear, "Your sister nearly killed me driving up here. I'm starting to think it's the *drivers* and not the roads I should be worried about."

I laugh.

"Do you think I will need a flash?" Mom asks.

"For what?" Fredrik asks.

"My camera," Mom says.

Fredrik looks to me.

"Yes, you need a flash. No, you may not use your camera," I say.

"But I'm taking the pictures. Elaine is handling the video."

Elaine enters the room.

"Where will I be?" Elaine asks, confused.

"In the waiting room," Peyton says, "with me. And my mother."

"Could you not use that tone of voice with me, please?" Mom asks.

"Take it outside. Dr. Mitchell is coming," I plead.

Dr. Mitchell comes in and Mom extends her hand.

"I am Mother Fox," she says. She takes off a cardigan

and reveals a shirt with a homemade appliqué iron-on that says MOTHER FOX111.

"I see that," Dr. Mitchell teases.

Peyton is—God, she is *so* obvious—checking out Dr. Mitchell.

"Everyone out," I order.

"OK, OK," Mom says. She comes to the side of the bed again and whispers, "I love you. I'm proud of you. You can do this." *Finally*. She walks out of the room with Elaine.

Peyton walks toward me and says, "I can't believe *this* is the guy you've been obsessing over." She winks.

And with that, they're gone.

Janice returns to the room and Dr. Mitchell does another check.

"You're at ten centimeters, Gretchen. Ready to start pushing?"

Janice nods to Fredrik. "Dad, stand there, grab a leg. I'll be on this side. When Dr. M. tells us, we'll tell Mom to push, and we'll count to ten. With me?"

"Let's go!" Dr. Mitchell shouts.

"PUSH PUSH PUSH PUSH PUSH! One. Two. Three. Four. Five . . ." Janice and Fredrik say.

"OH, MY GOD," I cry.

"Again now," Dr. Mitchell says.

My legs are shaking. I'm sweating. Dr. Mitchell is looking at the monitor. Fredrik looks, too.

"A drop in the heartbeat; let's give the baby a tickle."

"Again, now."

"PUSH PUSH PUSH PUSH PUSH PUSH! One. Two. Three. Four. Five. Six. Seven. Eight. Nine. Ten. Done, you did it," Janice says.

The heartbeat drops again. Another contraction is coming.

"Gretchen, do not push. I do not want you to push," Dr. Mitchell orders.

"Is the baby OK? I WANT TO PUSH!" I scream.

"The heartbeat is back up," Fredrik says.

Dr. Mitchell backs away from the southern hemisphere and stands up.

"The baby is still very high. The heartbeat is dropping with each push, which could indicate a problem. Maybe the umbilical cord. We have two options. We can push a few more times and hope the problem resolves itself. If it doesn't, we'll need to do a C-section and every minute would count. Or we do the C-section now."

Fredrik and I look at each other. I'm crying and nodding. He translates.

"Do it now," he says, his voice shaky.

Dr. Mitchell leaves the room as Janice starts to shave the top part of my pubic hair. *Please hurry! Please hurry!* I want to plead, *every second counts!* Another nurse hands Fredrik scrubs; he'll be brought into the operating room once we're ready. I'm wheeled out of the room, leaving Fredrik behind. We enter the OR and I have to squint, as the rest of the hospital is still dark. Two orderlies move me off the rolly bed and on to a table, where my arms are outstretched and strapped down. *Must remember to describe to Mom as crucifixion-like.* A green sheet is stretched across my stomach. The anesthesiologist sits at my head, gives me oxygen, and adjusts my IV.

"You might feel cold; the numbing will start at your chest and work down."

I have a shower cap on my head. I look to the right; an empty Isolette.

A new nurse, a large African-American woman, whispers in my ear, "You're doing great, honey. Dad will be here in a minute."

Fredrik walks in a door on my left. He looks ridiculous.

Dr. Mitchell remarks that my abdominal muscles are very strong and asks if I exercise regularly, do sit-ups, that kind of thing.

"I've *always* had a flat stomach," I lie, "until I got pregnant."

"Um, G?" Fredrik whispers to me "You're flirting with Dr. Mitchell."

"Am I?" I laugh.

Dr. Mitchell looks up at me, and smiles. I smile back. "You might feel some pressure and pulling. That's normal. If you feel pain, scream."

What? I stop smiling. I guess the OR is not a good place to kick off our relationship.

"It won't be long now," the nurse says.

Fredrik is looking over the sheet.

"What's happening?" I ask.

"Holy shit," he says. He looks down at me. "They are taking you apart."

"Let's stay positive, Dad," the nurse admonishes.

Dr. Wiley—I didn't see her come in—is now by the baby cart. I feel tugging, not pain, and digging.

"Almost there," Dr. Mitchell says. A sharp pull. "And it is a boy! A big guy! Whoa!! You sure about your dates? Want to cut the cord, Dad?"

I hear crying but I can't see anything. Then, to my right a nurse and Dr. Wiley are using a blue bulb thing on the baby's nose. DID THEY SAY "BOY"? He's covered in white stuff, and his arms and legs are flying everywhere.

"This is no preterm baby; he's EIGHT POUNDS THREE OUNCES! Someone had their dates wrong," Dr. Wiley says.

"I did not!" I shout.

She hands the baby, who is now wrapped in the hospital-issue blanket, to Fredrik. He lowers him to my face, but I can't even touch him; my arms are still strapped down. He is beautiful. A beautiful baby. Not *at all* raisinlike.

"You're a boy," I say.

*   *   *

After half an hour, I'm wheeled into the recovery room, and Mom, Peyton, Elaine, Karl, Andrew, Kim, and, God love her, Louisa, walk in.

"And what is my grandson's name?" Mom asks as Fredrik hands her the baby.

"Gregory," I answer. Dad's name.

POP. The lights turn back on.

"Oh." I'd forgotten about the electricity.

Mom's eyes tear up. "Looks like your dad was here after all."

"Yes, and great timing, as usual," Peyton says.

And I laugh. Even though it hurts like hell, I laugh.

Epilogue

One year later

I have officially stopped reading parenting books. I was getting frustrated by my inability to locate things in the index, for example: Nursing—there was no subcategory for *"supplementing with bottle feeding because you want to run to the CVS for shampoo—alone, just for forty-five minutes—without worrying someone's life hung in the balance."* Equally as unhelpful was the entry for Napping, as it did not include an answer to the question, *"Why does every child except mine sleep for four hours every day?"*

Though Gregory is asleep now, and I am trying to put the finishing touches on his first birthday party, he will likely not sleep for long. He is already stirring, only twenty minutes into it (I will ignore it, as the books suggest, and he will end up a more independent adult. There is a part of me that is desperate to disprove this theory—and all of the advice, really . . . only theories. So I have been asking everyone about their childhood napping habits and logging their answers in my Filofax. I don't have much.). By finishing touches, I mean I am trying to move the dust from the construction on the front part of the house to the outside, so we can celebrate the birthday near our partially completed patio, without needing a shower after.

I agreed to buy the farmhouse in a moment when I was clearly suffering from the cumulative effects of sleep deprivation, which Mom is constantly reminding me is a form of torture in many thriving dictatorships. For the first three months, all Gregory did was cry. He cried during the day, he cried during the night. So I started to cry, too, and then, it seemed like moving wasn't such a bad idea; it was something else to focus on. Then, when we sat down and thought about it, we realized we had a lot of EXTRA waking hours (seriously, the child never slept) now available to us. Why not use them constructively? The plan was for us to buy the farm and fix it up, while we got the other house ready for sale, etc. We could afford to do this as long as I was working. But less than two weeks after we signed the papers on the farm—and I still can't laugh about this—I got a call saying my position at the hotel had been eliminated, despite assurances to the contrary only a month or so before. So, Plan B (thank God Fredrik had mapped this out) went into action: we'd renovate and live at the farm at the same time. Fredrik and I survived the weeks of packing only by making jokes. "Storing stuff in my parents' basement—that *rocks*," he'd say "A sign to the world that we've made it." And I'd respond with, "I know, but it's just *not* as cool as going to your meeting with your state-appointed job counselor in maternity clothes, even though your baby is nearly three months old." "Awesome," he'd say in response. "We are fucking ON FIRE."

And then, the most amazing thing happened. *Gregory stopped crying*. He started smiling, and burping, and playing with his feet, and swinging at the three thousand brightly colored brilliance-inducing toys I strung on his stroller, his car seat, and his crib. He started to crawl, back-

wards, and then he started pulling himself up on tables
and chairs. And then, at ten months, he started walking.
Really, what happened was, he started to be fun (and by
fun, I mean *he finally knew who the hell I was*). And I
started to enjoy myself.

So today, we are *here,* in a house that is one-tenth finished, which is fine, as the renovation falls under "Facilities," which is Fredrik's responsibility. Whenever I get
asked a question about the house by Mom or by his parents (and they are constantly asking), I happily refer them
to that "department." After all, I am very busy managing
"Human Resources" and trying to learn "Food Services."
I am sure we will get lots of questions today—any minute
our friends and family are coming over for cake to celebrate Gregory's birthday. Mom arrived last night and right
now, Mom, Elaine, Karl, and Peyton are outside setting up
tables and chairs. Fredrik went to the store with Alexander to get beer (Fredrik didn't even tell me he was going,
which I find very strange. There is *no way* I'd leave Gregory without coordinating with Fredrik, Mom, Elaine,
and possibly the Emergency Broadcast System, but I guess
that is the difference between men and women.)

I look out the window. Peyton is fussing about and my
mom is sitting in a chair, eating. The doorbell rings. Mom
shouts, "I'll get it!" just as Peyton is starting to try and
reposition some chairs. Mom walks by me to the front
hallway, oblivious to Peyton's shouting her name, asking
her for help with a large Adirondack chair.

"Meredith is here!" she shouts as she opens the door.

I run out from the kitchen and then through what will
be the living room—in approximately six years—to shush
her. "Mom, *please*. Gregory is napping."

I hear a cry.

"Not anymore!"

Mom runs up the stairs to get Gregory while I hug

Meredith. Within seconds, Ryder takes off to look for Fredrik and his fancy lawn mower. It's called an X-wing fighter or an X-mark or something and Fredrik never tires of showing it off. Just then, Alexander and Fredrik show up with the beer. We all move to the back of the house (I considered putting a big sign up with an arrow, pointing to the back), and I offer everyone a drink. The boys, Mom, Gregory—everyone moves outside. Meredith stays behind with Hannah. She bends over her diaper bag and I notice her pants—they are elastic waistband. Huh. I wonder if she is pregnant.

"Meredith," I say. "Would you like a beer?"

"What? Oh, no—"

"Why not?"

"Just not in the mood for it, I guess," she says. She laughs.

"You're pregnant," I say. "Before you deny it, I saw the elastic."

She laughs, "I am. I didn't want to tell anyone yet because I'm RIDICULOUSLY early on. Definitely TOO EARLY for elastic waistband pants, but I am just so tired, I just grabbed these from the pile of fourth-trimester clothes I hadn't put away yet. Do I look awful?"

"No, you look great," I say.

"Please. I haven't looked 'great' in three years," she says a little wistfully.

"You are welcome to move in here. This house hasn't a single mirror."

"It doesn't?"

"Meredith, we barely have a functioning bathroom."

"And yet, you still won't stay with us. I don't understand it," Elaine says as she walks into the kitchen.

"Where are the boys?" I ask, changing the subject.

"They're carrying Gregory's present right to the back," she says.

Meredith raises her eyebrows at me. I shake my head. Who knows what it is? At Christmas, Karl gave Gregory a drill. A working drill. *For the 4-month-old.*

Hannah starts pointing to the outside. Elaine takes Hannah's hands to see if she will walk with her. But Hannah puts her arms up—she wants to be carried. Elaine brings her outside and Mcredith and I watch them for a moment.

"She has no interest in walking," Meredith says.

"Would you, if people were willing to carry you?" I ask.

"Probably not."

The front door opens and I hear Louisa's voice. "Hello?"

"Back here!" I shout.

Louisa walks in carrying two very large toy Mack trucks.

"I couldn't decide," she says. "So I bought both."

"Thanks," I say. "Where's Jason?"

"He is on the tractor thing with Fredrik. I am almost certain the ride will result in a trip to the hospital," she says. She looks out the window. "Who is *that?*"

"Oh, that's Alexander," I say.

"*That's* Alexander?" Meredith asks.

"Is he staying here?" Louisa asks.

"Yeah," I answer. "Why?"

"I just—I didn't know he was going to be so good-looking."

"I know," I say. "I try to ignore it."

"Well, I can't," Meredith says.

"Can't what?" Andrew asks, as he reaches for a cupcake.

"Um . . . those are for the kids," I say. "They're still cooling. They need to be room temperature before they can be frosted."

He takes one and pops it in his mouth. He starts fanning his mouth. "Hot! Hot! Hot!" he says as he grabs another.

"Where is Kim?" Louisa whispers as Andrew heads back outside.

"Still in the picture, from what I hear. Feel these—are these too hot to frost?"

Meredith nods her head yes, just as a man starts screaming. I hear my mom shout, "Oh! Oh!" and I run outside, thinking something has happened with Gregory and my heart is beating like crazy. But instead I see Jason hopping around on one foot. Louisa turns to Meredith and me. "Did I not predict this? Because it is *virtually impossible* for him to do anything even *remotely physical* without injuring himself," she says, smiling all the while. She then rushes off to him. "Are you OK, honey? Sit down. Right here. Let me look."

Meredith goes to join the others, and I nod at Fredrik, which was our previously agreed-upon signal that it was time to sing "Happy Birthday." I turn back to the house to get my platter of cupcakes, which I have stacked into a big pile. I come out of the house, and Fredrik takes Gregory on his lap, and everyone starts singing and taking pictures—it's like something out of a movie. *My movie.* And although I am nervous about falling, I don't, because I have locked eyes with my son. *My son.*

And as he looks at me, as I set down the platter of unfrosted cupcakes, he is all wide-eyed, and reaching out for me and I think, *He doesn't know that I can't find a job, or that the house is a mess, or that I can't figure out a good time to shower—and he doesn't care.* All he cares about is if I love him. And I do. More than I could have ever imagined. "Happy Birthday to you," we sing, hopelessly off-key.

Fredrik and I lean in to help him blow out the candle. Then Ryder—I think sensing an opportunity—is up at the side of the table, pulling a cupcake from the bottom, and before we even realize it, the whole pile of cupcakes is toppling down. Gregory starts clapping, and Ryder is shoving the cupcake in his mouth and we are all laughing. Meredith is apologizing but I reassure her, what's a little grass? I give both my boys big kisses and then I move to join the others, who are now sitting on the ground, eating cupcakes. Peyton goes to get the frosting from the kitchen.

"My daughter really knows how to have a party," Mom says to Elaine.

And as I hand my crumbled cupcake to my sister, with Gregory on my lap, and Fredrik now riding his tractor around in circles, I have to smile. I couldn't have planned the day any better.

NINE MONTHS IN AUGUST

Adriana Bourgoin

ABOUT THIS GUIDE

The suggested questions are included to enhance your
group's reading of Adriana Bourgoin's
Nine Months in August

DISCUSSION QUESTIONS

1. Despite Gretchen's father dying many years prior to the opening of the book, she still seems to be struggling with the impact of his death on her family. Her pregnancy sparks reflection and creates an opportunity to connect her past with her present. In your experience, what other life events have this impact?

2. After Gretchen reveals that she has shoplifted, does your opinion of her change? If so, how?

3. Fredrik's loyalty to his family riles Gretchen. Is she being reasonable, or does Gretchen need to accept that, for Fredrik, his family will always be a priority?

4. Meredith tries to provide a larger context for Gretchen around some of the challenges of balancing work and family. But Gretchen refuses to engage, focusing instead on her immediate situation. Should Gretchen care more about the cultural debate (and start reading all those articles)?

5. By her own admission, Gretchen has "fallen" into her jobs. In contrast, Eliza appears very driven. What, if anything, could they learn from each other?

6. Dr. Mitchell is a source of great comfort to Gretchen— a welcome distraction, even—throughout her pregnancy. Does the gender of an obstetrician matter to you?

7. Should Gretchen have kept Louisa's affair a secret from Fredrik? From Jason?

8. Gretchen and Louisa's friendship is strong but also somewhat rooted in nostalgia. Is it possible to maintain friendships, even as life circumstances change?

9. Gretchen has very particular ideas about how things should look—anything from her shoes to the paint on the bathroom walls—and can become distressed if she perceives that something looks wrong, or is out of order. Is Gretchen "just" a perfectionist, or could other factors have contributed to her obsession with appearances?

10. Is it hypocritical for Gretchen to attend church when she has significant questions regarding her faith?